A
Harlequin
Romance

OTHER
Harlequin Romances
by GWEN WESTWOOD

1333—KEEPER OF THE HEART
1396—BRIGHT WILDERNESS
1463—THE EMERALD CUCKOO
1531—CASTLE OF THE UNICORN
1638—PIRATE OF THE SUN
1716—CITADEL OF SWALLOWS
1843—SWEET ROOTS AND HONEY

Many of these titles are available at your local bookseller, or through the Harlequin Reader Service.

For a free catalogue listing all available Harlequin Romances, send your name and address to:

HARLEQUIN READER SERVICE,
M.P.O. Box 707, Niagara Falls, N.Y. 14302
Canadian address: Stratford, Ontario, Canada.

or use coupon at back of book.

KEEPER OF THE HEART

by

GWEN WESTWOOD

HARLEQUIN BOOKS

TORONTO
WINNIPEG

First published in 1969 by Mills & Boon Limited,
50 Grafton Way, Fitzroy Square, London, England.

SBN 373-01333-7

© Gwen Westwood 1969

Harlequin Canadian edition published September, 1969
Harlequin U.S. edition published December, 1969

Reprinted 1975

Printed in Canada

CHAPTER ONE

HER upbringing by an elderly North-country aunt had not only taught Vicky how to produce a Yorkshire pudding as light as a newly hatched chick and to turn the heel of a sock while reading Shakespeare's *Macbeth* aloud, but it had also ingrained in her a remarkable degree of self-control. No one of the cosmopolitan crowd hurrying back to work down the wide pathway of the Cape Town Gardens could have suspected that the letter she held had shattered all her hopes and dreams for the future.

She gazed unseeingly as a huge coloured woman swayed past, her flowered dress vivid as the contents of the basket balanced upon her head. A few yards away a Malay with grey beard and maroon fez conversed solemnly with a friend, undisturbed by the small newsvendors who dived amongst the crowd like swooping swallows. African nannies, in pink or blue striped dresses and white turban-like doeks and aprons, chased after their charges with many an admonishing shout, or wheeled gay pushcarts, laden with sleeping toddlers, whose heads drooped like top-heavy chrysanthemums.

Lightly clad typists, their legs and arms golden from the weekend's sunbathing, never looked Vicky's way, absorbed as they were in their shrill gossip, but several young men, in their regulation suits of bush jackets and shorts, glanced with interest at the girl with the warm golden hair and peaches and cream complexion, so startling to a South African eye. Encountering the blank, hurt gaze of Vicky's huge brown eyes, however, they seemed to give a mental shrug and hastened on to their shops, offices and banks.

Vicky's hands trembled as she unfolded the letter to read it once more, though already some of the phrases seemed to be burned indelibly in her mind: 'You must realize that in a new country a year is a long time ... I have never shared your sentimental idea of one woman destined for one man ... Don't think too badly of me. Even if this is not the grand passion we imagined we had for each other, my affection and respect for Eve are quite genuine. I wouldn't have become engaged to her otherwise, even though (since we said we

5

would always tell each other the truth) I must admit to you quite frankly that her father's influence will further my career, and you know how much that means to me.'

It was mid-November, and in the balmy warmth of a southern summer, the young girls' floating dresses made them look like a flock of gay butterflies, yet Vicky, who was still wearing the beautiful cream silk suit she had chosen so carefully for her first meeting with David, clasped her arms in a vain endeavour to sooth the trembling chill that seemed to have invaded her whole body.

'I must be fair to him,' she thought. 'Goodness knows, I never believed him perfect. I thought I knew his faults, my darling David. I knew he was ambitious for his career, but isn't that a good thing? But he never intended that I should be stranded in a strange country. That aspect is entirely my own fault. Elaine said I was foolish not to wait for a reply to my cable.'

Sadly she reviewed her own impulsive behaviour. A year ago, David, a geologist, had had a wonderful opportunity to obtain a post with a consulting engineer's firm in South Africa. Bitterly as they regretted parting, it was decided that he must go on ahead until he could send for her. They had decided against a formal engagement because there was also the problem of Vicky's aged aunt. It was impossible to know when they would be able to be reunited. But after a year, Vicky's aunt had died, leaving her a small sum of money, sufficient to make it possible for her to fly out to join David. She had written excitedly to him telling of her plans. It seemed that all barriers to their marriage had at last been removed.

When there was no immediate reply to her cable, Elaine, a distant cousin, had urged caution, but Vicky re-reading his loving letters felt sure that the delay must be due to David's being out upon field work. One letter of his particularly reassured her: 'If one day I could come back from work, walk in at the door and find you waiting – but how foolish of me – a lonely man's dream of bliss . . .'

A hundred times during the swift journey from London she had pictured this scene, but the reality was totally different. Sitting in the sunny gardens, she shivered again as she remembered the lonely arrival at the Cape Town air station, the journey by taxi to the hotel to which her letters had been addressed, where the information was coldly given that Mr. Thackeray had left six weeks before. No, there was no forwarding address. He had said he would call for his post, but so far he had not done so. If she was likely to see him perhaps she would take charge of these? And she was handed her own cable, a few letters she herself had written, and last, a letter to herself in David's handwriting, re-addressed from her own home. It had no blue airmail stamp and had evidently travelled by surface mail.

Obviously David knew nothing of her plans. He had become engaged to the daughter of his firm's managing director more than six weeks ago, just before he had moved to another hotel to be nearer her home, but the letter breaking this news to her had arrived, posted by surface mail, after Vicky had left for London, preparatory to her journey to South Africa.

How many hours had she been sitting here? The visit to the hotel had been made early this morning and, after leaving her suitcase at a left luggage office, she had asked the taxi-driver to drop her here, because in the midst of the city's hustle it seemed an oasis of green grass and fountains and trees.

She rose stiffly and walked like a mechanical doll towards the open-air café. Sitting in the warm sun, drinking hot coffee, she felt her numbed senses gradually returning and began to take in her surroundings without actually experiencing any process of realized thought. Through the barrier of her misery, she dimly realized that she had never before been in such a beautiful city. Her childhood had been spent in a grim, grey industrial town, where even the grass was gritty to the touch.

But here she looked over a wall of canna lilies, dark green and purple leaves topped by scarlet and orange flowers, towards a city of tall new buildings, intermingled with old, dignified churches and places of government, and at her back, behind the rhododendrons and palm trees and lovely pink camellias, the astonishing, lavender-hazed mountain seemed to brood over the noisy streets.

'We should have gone up the cableway today, for it's so clear you can see old Van Hunks and the Devil have given up their smoking.'

Somewhat surprised, Vicky glanced around and looked

straight into a pair of warm blue eyes surrounded by a cob-web network of laughter lines. The old lady's alert, kindly expression contradicted the effect of the severe suit in fawn tussore silk, the no-nonsense, straight-brimmed straw hat surmounting the wisps of iron grey hair, and the high-necked brown blouse fastened by a large cairngorm brooch. By her side, the small girl sedately sipping a milk shake looked as if she had come from another world than the one inhabited by the other shouting children with their sunsuits or brief dresses and boyish haircuts.

Her quaint, bunchy dress reached to her knees, her dark brown hair was severely plaited, and her grey eyes were large and solemn as she gravely considered the old lady's statement.

'Did you read that in your guide book, Gran?' she asked.

'Ay, it seems long ago there was a pirate called Van Hunks lived on the side of the mountain, drinking rum and smoking his pipe all day long. But one day a stranger came striding down the rocks, a tall ugly fellow, dressed in black velvet and carrying an enormous pipe.

'This fellow wagered that, if Van Hunks could smoke longer than he could, he would give him the kingdoms of the world. But if the pirate failed, he would lose his soul. How-ever, it turned out that, Van Hunks being the grand smoker that he was, it was the stranger who collapsed first, and as he fell he lost his hat and there were the devil's horns sprouting from his head!

'With that there was a flash of lightning, a peal of thunder and the two men vanished. All they left behind was a wee bit of scorched grass. But still when a black south-easter blows and cloud sweeps down over the mountain, people say it's the devil himself smoking with Van Hunks.'

'I don't like that story much, Gran. I'd rather think the cloud is a tablecloth over the mountain,' said the child. 'May I buy some peanuts and go to feed the squirrels?' she asked as a coloured vendor presented his basket.

'Yes, but keep within sight. I haven't the legs to go run-ning after you.'

The child walked away a little distance to a patch of grass where grey squirrels, spreadeagled upon the barks of trees, scrambled swiftly down when offered a nut and sat upright like small coffee-pots, munching rapidly, noses trembling and bright diamond eyes alert for sudden movements.

'They come to her quickly, you'll see,' said the old lady, addressing Vicky. 'She has a very gentle way with her – too gentle, I'm thinking, for a wee thing left without parents. It's a hard task to replace a mother when you are as old as I am.'

Vicky's brooding sadness lifted a little. It was the first time another person had spoken to her since she had read the letter.

'She seems a dear little girl,' she said.

'Susan, my great-grandchild,' the old lady informed her, taking Vicky's interest as an invitation to join her at her table. 'I've had the care of her since her mother died. Her father was an irresponsible boy who left my granddaughter shortly after Susan was born. I lost my own daughter and his children were brought up by their father and his relatives. It was only later in life that they turned to me.'

'Have you lived in this country long, Mrs. . . ?' asked Vicky, somewhat bewildered by this rapid recital, delivered with a strong Scots accent.

'Mrs. Grant, my dear. Bless you, no. We've only been here a wee while. It's getting too much for me, ye ken, to have the responsibility of a young child at my age. Eighty I am. So my grandson, Susan's uncle, Dr. Stephen Nash, offered us both a home here.'

'Does he live in Cape Town?' asked Vicky, not because she really wanted to know but because anything was better than thinking about the letter and her own future. Conversation with this talkative old lady put off the time when she must consider her own predicament.

'No, and it's a pity, for it seems a fine town and I've been used to Glasgow all my days. No, we're to go to a hospital in Pondoland, some outlandish place where the Africans live. I'm hoping I'll settle down there – my grandson says it's a wee bit quiet. I'm fond of my TV and a Saturday matinée and I'm not so keen on the country. They can show me the best views in the world, but what I always say is "Give me bricks and mortar". But I mustn't grumble. Stephen's been very good to me and it'll maybe no be so bad. It'll make a change.'

Vicky smiled for the first time since her arrival. There was something gay and indomitable about the eighty-year-old lady starting a new life in a different country at her age.

9

'I suppose you'll send Susan to boarding school?' she asked.

'Now there's a thing that's worrying me,' Mrs. Grant replied. 'We think she would be better staying with us just at first. But we don't know how to manage it. We have advertised for a governess, but few people want to bury themselves out in the wilds and the ones that have applied haven't seemed suitable. You know what doctors are like. My grandson, Stephen, is very particular. But I'm thinking we'll leave Cape Town without finding anyone to suit him.'

A wild idea zig-zagged through Vicky's brain and some kind of telepathy seemed to convey the same thought to Mrs. Grant.

'I don't suppose ... no ... you'd never be out of a job, then, a neat, nice-looking girl like you? Just got the afternoon off, I do suppose, or on holiday more like?'

The blue eyes peered hopefully at Vicky, who came to a lightning decision. Her immediate need, she felt, was to get away from Cape Town and to avoid the risk of meeting David.

'I do need work. I've only just arrived in this country and I must get something to do soon.'

'Would you be having any teaching experience? Stephen's that fussy you'd never believe it. I say a nice-mannered person, who could teach the child spelling and tables, is all we need, but he insists on someone who understands Shakespeare's plays. I ask you! Shakespeare's plays for a wee girl of ten!'

'It does seem a little advanced for that age,' Vicky agreed. 'But, Mrs. Grant, I have some teaching qualifications. I did a two years' training course in junior school teaching, but I was never able to take it up because I had to care for an aged aunt. And if it makes any difference to Dr. Nash's opinion of me, I read all Shakespeare's plays aloud to my aunt during the last year.'

'You don't say! Now isn't that a grand thing? It seems fate sent you specially to us this day.'

Vicky thought ruefully that it seemed rather a cruel trick of fate to send her halfway across the world just to oblige Mrs. Grant if it was meant she should lose David in the process, but she smiled hesitantly at the old lady's enthusiasm and cautiously tried to curb it a little.

'Your grandson might not think me suitable if he has interviewed so many people already without finding anyone satisfactory,' she suggested.

'Not a one like you!' said Mrs. Grant, her blue eyes shining and her chin determined. 'If Stephen doesn't take to you as soon as he sees you, for once I'll have something to say. To tell truth, Miss . . . now, there's a foolish thing, I don't even know your name.'

'I'm Victoria Scott, but people always call me Vicky.'

'Och, that's a pretty wee name. Vicky . . . yes, I like it. Well, Miss Scott or Vicky, as I was saying, Stephen's a mite set in his ways. A disappointment he had a while back seemed to harden him. But he's a braw laddie and a fine doctor. Susan thinks the world of him.'

Vicky looked across the grass at the quaintly dressed child absorbed in her task of feeding the squirrels. So eager had she been to seize the opportunity to get away from Cape Town and David that she had not even considered the nature of her task in taking over the care of this rather strange, sensitive-looking little girl.

The peanuts were finished now and the grey squirrels, their greed satisfied, had retreated back to the oak trees. Susan screwed up the paper packet, dropped it into the bin provided, then started to walk sedately back to the table, hardly glancing at the other more mobile children who swirled around her like whirlwinds.

One of them, a boy, taller and more heavily built than Susan, ran along the path, at the same time turning his head to shout wild admonishments to a smaller friend. Not looking where he was going, he crashed into Susan, who in a moment was sprawled at full length upon the gravel.

Vicky ran quickly towards her, but the little girl had already picked herself up. Her knees and hands were scratched and bleeding, her face white, her eyes large and brimming with tears, but she quickly wiped them away with the back of her hand and her mouth set firmly in an obvious effort not to break down. Vicky was amazed and somewhat shocked at the child's self-control. Recalling her own struggle with her emotions a while ago, she put her arms around Susan and said, 'There, darling, don't try too hard. It doesn't matter if you cry a little. Gran will understand.'

Susan gulped and gave a tiny pathetic sniff.

'Stephen wouldn't want me to cry,' she said, a slight

quiver in her voice the only sign of her distress. 'The children in his hospital are very brave. I have to be very brave too.'

'You are very brave,' Vicky assured her.

'Do you think so? Will you tell Stephen I was brave?'

'Yes, indeed I will,' Vicky said, wondering what kind of ogre Stephen could be to set such a rigid pattern of discipline for a small girl. She took Susan to wash the scratches, leaving Mrs. Grant sitting in the shade.

'There he is. There's Stephen!' cried Susan as they were returning. She seemed suddenly animated, a different child from the sedate companion to Mrs. Grant.

The first thing Vicky noticed was the slenderness of his hands as he gesticulated to Mrs. Grant, one foot on a chair, knee bent, the whole thin length of him bending towards her, blackbird's wing of hair falling forward over keen grey eyes.

'But who is this person?' he was saying. 'Gran, my love, you can't just pick up a governess in a park when you know how many unsuitable people we've rejected already.'

'That's exactly why I can,' Mrs. Grant asserted with determination. 'Wait till you see her. She's that bonny and she's got a mite of sense too, I'm thinking.'

'It hardly seems sensible to accept such a position from a casual encounter ...'

He broke off as Susan flung her arms around him.

'Hello, my girl. Now that's enough, Susan. You mustn't get too excited in this heat.'

Her arms dropped to her sides, and the words, obviously brimming on her lips, were choked back.

'This is Miss Scott, Stephen. My grandson, Dr. Nash. Even you must admit she's a bonny-looking lass, Stephen! You'll excuse me, my dear, but I've lived long enough to be able to please myself what I say.'

Vicky blushed as the cool grey eyes met hers in a frank appraisal.

'I'd prefer to speak to Miss Scott alone, Gran. I've left the car nearby. If you and Susan will start walking back, I'll follow you in a few moments. Meet me at the fish pond near the Art Gallery.'

'Ay, we'll do that, but mind your manners with Miss Scott, my laddie. You may be a fine doctor, but whiles you can be awfu' glum and no one knows it better than myself.'

12

Dr. Nash seemed quite unperturbed by the old lady's parting shot.

'Won't you sit down, Miss Scott?' he asked, as if they were in his consulting room. She sank down upon the bench, while he seized a small chair and draped himself around it, facing inwards, his arms around the back like a prosecuting counsel at the bar. A warm smile suddenly transformed his stern features.

'My grandmother is a delightful old lady, Miss Scott, but, as you may have gathered, she is occasionally a little impulsive.'

The smile was obviously directed at Mrs. Grant's foibles and did not include Vicky, for it vanished as quickly as it had come and was replaced by the former rather dour expression. Vicky's first inclination was to deny that she was interested in the post, but she had taken a liking to Mrs. Grant and Susan. Why should this arrogant doctor deter her?

'I understand that,' she said smoothly, 'but at the same time I would be interested if you could bring yourself to consider me as a governess for Susan. No doubt Mrs. Grant informed you of my qualifications?'

He eyed her up and down as if analysing her from top to toe, the perfectly set blonde hair, the beautiful skin with its subtle make-up, the cream suit of pure silk, the fine cobweb stockings and blond lizard shoes exactly matching the gold-clasped bag.

'Miss Scott,' he said at last, 'I'm not exactly experienced in the value of women's clothes, but I would hazard a guess that your present outfit is worth more than I could pay you in a whole year.'

Vicky could hardly explain how she had determined to meet David living up to his expectations of the perfectly dressed woman, and had recklessly spent far more than she should have upon the clothes she was to wear when she met him.

'That has nothing whatsoever to do with the fact that I would be grateful to have the post,' she responded rather sharply.

'Have you any experience of lonely places in Africa?'

'None whatsoever!'

'I thought as much.' The grey eyes were thoughtful. 'Gran talks too much. No doubt she told you that Susan is an heiress. If so, you can put that out of your mind. As far as we can tell the inheritance from her paternal grandfather may well prove worthless. For all we know the emerald mine may be unworkable.'

Vicky gasped indignantly.

'I had no idea ... I've discussed nothing of that kind with Mrs. Grant. If you think I could be influenced by ...'

'Everyone likes money or the idea of money, my dear Miss Scott. Even I myself.'

The grey eyes with their heavy fringe of black lashes and the dark quizzical brows gazed narrowly, rather cynically into her own.

'But I'm sorry to say, Miss Scott, I can offer very little pay for this work. You, I dare say, would hardly consider it enough to buy stockings.'

'The amount of money means nothing to me. I'm only interested in obtaining a post that will take me right away from Cape Town,' Vicky burst out desperately.

'I think I begin to understand.' The grey eyes were cold, a little scornful. 'Some love affair has gone wrong. There is some romantic complication you feel you must escape from?'

'Yes!' shouted Vicky. 'Yes ... yes!'

Goaded beyond endurance by the cool grey glance and the negligent stance of the man leaning over his chair like a prosecuting judge, she at last lost her carefully guarded self-control.

'I don't care what salary you pay me or how lonely the place is. I want to go far away from Cape Town because the man I love has become engaged to someone else. Now are you satisfied?'

And to her abject shame, she burst into tears.

Vicky woke to the sound of doves. 'Curoo – curoo ...' Their peaceful, bubbling conversation floated up from the courtyard below. She had noticed them last night as she entered the grounds of the hotel, softly feathered grey-blue birds so absorbed in each other's company that they failed to notice until the passerby was only a yard away, then soared in gentle flight to the new green of the oak trees.

Nearer than the cooing of doves was the quiet sound of someone breathing. She opened her eyes sleepily and saw Susan sitting quite still on a chair beside her bed. Her hands were clasped under her knees and she looked as if she must have been keeping this motionless pose for quite a long time, for when she saw that Vicky was awake she heaved a large sigh and her grave grey eyes with the long black lashes flickered once or twice as if released from a spell.

'You look beautiful when you're asleep,' she told Vicky solemnly.

'Thank you,' said Vicky. 'I'm glad.'

'Stephen says that if I like you and he likes you and you like us, we'll take you home to the hospital when we go in a few days' time.'

'Well, I like you, anyway, Susan, so I'll meet you halfway.' Susan looked a little puzzled.

'I think – I'm almost sure – I would like you to come, but Stephen doesn't like people very easily. If he could see how you look when you're asleep, I'm sure he would like you.'

Vicky's delicate skin flushed easily.

'Why are you so pink now?' asked Susan. 'Are you hot? Let's go out on to the balcony, shall we? It's like being a squirrel. You look straight into the trees.'

Vicky slipped into a buttercup yellow gown scattered with white daisies, and quickly combed through her shoulder length hair. Last night she had looked into the mirror at the sophisticated coiffure she had hoped would impress David and in a few seconds had devastated it with hard, savage strokes of her hairbursh. Now she drew it away from her forehead, tied it back with a white ribbon and followed Susan on to the balcony.

There was a delicate tracery of wrought iron enclosing the verandah which ran the whole length of the hotel's upper storey. The red floor tiles shone burnished in the early rays of the sun, and, as Susan had said, you looked straight into the leafy hearts of great trees from which birds burst forth bent upon frenzied vernal tasks. And once again, like the backdrop to a stage, there was that wonderful mountain, the upper slopes pink in the light of early morning, the lower kloofs shadowed by dark forest.

'Do you think we'll go up to the top today?' asked Susan.

'Do you want to?' said Vicky.

'Yes. Yes, if Stephen does,' Susan assured her. But Vicky noticed the child's delicate skin took on a greenish pallor and her eyes widened as she gazed up at the great masses of rock.

'The cablecar is like a tiny little birdcage, when you see it on the side of the mountain,' she informed Vicky. 'It goes up on a wire. Those wires couldn't break, could they?'

'Of course not. It's perfectly safe.'

'Stephen thinks I'm silly when I ask things like that. But it's just that I like to know. I'm not really afraid. You don't think I am, do you?'

'No,' said Vicky.

Already this quaint, nervous little girl was winding silken strands of love around Vicky's susceptible heart. She felt indignant that Stephen seemed incapable of meting out anything but strict treatment to his sensitive little niece who obviously longed for his affection.

As if in answer to her thoughts, Stephen's soft voice, that did not seem to accord at all with her impression of his personality, sounded on the verandah behind them.

'Why are you not dressed yet, Susan? It's almost time for breakfast. Hurry now. Gran wants to go to Kirstenbosch this morning.'

'Hello, Stephen!' Susan's grave, anxious face broke into smiles and she flung her arms around him. 'Oh, you do look so nice this morning. Doesn't he look handsome, Vicky? You look so lovely and brown in that white shirt ... like an advertisement for cigarettes.'

'Now stop this foolishness and go, Susan.' He glanced at Vicky as if to say, 'You too, Miss Scott.'

'Don't you think Vicky has a pretty gown?' asked Susan, making another determined bid for Stephen's attention.

'Very nice,' he said abruptly, glancing swiftly at Vicky and then away. 'And Susan, you must call Miss Scott by her surname. It's more respectful.'

'Oh, no, I don't want her to ...' Vicky protested.

'Susan must learn the correct way to behave. I'm afraid Gran has spoiled her,' said Stephen.

'Why, I think she's a remarkably well behaved child,' said Vicky indignantly.

'Indeed?'

His grey eyes studied her as if, she thought, she was a strange specimen upon the table of his laboratory.

'It depends of course upon one's own standards,' he said. 'I've always thought good manners very important in a child's upbringing. Don't you agree?'

'Yes, of course,' said Vicky, and could not resist adding, 'So long as they're ingrained sufficiently in childhood to become natural when one has grown up.'

'For yours could do with a little revision, Dr. Stephen Nash,' she thought, as he turned on his heel and abruptly strode away through the sun-filled loggia. She felt inclined to run after him and tell him what she thought of his ideas on bringing up children and of his own behaviour for that matter, but just then Susan slipped a small hand into hers.

'You mustn't be cross with Stephen,' she said anxiously, observing Vicky's stormy expression. 'I want him to like you. I know now that I want you to come with us.'

'But do I want to go?' thought Vicky as she quickly showered and slipped on a cool green linen dress. 'Oh, David, David, if you'd only told me sooner of your engagement! What am I doing here in a strange country, getting involved with people I don't know, an aged lady, a nervous child and an impossible doctor! What am I letting myself in for?'

But when she joined them at the table on the patio, she could not help but feel cheered by Gran's warm, welcoming smile and Susan's large shining eyes. Even the 'Dokertor,' as the coloured waiter called him, looked relaxed.

'He should smile more often,' thought Vicky to herself as she responded to his charming grin. It was true, as Susan had said, he looked very handsome this morning, not exactly 'like an advertisement for cigarettes,' for he did not have the look of a film star. 'But he has a very interesting face,' Vicky admitted to herself somewhat reluctantly. 'Emotions pass across it like the shadows of clouds on a meadow, and when he smiles everything seems brilliantly sunlit.'

His eyes met hers and the intent grey gaze made her feel a little breathless, then he turned to say something to Gran and for the moment his analysis of Susan's future governess was over.

'For that's why he looks at me in that way,' she thought. 'I hope this morning he's more satisfied with what he sees.'

For she had knotted her hair demurely, in an attempt to look older without appearing too sophisticated.

The white metal table, intricately decorated, was set on a paved patio on the ground floor of the hotel. Sunlight glittered through the leaves of a green climbing vine, striking sparks from the silver cutlery and shining glass. The honey, orange juice and marmalade glowed deep yellow as if they had taken to themselves a part of the sun.

'I can recommend the iced papaya with lemon juice,' said Stephen, spooning up golden sections from a plate decorated with green vine leaves.

'Och, it's an outlandish kind of fruit. I canna abide the taste,' declared Mrs. Grant, sprinkling salt on her mealie meal porridge.

'What's that like, Gran?' asked Susan.

'No so bad, but it needs a wee bit more body to make it as good as oatmeal.'

'I'll settle for bacon and eggs next,' said Stephen.

'What is boere ... boere ... boerewors?' asked Susan.

'It's a kind of sausage,' said Stephen.

'Can I try it?'

'No, child. With your nervous stomach, you'd much better stick to poached egg. We may go up the mountain today.'

'Not me,' said Gran. 'I'm thinking I'll go to the Kirstenbosch Gardens and sit there a wee while.'

'That place where we saw the silver trees?' asked Susan. She turned eagerly to Vicky. 'Do you know, Vicky, I mean Miss Scott, there are beautiful trees with leaves that are like the fur on a small silvery mouse?'

'I'd like to see the proteas again, and the heath,' said Gran.

'And what about Lady Anne Barnard's bath? Do you think she really did bathe in it?'

'They say not, but it's very pretty anyway with overhanging trees and ferns.'

'A bit cold, though,' said Susan, shivering.

'What a child you are for feeling the cold,' said Stephen. 'Look, even the thought of it has given you gooseflesh. The water there would be perfect on a hot summer's day. I want you to enjoy bathing on the Wild Coast near the hospital. There are lovely pools and you'll have fun there.'

'Will I?' asked Susan doubtfully. She looked crestfallen as she seemed to do when she thought Stephen was criticizing her.

When they met a little later in the foyer of the hotel, Stephen was speaking in a phone booth. He came out frowning.

'I'm afraid there will have to be a change of plan. I have to meet someone for a little while. However, I don't want Susan to miss the mountain. It may not be such a clear day tomorrow. You can take a taxi, Miss Scott, and I'll join you later when I can. I'll meet you at the tea-room which is at the top of the cableway.'

Vicky thought it would have been much better to call the expedition off, since Susan was obviously nervous about going in the cableway car, but Stephen was either very obtuse or wanted the child to conquer her fear. Vicky was torn between compassion for Susan and the feeling that she could do no good by protesting. Those keen grey eyes would see through any excuse she made to try to get Susan out of going.

As they drove up the winding streets to the Cable Station, the view of Cape Town unrolled behind them, the tall buildings in the town's centre, the dockside cranes stooping and bending like greedy giraffes, the faded shabby beauty of once grand old houses. Where in all this maze of buildings was David? Yesterday Vicky had felt drained of emotion, but now the dreadful ache started again. To be so near and not to be able to reach him!

'He must never know,' she thought. 'If I go to Pondoland, I'll be safe. He'll never know I followed him when already in his heart he had discarded me. It's the only way. I have plenty of clothes and I'll have no living expenses. I'll save my salary and then eventually I'll manage to get home again. By that time I'll be able to face my friends. Surely by then this heartache will have gone, though at the moment I feel it never will. Suppose I saw him now, this moment, in the street? What would I do? Would I shout "Stop!" to the taxi-driver and run to fling myself into his arms? But then suppose he looked at me coldly and said "There must be some mistake. Didn't you get my letter?" '

She strangled a little moan and woke from her dream to find Susan holding her hand and anxiously gazing at her.

'Have you got a pain, Vicky? You look so pale.'

Vicky smiled with difficulty.

'No, darling. I just had some rather painful thoughts. But it's over now. Let's not look back any more. Look up there. The sky's so bright and beautiful. We're going to have a glorious ride.'

They bought their tickets and walked from the platform into the cable car.

'It looks bigger than I thought it would be,' said Susan in a relieved tone.

Since it was a weekday, there were not many people going up. It seemed odd to see a couple of workmen with tins of paint, and there were three students and one or two people who had obviously come from ships in the harbour. Before they had had time to realize it, the cable-car was slowly climbing, hanging over the screes which did not really seem so very far below.

'There, it isn't so bad, is it, Susan?' asked Vicky, smiling at the solemn little face.

'Are you enjoying the ride, my girl?'

Vicky glanced round at the man who had addressed this remark to Susan. He was quite good-looking and spoke with an English accent, but there was an air of shabbiness about him.

'Not very much,' Susan replied. 'It's so high from the ground.'

'Oh, that's nothing. Look at the thick wires. They're tested regularly.'

'Look, Susan, we're higher than the birds,' said Vicky, not wanting to get too much involved in conversation with the stranger.

Below them, a large hawk was lying on the wind, scanning the countryside as it lazily cruised in the blue air. But only half Susan's attention was on the bird.

'We're getting awfully close to the cliff,' she said uneasily. 'Oh, Vicky, I'm sure we're going to bump it.'

The last part of the lift was the most alarming, for the wire rose almost vertically at the side of the cliff that formed part of the 'table'.

'It's all right, Susan, we're nearly there.'

But Susan clung to her hand, then buried her head in Vicky's skirt, letting out little whimpering noises like a frightened puppy. Vicky soothed her as best she could and it was not long before they reached the top. The stranger who had previously spoken to them helped Vicky step from the car, for she was hampered by Susan, who was clinging to her like a leech, her warm, damp face buried in Vicky's neck and her soft hair impeding Vicky's vision. She smiled gratefully, assuring him that Susan would be all right soon.

'Let me buy her a cool drink or an ice cream,' said the stranger, 'and perhaps you would join me in a cup of tea. That should soothe our nerves.'

'That's very kind of you,' Vicky responded, not wanting to appear ungrateful for the man's help. And they made their way to the tea-room, a picturesque building made from natural stone.

Susan was soon cheerful again.

'How quickly children forget their troubles,' thought Vicky wistfully.

Their new acquaintance ordered an ice for Susan and tea for the two of them.

'I suppose everything has to come by the cableway?' Vicky asked.

'Yes, all the provisions. It isn't difficult to climb the mountain. Just a long steady pull. General Smuts used to do it frequently even in his old age.'

'Oh, I hope next time I come I'll be strong enough to climb,' said Susan eagerly. 'I'd love that.'

The man smiled. Vicky had felt dubious about accepting his company, but he seemed quite a pleasant-mannered person and had certainly been very helpful with Susan. In her eagerness to console the child, she had forgotten to introduce herself and she supposed this had restrained him from saying his name. It hardly mattered now.

'Would you like to post a card from the postbox here?' he asked Susan. 'It will be stamped with the special Table Mountain postmark and everyone will know you've been here.'

'Yes,' said Susan, 'but who can I write to? I know, I'll send one to Stephen.'

'But, darling, he'll be here soon. Wouldn't you like to send one to someone else, a friend or . . .'

'To Gran,' said Susan.

'Well, all right,' said Vicky, reflecting that it was sad that Susan appeared to have no other relatives or friends. She watched the man help Susan to buy a postcard and wait while she painstakingly wrote her messages. Then they all went outside to look at the view that was stretched in breathtaking immensity at their feet.

Below them a deep blue ocean lapped the feet of the

Mother City. Beaches showed silvery below the dark green conifers and great ocean liners took their place in the harbour like graceful white swans in a vast lake. On the other side lay the hinterland, jagged blue mountains rising tier upon tier like the relief maps that children make at school.

'Can you see the dassies on the rocks?' the stranger asked Susan.

'What are dassies?' she asked.

'Small rock rabbits. They love the heat and sit all day sunning themselves beside their holes. See, there's one!'

At first they could see nothing, then suddenly made out the shape of the small animal almost the same colour as the brown rock, gazing intently towards them with bright dark eyes.

'It seems stupid, but their nearest relation in nature is the rhinoceros,' the man informed them.

They had wandered quite a way from the restaurant and now faintly in the breeze they heard a tinkling bell.

'What's that bell?' asked Susan.

'It's just to tell you a cable car is going down. There'll be plenty more.'

For some reason Vicky began to feel uneasy. All at once the day seemed to have lost its heat. She looked up and was alarmed to see gauzy veils of mist covering the sun.

'A mist seems to be coming down. Shouldn't we make our way back?' she asked.

'Plenty of time. It's quite usual for clouds to gather on the mountain. I'd like you to see the magnificent view from this rock before you go.'

By now great ragged streamers of cloud were being blown in upon a south-east wind. The bell tinkled again, this time sounding somehow muffled but urgent.

The man clicked his fingers as though he had suddenly remembered something.

'How crazy of me! I should have remembered they ring the bell to tell you that the weather conditions are deteriorating and everyone must go down.'

'Then we must hurry back,' said Vicky.

She did not want Susan to sense the sudden fear she felt, but it was difficult to hurry over the rough ground with the child clinging to her hand, for the moisture was making the rocks slippery.

'Let me take her,' the man said. 'My shoes are more adequate than yours. I'll go on ahead.'

'Don't go too fast,' begged Vicky.

She found it hard to keep up with him, even though she had relinquished Susan. The stony ground was difficult to negotiate. She felt as if she were walking upon ice and the mist was now so thick she could only see a few yards ahead. Every now and again she lost sight of them, but he called back reassuringly, 'All right? We'll go on ahead and shelter at the top of the cableway. I'll hurry with Susan, then she won't get too wet.'

Hurrying to try to keep them in sight, she failed to notice a large rock in her path and slipped to the ground, grazing her leg badly. By the time she had painfully recovered herself, Susan and the man were lost from sight in the mist. She called out, but there was no reply, and fear gripped her at the thought that she had left the little girl in the care of a stranger.

'But I can only be a few yards from the cableway now,' she thought.

The fall, however, had not only shaken her, but it had somehow muddled her sense of direction. After a few minutes of wandering she found herself back at the large rock she knew she had just left. She stood trembling, surrounded by cloud and not knowing in which direction to set out. To her distressed imagination hours seemed to go by, although it could only have been minutes before she heard a voice calling, sounding strangely disembodied in the midst.

'Miss Scott, are you there?'

'Here!' called Vicky.

'Stand still and I'll try to come to you.'

All at once the mist lifted a little and revealed Stephen some yards away, walking rapidly towards her, a worried scowl upon his dark, aquiline face. Childishly she thought of Mrs. Grant's story ... the tall dark fellow, striding over the rocks, who turned out to be the devil himself.

'I've left Susan at the cable station. I must say I was rather surprised to find her by herself there!'

'By herself?' said Vicky, 'but ...'

'She gave me some garbled version of how she came to lose you, but we'll talk about that later. We must hurry!'

He sounded so impatient that Vicky felt she could not tell him of her fall. Painfully she walked along beside him trying in vain to keep up with his long stride. At last he noticed that she was limping.

'Anything wrong?' he asked abruptly. 'Why are you walking with such difficulty?'

'I had a slight fall. It's nothing really.'

'You'd better hold on to me,' he instructed, and when she hesitated to take his arm, he gave an impatient exclamation and held her firmly around the waist, hurrying her with unrelenting speed towards the cable station.

Susan seemed none the worse for her adventure as they took their places in the small cable car. She seemed fully recovered from all her nervousness now that Stephen had arrived.

'We've had a grand time on the mountain,' she informed him, imitating Gran's accent. 'We saw dassies, and we met a man who bought us tea and icecream and helped me to send postcards from the café.'

Vicky was conscious of Stephen's quick, disapproving frown.

'Who was this man? I thought I'd always told you that you shouldn't talk to strangers, Susan.'

'He was kind and he liked Vicky, Miss Scott. He held me while I leaned over the edge of the mountain to see the dassies.' She turned to Vicky. 'But, Vicky, it was so strange. When we came to the cable station, there was a car just ready to go down and he said I should go in it with him and you would come later. He said we would wait for you at the bottom. But just then I saw Stephen. He must have come up the mountain in the same car, and I ran to him. When I looked again, the man had gone. I suppose he thought he needn't look after me any more because Stephen had come.'

Vicky thought the devil himself could not have worn a more menacing expression than Stephen at that moment, but he did not say anything. For the rest of the journey he avoided addressing Vicky, but every now and again she was aware of his cold gaze and was painfully conscious that she had been found wanting in her care for Susan.

When they reached the hotel, Susan ran into the garden to tell Gran of her adventures and Vicky tried to take leave of Stephen in the hallway. She longed desperately to go to her room, bathe her grazed legs, have a hot bath and brush her dishevelled hair, but his cold voice arrested her flight.

'I would like to speak to you, Miss Scott. Come into the small writing room. We won't be disturbed there.'

Unlike the other public rooms of the hotel, this was a small rather gloomy place, which, together with Stephen's frowning looks and her own depressed state, made Vicky's spirits reach an extremely low ebb. Her flushed pink cheeks, the silky tangled hair, golden as a silkworm's cocoon, and the warm brown eyes, large with emotion, made a very appealing picture against the background of dark wood panelling, but she was unaware of this, and only knew that Stephen was regarding her with a puzzled disapproving scowl.

He did not sit down nor invite her to do so and she was very conscious of his tall figure blocking out the light against the diamond-paned windows. She had a feeling of breathlessness, almost of fear.

'What's wrong with me?' she thought. 'How absurd that I should feel scared of him.'

'Miss Scott, I can hardly entrust Susan to a woman who engages in conversation with absolute strangers and accepts favours from them.'

'But, Dr. Nash, it wasn't like that at all.'

Ruefully Vicky realized that either she had to betray the fact that Susan had been panic-stricken on the journey up the mountain or be accused of uncircumspect behaviour herself.

Stephen strode restlessly up and down the little room, flinging back the dark hair that fell over his forehead and smoothing it with his long brown hands.

'Frankly, Miss Scott, I'm disappointed. Susan seems to have taken to you so quickly, and Gran likes you too. Although at first sight you didn't seem to me very suitable for this kind of position, I was hoping it would work out well. But if you're accustomed to such freedom of behaviour, I hardly think you're a suitable companion for a small girl.'

'Why must you put me in the wrong?' asked Vicky. 'I spoke to a stranger, but I could hardly do otherwise. The man was being kind. I could hardly snub him.'

Stephen's brooding frown swept over Vicky.

'You are not unattractive, Miss Scott. Surely you must have had experience in dealing with importunate men. It was unwise, to say the least, to let Susan go off on her own with him.'

Vicky remembered her moments of extreme fear when she lost sight of Susan and her anger towards Stephen cooled.

'I'm sorry, Dr. Nash. I'm not really in the habit of talking to strangers. Perhaps it was foolish of me. I certainly wish Susan nothing but good and I'm looking forward to caring for her. I won't take any chances again.'

Suddenly, to Vicky's extreme confusion, all the events of the day seemed to fuse together. She was aware that her bruised limbs were aching intolerably and that she needed to rest. The ornaments upon the mantel danced in front of her eyes, as she turned away from Stephen, whose face seemed to be receding into a black mist. She swayed and slid down to the floor.

She could see his face again now, as he knelt beside her. The grey eyes looked concerned. 'For me?' she wondered.

'My dear child!' Had she imagined that he said that? Now she was lying back in an armchair in her own room. How had she got here? And his hands were deft and skilful as he bathed and dressed the livid bruises. 'Why didn't you tell me you'd injured yourself?' he demanded.

'It was stupid of me, I know. I didn't want to alarm Susan.'

'You'd better rest for a while. I'll have dinner sent up to you.'

Vicky was left wondering at the transformation in him when he was doing his own kind of work.

'It was fun on the mountain, wasn't it, Vicky?' said Susan, when she came in to say good night.

'Yes,' Vicky agreed, making several private mental reservations.

'You didn't tell Stephen I was scared at first, did you?' Susan asked anxiously.

'No, of course not, darling. In any case, you were only a little scared. You soon got over it.'

'Yes, I did, didn't I?' She looked pensive. 'That man was nice when he bought me icecream and helped me with the postcards. Wasn't it strange that on the mountain we met someone who knew who I was?'

'What do you mean, Susan?'

'He knew me. He called me by my name.'

'Well, of course, he heard me calling you "Susan" in the

cable car.'

'No, I mean my other name. When we were buying the postcards, he said "You're Susan Osborne, aren't you?" How did he know that?'

Vicky thought rapidly. There must be some simple explanation, but that day Susan had not carried anything that visibly displayed her surname. No names had been exchanged at all. The man himself had remained nameless to them. How then did he know of Susan when she had only just arrived in this country? And why had he tried to get her to go down the cableway on her own? As she met Susan's inquiring gaze, Vicky experienced a small tremor of fear.

CHAPTER TWO

'THIS yellow dress would suit your little girl beautifully. She doesn't favour you at all, dear, does she? She's got a smile just like her daddy's.'

Vicky avoided Stephen's eye, while Susan suppressed her giggles. With surprising tact, Stephen had suggested to Gran that Susan's clothes and hairstyle were unsuited to the hot South African climate, and they were engaged upon an expedition to remedy this. Vicky had thought Stephen would be awkward in a children's dress shop, but he seemed to be able to adapt himself to the occasion.

She supposed that as a doctor he was used to talking to all kinds of people. Certainly the plump lady behind the counter seemed charmed by his smile and hurried to select the most attractive of her wares for Susan, shorts, striped sweaters, sundresses and brief pleated skirts in gay, clear colours. He left them in one of the big stores while they made a visit to the hairdressing salon, then rejoined them to buy doughnuts and lemonade in a grand celebration of Susan's emancipation from long dresses and hair.

'She looks charming,' he said in an aside to Vicky, as Susan went ahead of them. Her sleek dark boyish bob emphasized the pixie quality of her face.

'Why don't you tell her that?' asked Vicky.

But he shook his head.

'We mustn't spoil her. You mustn't think I approve of vanity.'

He glanced in what Vicky thought was a disapproving fashion at her pale orange lipstick which exactly matched the suit with its cream-coloured blouse that lent a glow to her golden skin. The few days spent almost exclusively out of doors had given her a slight becoming tan, but the faint blue shadows under her eyes betrayed her.

She was surprised when Stephen said abruptly,

'Did you sleep well, Miss Scott?'

'Oh, yes, quite well, thank you,' she stammered.

'You don't look as if you did,' he said sharply.

Vicky blushed under his scrutiny and hastily produced her

sunglasses from her bag.

'What a disconcerting man,' she thought. 'One moment he hardly seems to know you exist, then the next he notices something you would rather he didn't.'

'Only one more day in Cape Town,' she had thought thankfully when she awoke this morning. 'In a few days' time I'll be hundreds of miles away from David and he need never know I'm in South Africa.'

During the last trying days, at the back of her mind all the time had been the thought that in Cape Town she might accidentally meet him. Last night, in the dining-room of the hotel, her heart had thumped wildly because she caught a glimpse of a fair head, but in another moment she had realized that she was looking at somebody unknown to her. If in the street she saw the back view of someone similar in build to David she would think, 'There he is!' and her heart would be torn between relief and disappointment when she found herself mistaken.

Last night she had awakened at about three o'clock, a most depressing time to find oneself sleepless. Wild grief had swept over her again and she had wondered how she could go on. Had David really gone out of her life for ever? In the early hours of the morning, the thought that she would never see him again seemed hardly to be borne.

'Gran says we're going to Groot Constantia when we've finished our shopping,' said Susan, breaking into her thoughts. 'Where's that, Stephen?'

'It's not very far away, a short drive through beautiful forest high above Cape Town. There's a lovely great house, a typical seventeenth-century Dutch homestead. It was originally built by one of the Governors as a wine farm.'

'I'm looking forward to seeing it,' announced Gran, when they set out. 'Being a wee bit of an antique myself, I've got a fellow feeling for old things. I believe this place is beautifully furnished with old Cape furniture and pictures.'

Stephen had a car and soon they came out of the thick traffic and were climbing between tall pine trees. On their right, through the trees, were the purple slopes of the mountain and to the left, near at hand, the gardens of beautiful white houses overflowed with flowers and vivid blossoming shrubs, hollyhocks, dahlias, hibiscus and bougainvillea. Far below every now and again came a glimpse of hazy blue sea.

'How heavenly I would have thought all this if David had met me and we'd been planning to live here,' thought Vicky. 'Imagine living in a small white cottage on the slopes of a mountain, spending the day cultivating these strange lovely plants, baking and sewing and looking towards the city, knowing your love would be home by evening. That's all I would ever have wanted, not wealth or fame. But David was different. No, David would never have been contented with a small white cottage. He would want one of those mansions.'

And she looked at a white-pillared residence with green velvet lawns where a crowd of gaily dressed women were having tea under the trees. She looked at the tennis court and the blue kidney-shaped swimming pool.

'That's more the kind of house he would have liked,' she thought.

Soon they were driving through the avenue leading to the great house. On either side the young leaves of the vines showed green along the low rows of twisted branches and at the winery there was bustling activity.

'I didn't realize wine was still made here,' said Vicky.

'Och, yes,' said Gran. 'The tradition of wine-making is still carried on. I can tell you all about it. A lady at the hotel kindly gave me a guide book and I studied it a wee bit.'

'Isn't it the good Scots Gran we have to get us a free guide book,' scoffed Stephen.

'When he smiles, he looks a different person,' thought Vicky. 'Maybe it won't be so difficult after all.'

'Och, away with your teasing,' cried Gran, her eyes sparkling. 'Like it or not, I'm going to give you some information about this grand house.'

'Must you?' asked Stephen, pretending despair.

'Now hold your noise, laddie, and listen. The land was given to the Governor Simon van der Stel by the Dutch East India Company in recognition of his fine work at farming, for you ken he had a green thumb and had got the farmers going in this new land. The sweet dessert wines of Constantia soon became well-known even in Europe and it was the last thing Napoleon asked for as he lay dying at St. Helena.'

'What a morbid recommendation!' laughed Stephen.

The gaiety of his mood put them all in a good temper, and Vicky's spirits lifted as the white house came into view, serene and lovely at the end of its avenue of trees. The dazzling whitewashed building had gables at each end which followed the lines of the thatched roof, but the gable that gave importance to the whole house was the beautifully proportioned one directly in the middle above the front door.

Walking across the open paved stoep, they were admitted to a high cool hall, on either side of which were tall rooms furnished with old chests, tables, chairs and cupboards in mellow polished wood, and ornaments of old blue and white Oriental china. The house breathed the dignity of the seventeenth century, yet, as Gran informed them, it had been burned down in a disastrous fire in 1925. However, the walls remained and the building had been lovingly reassembled, an exact reproduction of the old one.

Gran was fascinated by the huge carved clothes presses made from stinkwood, the fourposter beds with acanthus carved posts, and Susan exclaimed with delight over a small child's cane-seated armchair and a swinging wooden cradle, exquisitely made, but Vicky loved the small fragile things that had miraculously survived the years, like the cracked Delft plaque in blue and orange with a sedate lady in period costume, seated with her fishing rod on a river's bank and accompanied by a hopeful cat.

While Stephen and Susan studied maps and deeds of sale in the Museum Room, Gran and Vicky exclaimed over the huge cool kitchen with its old gateleg table, the enormous open fireplace and all the intricate kitchen equipment so far removed from modern housekeeping, the mortars and pestles, the brown glaze spice jars, the teak waterbutt, the copper stew pans, the oak butter tub bound with shining brass, the huge copper kettles, the wooden brassbound buckets and the green Wedgwood plates with embossed vine leaf pattern.

After this, Gran declared that she needed her tea before she could go a step further.

'You're getting to be a real South African already, always needing your morning tea,' chaffed Stephen, but he led the way to the tables beneath the oaks and ordered the tea and apple pie with cream that was being served by a smiling coloured girl.

'How lovely the air is up here,' said Vicky.

'Yes,' said Stephen. 'It's because Constantia is cooled by

the sea breezes that its wine is so good. The vintage comes later than it does in the hotter vineyards and the wine of early autumn is a little superior to that made from grapes ripened in the full heat of summer.'

This morning Vicky felt she was content just to exist. The beautiful house with its atmosphere of tranquillity, the mellow golden light and the fine clarity of the air combined to give her a sense of well-being she had never experienced before. For the first time since she had arrived she felt, 'Perhaps one day I'll be happy again.'

'There are quite a few visitors here,' remarked Gran, looking round at the other tables with lively curiosity. 'I love to watch people and wonder where they all come from. Yon couple are from Germany, I can hear by their speech, and by her accent the girl in the bright trews hails from America without a doubt. But I canna tell whether that pair are English or South African. The man has an English look, with that fair hair.'

Vicky looked around, straight into the eyes of David Thackeray. He was sitting at a nearby table with a slim, sweet-faced girl, who was gazing at him as if for her no other person existed in the world. First David looked puzzled, then astonished. He spoke to the girl beside him and strode swiftly over to stand beside Vicky.

'Vicky, my dear, what are you doing here?'

She had risen in agitation and he seized both her hands in his, turning to the girl who had followed him from their table.

'What an amazing surprise!' he exclaimed. 'Vicky is an old friend of mine from England,' he explained to the girl. 'This is Eve Bowman, my fiancée.' Turning aside, he whispered, 'I must see you alone.'

Only Stephen who had also risen caught the softly spoken message and his face became blank as he comprehended the situation. The girl, Eve, gazed curiously at Vicky. The picture Vicky had conjured up of a fascinating, glamorous rival faded before the sight of this slight girl with fine wispy mouse-brown hair arranged in a rather unbecoming style, her one beauty the large hazel eyes that were once more fixed upon David as if she wished to comprehend his every change of expression.

'Och, Vicky, how nice for you to meet someone you know,'

32

said Mrs. Grant. 'Nae doot you'd like a wee bit of a crack together. Stephen, take me to see the wine cellar while these young people talk. I'm anxious to see it, because it's the old original one, it wasna burned down with the homestead.'

'We haven't seen it either. Let's all go,' declared Eve nervously.

She had obviously sensed the waves of emotion flowing between David and Vicky and wanted to avoid being alone with them.

'Very well, let's go,' said David abruptly. He shook his fair head as if dispelling some misty dream and they all made their way through the old house and into the courtyard where the beautiful pediment above the wine cellar flashed white in the brilliant sunshine.

'Isn't it a fine work of art?' asked Gran, enthusiastically. 'It was made by Anton Anreith in 1791 and it shows Ganymede and his swan. Those children throwing bunches of grapes at wild animals may have been done to show that leopards still came into the vineyards in those days. It says here he made it behind a screen and wouldn't let anyone see it until it was finished.'

Susan was the only one who displayed any interest. David, Eve, Vicky and Stephen received the information in stony silence. They proceeded to inspect the huge old vats in the whitewashed vaults. Gran and Susan made suitable exclamations of surprise and interest, but after the heat of the courtyard, the temperature of the cellar seemed almost arctic, and Vicky, emotionally disturbed almost beyond bearing, found it difficult to repress the shudders that threatened to betray her distress.

She purposely lagged behind the others and escaped into a small side room. Her eyes felt hot with unshed tears, but the rest of her body was ice cold. Leaning her throbbing head upon the wall, she breathed in the dark, desolate smell of whitewash. It was like being in a tomb.

'Vicky!' David's voice came from the passageway and in a moment he came into the little room. As he grasped her by the shoulders, she had to turn reluctantly to face him.

'Are you all right?'

'Yes, yes, of course.'

'Whatever are you doing in this country? Why didn't you let me know you were coming?'

R—K.O.H.—B

Vicky said the first thing that came into her head.

'I'm working for Dr. Nash. I've taken a post as governess to his niece.'

David looked puzzled and incredulous.

'Vicky, did you get my letter? You didn't come ... ?'

Vicky pulled herself from his grasp and gathered up the scattered remnants of her pride.

'Don't be afraid, David. I won't interfere with your engagement. My aunt died and I was offered the opportunity to travel. South Africa is a big country. I hardly thought I would meet you so soon.'

'I don't understand. How did you meet these people? Are you interested in this Dr. Nash?'

Vicky suddenly saw a way out of her dilemma.

'Yes, yes, I am.' She laughed rather hysterically.

'But up to a few weeks ago, you were writing loving letters to me!'

'So were you to me, David. But, you see, my ideas of romantic love have changed too.'

'I would never have believed it. He isn't your type at all.'

'David!'

Eve's sweet shrill voice echoed through the vaults.

'I must go now. But we must talk again. Meet me this evening. Where are you staying ... Yes, I know the place. I'll wait with the car at the end of the road. Meet me at eight.'

'No, David, it's impossible.'

'You used to be fond of me. What's a meeting between old friends? We've got to talk some more.'

'David!'

Eve's voice sounded only a few yards away.

'I'll try to get away,' Vicky promised.

Susan had gone to bed without protest, tired out by all the day's activity. At dinner when Vicky mentioned she might go out for a while, Mrs. Grant patted her hand approvingly.

'Of course, child, there must be people you want to say good-bye to. Go, by all means. I wouldn't be too late, though, my dear. We've got a long day's travelling tomorrow.'

'No, I won't, Mrs. Grant,' said Vicky, feeling guilty under Gran's affectionate blue eyes and her crinkling smile. Since the meeting with David, Stephen had withdrawn again and

34

she found herself avoiding his frosty glance. She was wearing a light silk dress in a pattern of pastel flowers, and now she slipped on a fluffy cream coat, lightweight but warm enough to protect her against the cool evening breeze. The garnet ear-rings and pendant in antique gold setting, which she had inherited from her aunt, emphasized the glowing apricot of her sun-touched skin and the fairness of her hair. She had not been able to resist drawing this up into the sophisticated French knot style that she knew David preferred.

David had drawn up his car close under the shade of the trees at the end of the road. She had imagined he would have an old mini car and was surprised to see he was driving a sleek Alfa Romeo, with silver bodywork and red upholstery.

'David, what a beautiful car!'

'Yes,' he said. 'Just the kind I've always wanted.'

She thrust aside the thought that in his letters he had constantly bemoaned the fact that he could not yet afford to marry. That had nothing to do with her any more. He was engaged to someone else, someone whose parents' influence would lead him along the paths he wished to take.

There was not much opportunity for conversation. The theatre-going crowds were hurrying towards the city and David had to concentrate on his driving as the high-powered car strained under his hands like an elegant racehorse slowed down to a walking pace. They passed Sea Point where hotels and huge blocks of flats like dazzling pigeon lofts towered above the Atlantic Ocean, and where in the balmy night even at this hour people dived into the enormous swimming pool.

'Where are we going?' asked Vicky.

'To a little place I know, a quiet place where we'll be undisturbed.'

'David, I don't want ...'

'We'll talk later, Vicky. Just concentrate on the view and I'll attend to the driving.'

They swept along the Marine Drive that seemed more like the French Riviera than a place in Africa. On one side it hugged the base of the mountain range and on the other far below the dark ocean creamed and churned in small bays. Houses perched like goats upon every ledge of rock, their curtains open to the breeze, windows gay with lights. But however enchanting the drive was, Vicky was relieved when they drew up at a small restaurant.

When they were settled at a candlelit table in the corner of the quiet dining-room, David concentrated his gaze upon Vicky until she was forced to turn away, unaware that a lovely flush of colour heightened her radiant appeal.

'I must have been mad,' David murmured as if to himself.

'Oh, David!' Unshed tears gathered in Vicky's brown eyes. She felt she could not reproach him, for if she did she would break down altogether.

'I'd forgotten, my dear, how lovely you are. What a fool I've been!'

In the turmoil of emotion sweeping across her mind, Vicky could not think clearly. She only knew that David, her David, was sitting across the table from her. She had only to reach out in order to touch his hand. Nothing else mattered now.

A dark-skinned waiter brought them Crayfish Thermidor, small Cape lobsters served in their shells in a creamy sauce, and this was followed by Pêche Flambée, the chef taking a proud delight in cooking the flaming dessert beside the table. The delicious food and the chilled, slightly sparkling white wine which accompanied it lulled Vicky into a sense of security. She was content to be charmed by David as she had so often been charmed before. She cast aside all thought of his engagement. Almost she felt as if she had dreamed the last sad days.

It was only when they were sitting upon the patio, drinking coffee and sipping a delicious liqueur tasting of tangerines, that David became more serious.

'Dearest Vicky, it's lovely seeing you again. I must have been mad to write that letter. But now we're reunited we must plan our lives again. You aren't serious about going on with that crazy job, are you, my sweet?'

'I – I don't know, David. I must find some kind of work. What else would you suggest?'

'Quite frankly I think it's crazy for a girl as lovely as you to bury herself at a hospital in the wilds with an old woman and a child and a fanatical doctor. Sorry, Vicky dear, I forgot you said you were interested in him.'

Vicky bitterly regretted the lie forced upon her by pride, but she let it rest there.

'What do you think I should do?'

'You could easily get work in Cape Town. With your face

and figure, you could get a modelling job quite easily. Then we could continue to see each other.'

'But, David,' said Vicky, for the first time experiencing a small niggling doubt, 'what about Eve?'

David smiled, but there was no kindness in it.

'Surely you could see for yourself when you met. Eve's easy. She adores me. She'll do anything for me. She'll never object to our friendship.'

'Do you mean you would remain engaged to her?' Vicky tried to remain calm, but her voice trembled.

'Sure, why not? For the time being at any rate. Look, Vicky, I have to be frank with you. In any profession you have to grab opportunities if you want to get on. I work for Eve's father. If he thinks I'm going to marry Eve, I'll get sure promotion. I have talent, but with a bit of influence and that extra push there'll be no stopping me. I could never marry on a shoestring. I'm not that kind. You couldn't do without money either. Look at you. You need lovely clothes to enhance your beauty. I'm too involved with Eve's father now to pull out. It's too difficult. Why, he even bought that car for me as an advance wedding present to us both. But this needn't really make any difference to us, my sweetheart. It's only for a while. I'll string Eve and her father along until I become well known. Then I can leave that firm and get a good job with someone else.'

'I understand now,' said Vicky. Her hands and feet were like ice.

'I knew you would see reason, sweetie. Why are you shivering? Too cold out here for you? Let's dance, shall we?'

Vicky thought anything would be better than sitting here in this wretched state of mind. She rose and they joined the few couples on the small dance floor. It was agonizing to be in his arms again and know what she now knew, that David was utterly selfish and had become engaged to someone else merely to promote his career. She thought she could have forgiven him if he had genuinely fallen in love with Eve, but this coldblooded planning of their lives revolted and dismayed her.

On the darkened dance floor, David held her closely, his hands caressing her, his mouth seeking hers.

'What's the matter, sweetheart,' he asked when she turned her face away. 'Too crowded here for you? It would be better if we were alone, I agree. Let's go.'

They drove back along the winding road between sea and mountain.

'All those lights,' thought Vicky, 'and every one lights a room where people are happy or sad, in love or merely existing.'

She thought of the happy anticipation with which she had looked forward to coming to South Africa. All over now. She would never marry David at the expense of that gentle girl's happiness.

'Why are you so quiet, my lovely?' asked David. He put an arm around her and drew her close as he was driving.

'No, David, it's dangerous.' She quickly withdrew from the circle of his embrace.

'Don't you trust me?'

He was wearing that reckless smile which had often half-scared, half delighted her in happier days. They were on the de Waal Drive high above the city. Ships like illuminated toys rested in the harbour far below and black spaces enclosed in glittering lights defined the limits of the water.

Vicky was sure David was exceeding the speed limit, but whereas normally she would have been terrified, she felt benumbed by the events of the last few days, culminating in David's conversation in the quiet restaurant. Lines of light swept towards them from approaching cars and her fair hair, loosened from its precise knot, streamed out in the warm wind.

'What a sport you are, Vicky!' David shouted, as the speedometer needle swayed around the highest numbers. 'Eve can't stand my driving like this. I can see we'll have lots of fun together. You must stay in Cape Town.'

With a shriek of brakes the car swept into the drive of the hotel, narrowly missing the uniformed guard who was watching the parked cars. The throbbing engine ceased and to Vicky it seemed as if the resulting stillness should never be interrupted. She leaned wearily towards the door, fumbling with the catch, but David had already slid across the seat and was now holding her in an urgent embrace.

'You have decided to stay, haven't you, darling? You wouldn't let me down, would you? We suit each other so well, and Eve need never know.'

For a moment the old magic was there. Vicky found herself responding to the touch of his hands and the warmth of his lips. Instinctively she relaxed in his embrace – and then reality intruded. How *could* he? This was their first meeting since he had so casually discarded her for the girl who was now his fiancée, and yet he expected Vicky to behave as if nothing had changed. Indignation rose in her and she wrenched away from him.

David's arms dropped away from her and he demanded crossly, 'Why the sudden change of heart, my sweet? Why else did you come here with me?'

'I didn't . . .'

'Oh, come off it, Vicky. That's a lot of nonsense about this job of yours. I can't see quite where Dr. Nash fits into the picture, but I'm sure you really came to meet me. It's quite plain. Well, that suits me. Now I've seen you again, I'm not going to let you go so easily.'

Vicky's hand had been fumbling at the car door and now she found the catch, opened it, and tore herself free. The sudden move took David by surprise and it was a few seconds before he followed her. Meanwhile she was running towards the open door of the hotel foyer, apparently deserted at this late hour. But a few yards from the door David caught up with her. He blocked her way, grasping her by the waist and forcing her to face him.

'What's wrong, Vicky?' he asked, genuinely puzzled. 'What have I done to offend you?'

Vicky could not restrain her tears.

'Oh, David, David, just leave me alone. You're engaged to be married. I have no further claim on you. I'm going to take this job. I wouldn't dream of staying in Cape Town now. Maybe Dr. Nash is peculiar and a fanatic, but at least he'll help me to get away from you!'

'I think you'd better go, Mr. Thackeray. You seem to be disturbing my employee,' said a voice from the shadows. Stephen was standing in the driveway, a pipe clutched in his hand.

'And what right have you to interfere between myself and my . . .' David hesitated.

'Your what? Even in Africa, it isn't customary to have more than one fiancée, surely, Mr. Thackeray?'

David looked annoyed and sulky.

'I won't stay to argue. I'll phone you tomorrow, Vicky.'

'You'll have to do so rather early, I'm afraid. We leave at six in the morning,' said Stephen.

'Don't go, Vicky. Stay with me. Remember I still love you,' David pleaded, ignoring Stephen. He had his appealing little boy look and his blue eyes gazed directly at her.

'I must, David. Let's just forget this evening ever happened. Let's only remember the happy times.'

'There'll be more of them, you'll see. I'm not letting a little country doctor take my girl.'

Stephen stepped towards him, but with a last baleful look at him, David turned on his heel and strode away. The engine sprang into noisy life and the silver car shot like a thunderbolt down the drive and along the deserted street.

'Not a very pretty scene, Miss Scott,' Stephen commented grimly. 'I must confess I'm astonished that you should have decided to meet this young man this evening, but doubtless you know your own business best.'

Vicky shook her head sadly.

'Please, Dr. Nash, I can't stand any more. Let me go in.'

'Before you go, Miss Scott, I feel I must tell you that a young woman of your temperament is likely to find the hospital extremely quiet. There's very little gaiety.'

'I don't need gaiety, Dr. Nash, I assure you.'

'Sound carries well in this clear air. Apparently you've already decided that I'm peculiar and a fanatic. I should hardly have thought you would like to entrust yourself to such a strange character in the wilds of Pondoland.'

For a moment Vicky was tempted to give up before she had even begun, but the thought of Susan and Gran restrained her.

'Gran seems to have taken a fancy to you,' said Stephen, as if reading her thoughts. 'I wouldn't like to upset her. She's looking forward to your company at the hospital. I hope she won't be disappointed.'

CHAPTER THREE

'I DON'T like it here much, Vicky. Will there be lights inside the caves?'

'Yes, I believe it's very well lit up. It's just that our eyes aren't used to the half light. We'll soon be able to see properly.'

Vicky and Susan were putting on their slacks and sweaters in the changing rooms of the Cango Caves, which was on the route they were taking through the Western Cape. It seemed very strange to see a sign saying 'Cloakroom' and find yourself in a vast dimly lit cave equipped with washbasins and mirrors. Gran had decided the journey through the caves might prove too arduous for her, but Stephen was taking Vicky and Susan in a guided party.

'You will hold my hand, won't you, Vicky? It looks awfully spooky,' said Susan as they emerged from this troglodyte's dressing-room and joined Stephen.

'We're going through with a guide and a crowd of people, Susan,' said Stephen, somewhat impatiently. 'There isn't the slightest reason to be scared. It's well illuminated now,' he added. 'I hear it's so well lit, we'll feel as if we're in the middle of Piccadilly Circus. Think of the early days when they first started exploring here. They must have done it with candles and lamps.'

'They must have been very brave,' said Vicky. She held the little girl's hand firmly as they joined the crowd following the guide. It might be well lit, but she wasn't taking any chances on Susan's being frightened. There was something very weird about the idea of vast caverns existing underneath the ground.

The crowd of tourists straggled down a long gently sloping flight of steps. Nothing in the rather gloomy monotonous walk downwards prepared them for the sight that they came upon as the stairs ended. They were in a huge hall, the walls of which were almost completely hidden by magnificent stalactites and stalagmites in glittering curious shapes.

The flat accents of the guide described the different formations by the names people's imaginations had given to them through the years. Susan was charmed to trace the resemblance to a camel surmounted by a man in flowing robes with both hands raised above his head. Then there was the magnificent system of stalagmites and stalactites that had joined in columns against one of the walls to resemble a fantastic organ.

Vicky closed her ears to the facetious comments of the guide. She did not care what the shapes resembled. She was content to admire the beauty of these creamy forms of glittering crystal that had been slowly, secretly growing in their dark home for hundreds upon hundreds of years. Over the curving roof beautiful folds of grey limestone flowed like the waves of the sea.

'Who was van Zyl?' she asked Stephen, catching his last words as he told Susan that this was 'Van Zyl's Hall'.

He grinned teasingly. 'The guide has just told us he was the man who discovered the caves. He found them while hunting a buck.'

In this vast cavern, surrounded as she was by strangers, Vicky felt a strange kind of security with Stephen by her side. Since leaving Cape Town he had been courteous and kind and some of the warmth he showed towards Gran seemed somehow to brush off upon Vicky. She still felt he could be less strict with Susan, but she supposed it was difficult for a man of Stephen's temperament to understand the feelings of a small girl.

She had tried hard to bury the memory of that last night in Cape Town and she supposed, now she was travelling with them towards the hospital, that Stephen had decided to forget his disapproval, or at any rate he did not voice it any more. During the last days she had put aside the thought of David and had determined to enjoy her first sight of this beautiful country.

The crowd of tourists surged around her and Susan, and she was glad when Stephen took her arm to steady her. Susan was not clinging to her quite so tightly now. She had forgotten her nervousness and was utterly absorbed in the strange sights unfolding before them, Botha's Hall with its splendid throne room, and its Madonna and child, touchingly surrounded by stalagmites that one could imagine were worshipping figures.

The Rainbow Room with its varied coloured lighting was

greeted with murmurs of admiration and then they had to cross a narrow bridge above a deeper cavern. Vicky found herself being jostled on both sides and found it difficult to protect Susan in the crowd. She looked around for Stephen, but found she had become separated from him. The flat-voiced guide announced that they had now come to the Bridal Chamber and pointed out the old-fashioned fourposter bed formed from grouped stalactites, extracting the last ounce of mirth from the crowd with his double-edged comments.

Tiring of the commentary and the sense of being hemmed in by the crowd, Vicky edged her way to the back and with Susan walked on into the Fairy Palace, which got its name, she supposed, from the myriad tiny crystal formations in the cave. A few other people had also wandered on away from the main party, so she was not alone and they were not left in peace for long. In a few minutes the crowd surged through the sparkling cave.

Trying to keep ahead of them, Vicky and Susan came to a cave that was smaller than the rest. For the first time while exploring the place, Vicky felt a hint of claustrophobia. The other caves had been spacious, but this one was dark and had large curtain-like formations hanging from its roof.

'I don't like this cave,' said Susan. 'It feels ghostly.'

'We'll be out soon,' Vicky reassured her.

'Where's Stephen?' asked Susan anxiously.

Vicky looked around, but the crowd of people spilling out from the other cavern seemed to be vague shapes, unrecognizable in the gloom.

'Now I'm going to show you something of real interest to you travellers,' said the guide. 'African sunset!' he announced. Suddenly the lights were extinguished and then a red glow gradually appeared, bathing the small cave in lurid light.

'I don't like it,' whimpered Susan. 'It looks as if it's on fire. Where's Stephen?'

'Sh!' said Vicky. 'We'll go back as soon as this is over.'

She disliked intensely the sense of being in a small gloomy cave surrounded by people who were only vague presences.

'Darkest Africa!' announced the guide, in sepulchral tones.

The cave was drowned in Stygian darkness and through the sudden night came a sound, primaeval and evocative, the

43

mysterious, resonant thunder of deep-toned drums. In the darkness, the tension became almost unbearable. Somebody laughed hysterically. Then all at once Vicky felt someone thrust her aside, and, as she lost her grip on Susan's hand, she heard a shrill scream coming from the terrified child.

'Turn the lights on, please,' she implored, but the guide, used to a little hysteria at this stage, was determined not to lose his dramatic moment. He continued to strike the 'curtain' and the weird, drumlike reverberation went on. Then: 'Africa awakes!' he announced, and a pink light heralded an artificial dawn.

'Susan!' Vicky cried, almost beside herself with fear. 'Where are you?' She searched frantically around the crowd. There were few children and a small girl should have been easy to find, but minutes passed like hours before she caught sight of Stephen holding a weeping Susan.

'I have her,' he said. 'But how did she come to be alone? I thought you were with her.'

Susan clung to Vicky, sobbing.

'Someone tried to take me away from you. Someone got hold of my hand and said "Come with me . . . hurry!"'

Stephen shook his head.

'My girlie, you imagine things. Who would want to take you away? Specially in a place like this. You shouldn't have left Miss Scott.' He turned to Vicky. 'We'd better go back. I didn't realize how nervous she was.'

'But what was she doing when you found her?' asked Vicky. 'Was she alone?'

'No, not exactly. One or two people were trying to calm her. They said she was alone when the lights went up. They thought the darkness had scared her.'

'Someone did try to take me, Vicky. It's true,' Susan persisted.

Vicky was puzzled. Susan had a vivid imagintion and the darkness would certainly have frightened her. Someone might have held her to reassure her when she screamed and let her go when the lights were restored. But then why was she so far away from Vicky when she was found? Certainly the Drum Room had been terrifying even to the grown-ups. It would be better to go back now before Susan became more frightened.

Later that afternoon, they visited an ostrich farm and the

sight of the ludicrous birds and the fluffy large-eyed chicks made Susan forget her frightening experience. Next day she was excited because Stephen had told her they were to stay at an inn in the heart of a forest.

'It will be like *Snow White,* won't it, Vicky?' she said, her small eager face alight with interest.

Because Gran was not used to long car journeys, they were travelling slowly along what is known as the Garden Route from Cape Town to the eastern part of the Cape Province. They had left behind the vineyards and fruit orchards of the Western Cape and were now in a country of tall forests and bubbling peat brown streams. But ever present beyond the forests were the high misty blue mountains.

'This reminds me a wee bit of Scotland,' said Gran, 'but on a larger scale, ye ken, and it hasna got Scotland's lakes.'

'Ah, I knew you'd find something lacking,' said Stephen, laughing at her. 'But I'm taking you to see an engineering feat that's as good as any in Scotland, you'll see.'

Soon they drew up beside a long bridge and Stephen indicated they should walk across it on foot.

'What's so wonderful about this?' asked Gran, casting a longing glance at the tea-room to the left. 'Can't we have tea first, Stephen? We'll see what those cream scones are like that they advertise in such big letters.'

'Sightseeing first, tea next,' said Stephen, adamantly.

Vicky gasped as she looked over the railing of the bridge. Hundreds of feet below, the Storms River picked its way through a deep rocky gorge. The rugged chasm with its precipitous grandeur of rocks and trees seemed in startling contrast to the modern main road that passed over the scene.

Vicky turned to look for Susan and found that Stephen had picked her up and was holding her as she leaned over the railing gazing into the gorge below. Her face was half excited, half terror-stricken. Vicky was overwhelmed by the memory of her feelings when she had missed Susan in the Drum Room. Without thinking she rushed towards them, saying, 'Please, Dr. Nash, put her down. It looks so dangerous. I'm so scared she might fall.'

Stephen looked surprised, but gently replaced Susan on the ground saying. 'You sound a little overwrought, Miss Scott.'

'These long journeys are very tiring,' said Gran, who had

heard the interchange and was looking a bit puzzled. 'We all need our tea. Susan, help your old gran back across the bridge.'

She took Susan's hand and they went on ahead.

Vicky found herself alone with Stephen. He was frowning and his dark brows seemed to hide the shining intelligence of his grey eyes and make him look gloomy and withdrawn.

'Miss Scott,' he said, 'you've probably gathered by now that Susan is an exceptionally timid, highly strung child. You saw what happened yesterday at the caves, when a particular set of circumstances played on her vivid imagination. I'm trying to remedy this fault in her character and though, naturally, I want you to care for her well, it won't help it you're over-cautious about her.'

'I'm either neglectful or overcautious,' thought Vicky, in despair. 'I always seem to be in the wrong as far as he's concerned.'

'Susan is a very lovable little girl,' she said. 'I've become very fond of her already. Any woman would be terrified to see a child held over such a deep gorge. An accident could happen so easily.'

'Oh, come, Miss Scott, surely you can trust me to look after Susan. Believe me, I'm only considering her welfare when I ask you to be strong-minded with her.'

'If you expect me to play the stern governess, you'll be disappointed. Susan is a gentle little girl. You can't make a tough cabbage out of a harebell.'

'But if she develops in the way she seems to be going, she'll have a very difficult future. I think I mentioned once before that by a rather indeterminate will she has inherited her grandfather's assets. The extent of these is still to be investigated, but if it should prove that she is to be rich, she will have a great deal of responsibility and will need a strong character. I want to try to make her able to resist life, to be able to stand up to hurt and disappointment.'

'That seems rather a gloomy way to look at a young girl's future,' Vicky protested.

'I hadn't noticed before,' she thought, 'that his mouth is sensitive like Susan's.'

'Surely you should know from your own experience that most people have to face grief, if not in tragedy then in disillusion with life or disenchantment with a loved one.'

Vicky felt deeply troubled by Stephen's speech. There was

46

a wretchedness in the set of his mouth that seemed to betray grief deeply hidden. It was not all caused by concern for Susan. Hard as was her own disappointment in David, she had an inherent resilience of spirit which forbade bitterness. In her case, disillusion with the loved one had not shattered her deep belief in the validity of romantic love. Impulsively she put out her hand and took his.

'Believe me, Dr. Nash, I want nothing but good for Susan. But if you bring her up to expect disillusion, you'll be doing more damage to her spirit than if she faced life too timidly.'

He held the hand she had placed in his and for a few moments some strangely heightened emotion seemed to flow between them. He looked young, troubled, defenceless, his grey eyes puzzled, the dark lock of hair falling over his forehead. Vicky felt a warm surge of something that seemed almost affection.

'Why, I could like him,' she thought. 'He isn't really cold or bad-tempered.'

Then he laughed as if ashamed to show emotion and the slender bond of sympathy was shattered. He dropped her hand and strode quickly towards the tea-room, leaving Vicky to follow, feeling rather shaken by the argument but more convinced than ever that she was right in her ideas of bringing up Susan.

When they had prised Gran away from the tea-table, Stephen drove back to where a small motor road led them to the inn in the forest. The buildings were of the chalet type set around a beautiful garden of lawns and flowering shrubs. Susan was delighted to find that she and Vicky were to share a small cottage, furnished with wardrobe, beds and dressing-table made from the indigenous woods. The resinous smell of the forest seemed to linger in the room and Vicky was not sure whether it came from the open window or from the new unpolished wood of the furniture, but it had a tranquillizing effect upon her troubled mind and she felt more cheerful as she went to see if she could help Gran.

'Stephen says he'll take Susan for a walk in the forest to see the Big Tree. We'll bide here a while in this bonny garden. Do you think one of yon gentlemen would bring us tea, Vicky?' asked Gran, indicating a white-coated waiter.

Vicky hurried off to see that Susan was adequately equipped for a walk in the forest. Stephen watched rather disapprovingly as Vicky insisted on Susan's wearing heavier shoes and carrying a sweater. Obviously he thought she was making too much fuss. Susan was wild with excitement at the idea of being taken to the Big Tree and behaved rather badly, shrugging off Vicky's efforts to help her until called to order by a stern word from Stephen.

After all this, Vicky was quite relieved to find herself sitting sipping tea in a deck chair in the shade of a blossoming tree and admiring the arum lilies that grew thickly around the stream running through the garden.

'I remember when my daughter first came to Africa,' said Gran, 'that was one of the first things that impressed her. She wrote to tell me about the fields of arum lilies, growing like weeds. So astonishing, when at home we only see them at weddings and funerals.'

'Was that Dr. Nash's mother?' asked Vicky.

'Och, yes, my puir Jeannie. She was the gentlest creature you ever did meet and yet whiles she could have a will of iron. It was like that when she fell in love with Andrew. He was fifteen years older than she, stern and dour, but a handsome man enough to turn the head of any girl. Dark – Stephen favours him. She was only eighteen at the time and she knew he was determined to go as a missionary to Central Africa, but she didna care. Indeed it made her think of him like a god. Whiles I thought he should never have married. He was dedicated, almost fanatical, nae what you could call a family man, and my puir Jeannie was always a wee bit delicate.'

'Did she go with him?' asked Vicky.

'There was nae stopping her. She never said much, but it was a hard life for such as she. "I love him, Mother," she said, the last time she spoke to me. "I've always loved him all my life. It's all been worthwhile, all of it." But I knew it near broke her heart to have to part with her bairns. She lost her first babies in those unhealthy tropical jungles so she had to send Stephen and little Jean home when they were very young. Not long afterwards she died having another babe and the wee thing died too. Whiles I think it was her heart was broken. The bairns were puir pale wee creatures when they came to Scotland and Andrew insisted they should be brought up by his sister and brother-in-law. I was allowed no part in it.'

'That must have saddened your daughter before she died.'

48

'If it worried her she never told me,' said Gran. 'She was completely loyal. She thought everything Andrew ordered was right. And at the time my husband was ill so it seemed for the best, but the children suffered as much as she did from the parting, for this sister was flint-hard. She brought them up well according to her lights, but it was a life without love for both of them. It's had a lasting effect on them both. Susan's mother ran away with the first handsome man who offered her love and he turned out to be irresponsible and a ne'er-do-well who left her when Susan was born, and Stephen . . .' She sighed. 'Ah well, I'm gey fond of Stephen. He has his faults, but he's a good lad. I've tried to make up to him for that barren childhood, but there's not a lot an old woman like me can do, is there?'

'I think you've done a great deal,' Vicky protested, once more touched and impressed by the old lady's sturdy spirit. 'You've done a great deal in caring for Susan and giving up your home and joining Stephen here.'

'I'm afraid he's not quite the right kind of person to bring up a little girl like Susan. That's why I'm so pleased we found you, my dear. I hope you will stay with us for a long time.'

She gazed with undisguised affection at Vicky and, looking at those trusting blue eyes, Vicky's determination to succeed in her new life was renewed once more. She felt she must try to be patient with Stephen's irascible temperament since Gran had explained the circumstances of his upbringing.

But her new resolutions were somewhat short-lived when some time later Susan came running across the lawn, happy, vivacious and very pleased with herself.

'We walked all the way to the Big Tree. It was miles and miles, wasn't it, Stephen?'

'One mile, Susan. You mustn't exaggerate.'

Susan looked crestfallen, then she brightened.

'But I walked very well, didn't I, Stephen? You never thought I'd be able to walk so far, did you?'

Vicky sensed she was painfully anxious for his praise and silently willed Stephen to say a kind word, but all he said was, 'If I had thought you couldn't walk so far, Susan, I would never have taken you.'

'Stephen Nash, sometimes I get close to hating you,' thought Vicky, all her sympathetic thoughts swallowed up in a wave of hostility as she looked at Susan's sad expression.

' "We had to take root and grow, or die where we stood."
That's what one of the settlers said, speaking of their first
days in the Eastern Cape.'

Stephen was anxious that Gran and Susan should grow to
like this country and was constantly thinking of stories to
tell them about their new surroundings. At these times he
was charming, intelligent, informative, and Vicky found she
could forget his faults. Now, in Port Elizabeth, they had been
admiring the Campanile, erected to the memory of the 1820
Settlers, and from there had made their way to the obelisk on
a grass lawn high above the sea.

As Stephen spoke, in Vicky's imagination, the busy port
vanished, to be replaced by a turbulent bay surrounded by
bleak sandhills and a barren hinterland. She saw the little
sailing ships with their cargo of human beings, brave and
hopeful, yet somewhat scared by the rugged conditions they
must face in this strange wild land.

'How brave people were then,' she mused. 'Once here there
could be no turning back.'

Her own doubts and hesitations paled into insignificance
before the indomitable courage of the folk who lived more
than a hundred years ago.

'Nae doot a few of them were Scots,' said Gran.

'Of course,' said Stephen, twinkling. 'Thomas Pringle,
South Africa's first poet, was Scots.'

'A poet?' exclaimed Gran, somewhat taken aback.

'And a brave man,' Stephen assured her. 'A man who
valued freedom above all else.'

'What's this queer memorial here?' asked Susan, examin-
ing the rough stone pyramid near at hand.

'Sir Rufane Donkin, the Governor, who was here to help
the settlers, had it erected to the memory of his wife. It's a
strange thing that Port Elizabeth is called after a woman who
never even saw this country. She died in India in 1818.'

Vicky went to read the inscription.

'To the memory of one of the most perfect of human beings, who has given her name to the town below,' she read.
'Erected by a husband whose heart is still wrung by undim-
inished grief.'

Quick tears sprang to her eyes as she stood on the windy
hill, reading this testimony of a love that survived death.
Susan took her hand and squeezed it anxiously.

'What is it, Vicky? You look so sad. You have tears in your eyes.'

'It's the wind,' she assured the child, trying to avoid Stephen's curious gaze. Then, repenting of her fib, she declared, 'No, not really, Susan. I was touched by these words. It seems so tragic to think of this poor man still breaking his heart at the loss of his wife. If he felt like that, they must have had so much happiness, even if it was only for a little while.'

'Perhaps they hadn't had time to tire of each other,' said Stephen brusquely. 'Doubtless that would have come later.'

'No, no,' protested Vicky. 'Don't spoil it for me.'

He gave her a quizzical look.

'What a strangely romantic young woman you are at times, Miss Scott. I find you an odd mixture.'

'Indeed and she's not,' Gran asserted stoutly. 'Every young woman has a right to expect romance in life. It's only dour bachelors like yourself, Stephen, who canna see what's good for them. And now what about going to see these dolphins I've heard so much about? Even they pine for romance, I'm told. The lady at the hotel said they are looking for a husband for Haig.'

'Haig's a funny name for a girl dolphin,' said Susan. 'What's the other one called?'

'Lady Dimple,' said Gran.

'That's better,' Susan approved.

They drove along the wide road beside the beach-front. There was no mistaking their place of destination for a huge skeleton of a whale towered above the Oceanarium, visible from all sides. In the Museum, Susan quailed at the huge models of prehistoric reptiles and clung to Vicky's hand, but once seated in the front row beside the dolphin tank, eating an iced lolly, she quickly cheered up and waited patiently for the performance to begin, gazing with bright-eyed interest at the other children, but resisting any attempts at communication when one of them approached her.

'What a pity she will be so isolated at the hospital,' thought Vicky. 'She needs to get to know other children. It's not good for her to be with grown-ups all the time.'

In a little while they were all lost in the enchanted world of the dolphins. These, as soon as their trainer appeared, were transformed as if by magic from lazily swimming mammals into performers as brilliant as ballet dancers. They swam eagerly to the trainer's platform, nuzzling against him, anxious to be the favoured one.

The clownlike grin which is a permanent part of a dolphin's appearance gave them enormous appeal because it made them look so happy. Their strong sleek bodies hurtled streamlined through the air as they jumped through hoops or quivered vertically in mid-air, catching fish with split-second timing.

The crowd, by turn thrilled and amused at the acrobatic tricks, gasped then laughed as Haig obligingly carried a shopping basket in her flipper or balanced a pair of sunglasses on her nose. At last it was over. Haig, instructed by her trainer, gobbled a last titbit of fish and waved farewell to the crowd with one flipper out of the water, then they were sea creatures again absorbed in their own swimming, the cheers of the crowd forgotten for a while.

'Oh, Vicky, wasn't that beautiful!' said Susan, her eyes wide and shining.

'Yes, it was one of the most charming things I've ever seen,' Vicky agreed.

They were walking ahead of Stephen who had stayed to protect Gran from the hustling crowd.

'Did you see that man sitting quite near to us? I was going to tell you, and then the dolphin came and I forgot.'

'What man?' asked Vicky, not concentrating very much on Susan's chatter because she was still thinking of the dolphins.

'The man who knew my name – the one we met on Table Mountain,' said Susan.

A small cold shocked feeling spread itself inside Vicky. Then she laughed disbelievingly.'

'Oh, Sue, I don't think it could have been the same man. We're so far away from Cape Town now.'

'Yes, it was. It was the same man. He was looking at me too. Every time I looked up from the dolphins he was staring at me across the water.'

'Susan darling, I do think you've imagined this. There were so many people there. Whoever it was could have been looking at anyone.'

'He was looking at me,' said Susan stubbornly.

Vicky looked around. The crowd was dispersing now. There was no one who looked in the least like the stranger on the mountain.

'It's just Susan's vivid imagination,' she thought. But she felt puzzled and again there came that faint cold thrill of fear.

'Almost home,' said Stephen, when they booked in at the hotel on the beach-front at East London, the following day.

'I'll be glad to have done with all this travelling,' said Gran. 'Though I must say, Stephen, we've seen an awfu' big piece of Africa.'

'You're only just coming to the interesting part – at least it's the part I like best,' said Stephen.

'Then I'll like it too,' said Susan, sliding her hand into his.

'I hope so Susan. Don't forget you and Miss Scott will have to start work. It's been all holiday up to now.'

'I'll love school work with Vicky, I know. She's promised to take me to the aquarium across the road to learn about fishes and crabs. May she take me now, Stephen?'

'Yes, go, by all means. I have a few phone calls to make.'

They spent an hour contemplating the weird creatures in the tanks, octopi, small squid, rays and smaller things like hermit crabs and various other crustaceans. The hermit crabs scuttled around the bottom of the tanks, mistrustfully peering out from their purloined homes made of exotic convoluted shells.

Fiddler crabs waved one enormous red claw while rubbing the smallest one against it as if playing a violin. Sea anemone spread out exotically coloured fronds, while large starfish clung to the rocks in this fascinating underwater world.

'Look, here's some walking fish,' said Susan. There was a tank full of gurnards, a fish equipped with such stiff fins that it is able to use them for walking under water. They looked rather ugly, with brindled brown bodies and tadpole-shaped heads, but when they swam they were miraculously transformed into creatures of breathtaking beauty, for their fins were lime green and navy with white spots and a brilliant cobalt blue edging so that they looked like a flock of gorgeous butterflies.

But the sea-horses were the things that fascinated Vicky and Susan most. They spent a long time gazing at these odd, magical little creatures which propelled themselves from one weed to another with much fluttering of tiny fins and curling of their prehensile tails. They looked like finely wrought knights from a carved chess set, and Susan was charmed with

53

them.

Afterwards Vicky walked with Susan along the promenade, admiring the clean-cut sweep of the coastline, blue water and blue sea sweeping away to sand-dunes on the left, but to the right the small harbour with its busy tugs and its long breakwater looking like a scene from some Dutch painting.

When at last they turned, laughing and windswept, into the foyer of the hotel, Vicky was surprised to see that Stephen and Gran, who were sitting having tea, were not alone. Before they could escape to tidy their hair, Stephen called to them and Vicky reluctantly propelled Susan to the table.

The woman who sat next to Stephen on the settee was dark and graceful. Vicky's first impression of her was one of smoothness, dark well-groomed hair, parted above the oval face and drawn back in a classical knot on the slender neck, skin like the creamy heart of a magnolia, slender hands tipped with rosy mother of pearl, simple, dear expensive suit that made all the other women in the lounge appear overdressed.

Vicky, dressed in the striped cotton shift she had worn to the aquarium and with her hair tangled by the wind, felt naïve and ill at ease as the curious emerald eyes were lifted to inspect her.

'Here's a wonderful surprise,' said Stephen, who for once appeared smiling, relaxed and happy. 'This is Olivia Chazal ... Vicky Scott, and this is Susan. Olivia does secretarial work for us at the hospital. She has come to take delivery of her beautiful new car and is proposing to take us back in it. She has brought a driver with her to get my old heap back to the hospital.'

'But, Stephen, I love driving in your car. I don't want to go in any other one,' Susan burst out.

'Don't be foolish, Susan, and say how d'you do to Miss Chazal.'

Susan mumbled indistinctly and went to sit near Gran, a rather sulky look spoiling her usually sweet expression. Vicky could not help sympathizing a little with Stephen, thinking that children inevitably let you down when you want them to make a good impression, but Olivia seemed more interested in herself than the child.

'Stephen tells me that you've not been in South Africa long, Miss Scott?'

'Only a little while,' Vicky agreed placidly.

'I wonder how you're going to like the hospital?'

'I'll soon find out, I suppose,' said Vicky, somewhat irritated by the dubious tone Olivia had used.

'Yes, indeed. One either loves or hates living in Pondoland, isn't that so, Stephen?' Her feline eyes had a tender teasing look when she gazed at him and she put a possessive hand on his arm. 'Either you have to be like Stephen, deeply devoted to the people there, or like me, who was born there and know it well. I'm afraid it's difficult for a stranger with no ties to settle down there, Miss Scott.'

'Vicky will love it there and I will too,' asserted Susan, who had been listening to this interchange. 'Because Stephen's there.'

'Indeed?' Olivia said coolly. She glanced speculatively from Vicky to Stephen.

Vicky felt a hot blush coursing over her thin tell-tale skin. 'Oh, dear, trust Susan to make things worse!' she thought.

'I hope to see a lot of you, Susan dear,' said Olivia, turning the full light of her deliberate charm upon the child. 'My brother has a trading station where there are horses to ride. We must find you a pony.'

'I don't like riding,' said Susan ungraciously.

'Susan's a wee bit scared of horses,' said Gran, coming to the rescue. 'But it's gey kind of you to offer.'

'I'm sure she'll like these, Mrs. Grant. We'll find a tame one for you, Susan.'

Stephen was beginning to look annoyed at Susan's lack of response, but before he could say anything Olivia fumbled in her beautiful handbag made from leopard skin.

'I'd quite forgotten – I brought you a present.'

Susan brightened at the sight of the small gaily wrapped box, thanked Olivia very politely and proceeded to open it. Then she gave a gasp of disgust and flung it down on the table.

'Ugh, it's a sea-horse! Oh, Vicky, it's one of those sweet little sea-horses, and it's dead!'

It was a brooch made from a petrified sea-horse. It had been covered with bronze paint, but it did indeed look very dead.

'Susan!' Stephen reproved in a voice like thunder, but

55

Susan had flung herself against Vicky, tears coursing down her cheeks.

'I'll take her to her room,' said Vicky quietly.

'Yes, do that. She certainly behaves too childishly in our company.'

'Don't worry, Stephen dear. It's nothing, nothing at all,' she heard Olivia say as Susan sadly accompanied her upstairs. 'It was just a small gift. I thought a child would adore it.'

'And so they would,' Stephen replied grimly. 'Any normal child.'

'Forgive me, Stephen, but is that Miss Scott quite the right person . . . could so easily spoil Susan . . .' Olivia's penetrating voice died away as they turned the bend of the stairs.

Vicky ordered supper to be brought to Susan in her room that evening. She seemed tired and overwrought and it would be better to avoid another encounter with Olivia. With an hour to spare before dinner, she herself enjoyed a fragrant bath. Without admitting the real reason for her desire to look more sophisticated, she chose a simple well-cut dress in a colour like the dark flash of a starling's wing. It enhanced her fair skin, but nevertheless she spent much longer than usual before her mirror, shading silver-jade eye-shadow on to her lids, emphasizing the poignant sweep of her brows with a dark brown pencil, brushing a peachlike bloom on to her naturally beautiful complexion so that the effect was even more breathtaking. The shining fair hair obeyed the twisting and turning of her brush until it was piled in smooth waves above her brow.

'Ooh, Vicky, you look simply gorgeous tonight,' said Susan, eyeing her from her bed where she sat eating roast chicken, her good spirits quite restored by their gossiping chatter. 'You look much nicer than Olivia.'

Secretly that was what Vicky had hoped, but she did not admit this even to herself.

Gran was equally flattering.

'Och, Vicky, you look real bonny for our last dinner in a hotel. It's to be hoped there'll be a little gaiety for you at the hospital, my dear, so you can wear your pretty dresses.'

They joined Stephen at a table on the verandah where he ordered aperitifs. Olivia was nowhere in sight.

'Doesn't Vicky look bonny, the nicht?' Gran demanded of

Stephen.

'Very charming,' Stephen agreed. This time he looked at her properly and his eyes seemed to approve what they saw. For a few moments there was a warm feeling of friendship and familiarity between the three of them.

'The end of the journey,' sighed Gran. 'And a new beginning tomorrow. Here's to us!'

She raised her glass of grape juice.

A shadow fell across the table and Olivia stood there, smiling sweetly. She wore a grey and silver dress, the shining thread woven in intricate design upon the heavy fabric. Diamonds shone at her ears and throat and she carried a mink stole of a hazy pearl colour.

'Good evening, Mrs. Grant. Sorry to keep you waiting, Stephen dear. How nice you look, Vicky. You don't mind my calling you Vicky, I hope. Doesn't she look sweet tonight?'

Her saccharine tone of voice made Vicky feel she wanted to crawl under the table, but Stephen did not seem to notice her embarrassment. He had sprung up and all his attention was concentrated upon Olivia.

'I hope you two don't mind,' Olivia said gaily. 'I'm stealing Stephen away from you this evening. He's taking me out to dinner. We have so many things to discuss alone, haven't we, Stephen? I'm afraid it might be boring for anyone else.'

Her green jewel-like eyes seemed to caress him, as she put a hand on his arm, her face sparkling with conscious allure. Then she turned her beautiful shoulders towards him and handed him the mink wrap, shrugging herself into it with a small murmur of sensual delight.

'Stephen's so stern with me about my passion of furs,' she turned informatively to Gran and Vicky. 'He doesn't approve at all of animals being killed to adorn females, but, Stephen, you must admit this one looks beautiful, and minks are such horrid little beasts anyway.'

Stephen grinned and shook his head in seeming despair.

'I suppose it's no use pointing out that the cost of your furs would practically buy me a new ward at the hospital,' he said.

'Oh, Stephen, don't be like that,' Olivia pouted. 'You know I work hard for your old hospital. Who has to charm the visitors into giving you donations?'

'I must admit you do that part of your work very well. It's quite outside my ability. I hate having to ask for money.'

'Who knows?' said Olivia. 'One day you may have more than you imagine.' She took his arm, and they hurried, laughing, down the steps of the hotel.

'She seems a gay one,' said Gran. 'I've never seen Stephen so bright with a woman before, leastways not for a long time.'

'She's very good-looking,' agreed Vicky.

She sighed. The feeling of togetherness that she had just now experienced with Stephen and Gran had disappeared. She chatted brightly to Gran as they dined together, but afterwards Gran, yawning, declared she was ready for bed and for Vicky the long, lonely evening seemed to stretch drearily ahead.

She sat at the open window of her room trying to concentrate on a book. But, quickly tiring of it, she went to stand on the verandah facing the sea. Strings of coloured lights stretched across the promenade, yet they only seemed to emphasize the darkness of the pulsing waves and the deserted appearance of the beach-front. The wind had risen and there were very few people about. Only directly across the road the figure of a man stood motionless, chin huddled into the turned-up collar of his coat, hat pulled well down. He seemed to be staring at the hotel as if he were waiting for someone to come out.

As she watched, he walked down the steps towards the pool below the aquarium where the sea-lions still grunted and splashed, glossy shining black forms against the blacker water. 'Rather an odd time to look at sea-lions,' thought Vicky.

She resumed her reading, but finally gave up and went to bed. Some time later, however, she awoke to the sound of the sea crashing upon the rocks below. The tide was high now and the noise seemed to thunder into the room. It was impossible to sleep again and, putting on her fleecy coat, she quietly let herself out on to the verandah and sat in a cane chair, rather enjoying the wild din of the waves and the salt-laden breeze that rustled through the potted hibiscus shrubs.

The crashing of the sea had blotted out any smaller noise, but then, in the sudden hush caused by a retreating wave, she was aware all at once that she was not alone. At the end of the verandah, only a few yards from where she was sitting, there were two figures, standing looking out to sea, apparently absorbed in conversation.

Disjointed fragments of their talk floated across the intervening space, interrupted every now and again by the louder noise of the waves. The man spoke in a low voice, but the woman's was more audible. Vicky had heard that voice for the first time today, but there was no mistaking the clipped cultured tone ... Olivia! Then she must be talking to Stephen. Vicky shrank back in her chair, terribly embarrassed at the idea of interrupting what looked like an intimate conversation by her untimely appearance.

They seemed to be arguing about something, for once she heard Olivia say quite sharply, 'Don't be foolish – think what you could do with the money.' She saw Olivia turn her lovely profile towards the other's shadowy figure, and put two slender hands on his shoulders, her head tilted at a laughing, persuasive angle.

Stephen seemed to hesitate for a moment, then Vicky, an unwilling spectator, saw him gather her to him in a passionate embrace. Feeling desperately that she must get away, she got up at the next crash of a wave and slipped silently back into her room.

For a long time she lay awake, staring into the darkness, feeling as lonely and desolate as the sound of the moaning sea.

CHAPTER FOUR

'AH, it's a bonny country, this,' said Gran.

'Not much like Scotland, though,' said Stephen.

'No . . . no . . . a wee bit like the downs.'

Olivia, in a beautifully cut slacks suit, was driving smoothly and efficiently in her silver-grey Mercedes through rolling green country with blue hills in the distance. On every hillside could be seen the round beehive-shaped African huts, with mud walls painted white, and roofs neatly thatched. Near the huts were square cattle kraals, fenced in with live aloes, and on the hillsides small naked herdboys tended flocks of sheep and cattle.

In patchwork squares of mealie fields, women sang as they hoed the red earth. They were dressed in orange coloured blankets draped into long full swinging skirts, decorated with rows of black braid. On their heads were large black turbans, and it seemed the older the owner the bigger was the turban. Copper and wire bangles clanked upon their wrists and ankles. Now and then the car passed a man also draped in a red blanket, contentedly smoking a long pipe as he peacefully contemplated his cattle.

'It evidently pays to be a man here,' Gran observed, for the women alone seemed to be working hard. They met them along the road balancing enormous bundles of firewood or buckets of water upon their heads. They smiled in shy greeting as the car passed by, their eyes brown and gentle as those of a gazelle.

Quite often Olivia had to brake suddenly because of a flock of goats or a fat black pig in the road. Then small, dark-skinned children would emerge from the huts, laughing, shouting, waving sticks, and would scatter the animals in all directions until it became even more difficult to drive through them.

'These are my patients,' Stephen explained to Gran. 'They walk miles from remote settlements to get treatment at the hospital.'

He was sitting next to Susan and Vicky in the back of the enormous car. He had insisted that Gran should take the front seat. Vicky thought Olivia had looked a little displeased when he proposed this seating plan, but she had smiled gracciously and been at her most charming to the old lady.

Since Olivia's arrival, Stephen's darker mood seemed to be a thing of the past. He was all eagerness to return to his hospital and pointed out interesting things to Susan as if he had never felt any annoyance with her. Eagerly responding to his mood, she chattered happily about the people and animals she saw until Olivia lifted slender fingers to press her forehead and say, 'Please, Susan, would you mind if I asked for a little quietness?' Then hurriedly explained, 'It's not easy to drive a new car – I find I need to concentrate.'

Vicky could understand she had reason on her side, but wished Susan need not have been quietened when for once she and Stephen were getting on so well.

Arriving at a small village, Olivia drew up in the shade of a large kaffirboom tree in front of the hotel. The one main street consisted of a few one-storeyed houses with white-painted walls and iron roofs, a garage with three petrol pumps, and two or three African general stores, their windows filled with coloured blankets, tin buckets, patent medicines, bright plaid shirts and cheap watches. The main road was bitumenized, but the few side roads leading to houses were dry and dusty with red earth.

The hotel was a long low one-storeyed place built around a central courtyard. Unlike the rest of the village it looked sparklingly clean and well cared for. Someone had painstakingly cultivated a small green lawn in the middle of the quadrangle and this was bordered by gay beds of red and pink petunias. Painted benches and multi-striped umbrellas offered inviting shelter from the hot sun.

As they came in, the sleepy atmosphere of the hot afternoon seemed to be swept away and African voices were heard from all directions shouting the good news that, 'Igquira u fikile!' – 'The doctor has come!' Vicky was fleetingly sorry for anyone who was trying to rest in any of the rooms opening directly on to the paved stoep, for the African waiters laughed and shouted, clapping their hands and making a great noise to welcome them. But then, shouting louder than any of her African servants, an enormous woman burst through the swing doors leading from the kitchen, her arms flung wide, a pleased smile creasing her glossy red cheeks. Two magnificent blonde plaits circled her head and very elaborate silver ear-rings swung as she talked. Flinging aside a floury apron to display a dress of bright pink, patterned with enormous roses, she advanced towards Stephen and rather to Vicky's surprise planted a kiss upon his bony cheek.

'Well, how goes it? I said to Gumede here, "I wonder when Doctor Stephen is coming," but we didn't think you would make it until tomorrow.'

'Ah, but we had a good driver today. Laetitia, meet Gran, Mrs. Grant, and my niece Susan ... and this is Miss Scott. You know Miss Chazal, of course.'

'Yes, we have met,' Mrs. Honeywell said rather shortly. Then turning to Gran, 'What you'll be needing, Mrs. Grant, will be a nice cup of tea, and some date scones straight from the oven. And you, ducky, what d'you say to an orange squash? Hang, man, but it's good to see you folks!'

Mrs. Honeywell radiated warmth like a sun and, like the sun, the whole world of her hotel seemed to pivot around her. They were ushered into her private sitting room, a place over-flowing with fat red velvet chairs and satin curtains with padded pelmets and elaborate tassels, most unsuitable, Vicky thought, for the African climate, but displaying in a way their hostess's expansive nature. Grinning African waiters quickly brought the 'Specially nice pot of tea' ordered for her guests, and date scones dripping with butter appeared from the kitchen within seconds.

'No, no, I couldn't eat a thing,' Olivia said, when pressed to eat these.

'Why ever not?' said Laetitia bluntly. 'There's good stuff in these, and you could do with a little fat on those bones, my girl!' critically eyeing Olivia's slender elegance.

'Dear Mrs. Honeywell,' said Olivia, all sweetness, 'you should know me by now. I never eat between meals.'

'Well, I do,' said Gran. 'And I must say, Mrs. Honeywell, these are the best scones I've tasted since I left Glasgow. I couldn't do better myself.'

'And let me tell you that's a very big compliment,' Stephen informed her.

Mrs. Honeywell turned frankly inquiring eyes upon Vicky. 'And what do you do, Miss Scott? Are you a nurse?'

Vicky smiled.

'No, I'm going to help with teaching Susan.'

'Ah, that will be a good thing, then. I've been wondering how they would manage about her schooling. It's a bit remote here. All the children in the neighbourhood have to go to boarding school quite early. My three are away at school. We have lots of gay parties during the hols, but it's far too quiet when they've gone back.'

'Do you have a lot of people staying at your hotel, Mrs. Honeywell?' asked Vicky.

'Call me Laetitia, dear. I'm kept busy with commercial travellers and so on ... representatives they call themselves these days, and twice a week I cater for a tourists' bus. They bring people from cruise ships to see how the Africans live in the reserves. None of them stay very long. That reminds me,' she said, turning to Stephen, 'a man phoned to ask if I had accommodation to offer for a few weeks. He seemed interested in the hospital. Asked if it was far away from here – if he could get there easily – what the road was like.'

'That's strange,' said Stephen. 'But perhaps there'll be a letter when I get back. Maybe it's someone wanting to do research. We'll see.'

'I told him he could get a room any time here. We're never so full that I can't push him in.'

'We'd better be on our way. It's a rough road down to the hospital and it's getting late.'

Mrs. Honeywell pressed Gran and Vicky to come to visit her any time they felt lonely and, with many expressions of good will, they parted.

Evening was approaching, and there was a blue mistiness in the deep valleys with a rosy diffused light spreading across the sky. Small fires flickered like glow-worms upon the hillsides. The road was rough, dusty and winding. Stephen took the wheel from Olivia and she sat next to him, directing him with an intimacy that had the effect of excluding the passengers on the back seat.

'There's a bump here ... remember when we were coming home late that night, we broke a spring on it. What a lovely party that was, wasn't it? The Singletons always give divine parties, don't they? It was worth the broken spring, wasn't it?'

'If you say so,' said Stephen, laughing. Then turning to Gran, he said, 'Nearly there now.'

They turned another winding bend in the road and there before them was a group of neatly thatched, whitewashed buildings. It did not look very different from the African villages they had passed on the way, but the cattle and pigs were absent, though several hens ran squawking from under the wheels of the car as it approached the hospital.

A smiling African child ran to open the gate and squirmed with shyness and joy as Stephen greeted him. Then they were in front of the main building and, as Stephen braked quietly, it seemed as if they had arrived at a large aviary, for the stoep of the hospital was screened with wire to keep out flies, and behind it there was a loud twittering as if a hundred mynah birds had been caged together.

But as Stephen stepped out of the car and turned to help Gran, there was a sudden hush, followed by a grown-up's voice giving rapid instructions, then the tap of a baton, and all at once the mynahs became transformed into nightingales. Clear, sweet, heartcatching, the voices of the African children sang out from the stoep. Those who were convalescent moved forward with their teacher on to the grass. They stood in a ring around Stephen, Gran and Susan, their dark eyes solemn, singing a song of praise and welcome.

The children's dark faces were luminous in the last yellow light of the rapidly darkening sky, their voices ringing pure and joyous as some angelic choir. Stephen's expression was full of warmth and laughter. One could hardly believe in the dour man Vicky had encountered so often during the homeward journey.

Vicky found that Olivia was standing beside her.

'How did they know he was coming now?' Vicky asked.

'Word travels quickly from hill to hill along the way.'

Olivia wore an amused smile as she realized Vicky's eyes were brimming with tears.

'Vicky dear, tell Stephen I'll see him tomorrow. I can't wait now. I must go. These African welcomes always take ages. If the old Umfundisi, the clergyman, starts to make a speech, we'll be here for another half hour.'

'Don't you stay here, then?' asked Vicky, somewhat surprised.

'Good heavens, no! Can you see me in one of these primitive cottages? I help Stephen with his administrative work during the day, but I stay with my brother who has a trading station about a mile away. No, my dear. I only consented to return here when he'd promised to build a new house for me. You must come to see us soon. We'll arrange something tomorrow.'

The car slid quietly away as an old African minister started declaiming loudly. Vicky did not find this part of the welcome boring, though it was true, as Olivia had predicted, that the old man spoke for a long time. However, she was so interested in the scene before her that it did not seem to matter that the old man was speaking in an unknown language.

It was obvious that he was telling his audience what a fine man the doctor was and how glad they were to welcome him back. This audience, agreeing with him in loud assenting cries, varied from trim little African nurses in spotless uniforms and small starched caps perched upon glossy, straightened hair, to women wrapped in red blankets, their faces painted with white clay. Some of them carried babies slung upon their backs and grasped pipes about two feet long.

After the speech, Stephen moved amongst them, questioning them, laughing, greeting them in their own language. At last the gathering broke up and Stephen took Gran, Susan and Vicky to show them where they were to live. It was a charming cottage made after the fashion of the African huts with white-painted adobe walls and thatched roof, but the design was a little more elaborate.

The door of the small verandah or stoep at the front of the house led straight into a large living room furnished with simple cane chairs and settee upholstered in bright hand-woven linen. The blue and red striped rugs on the light polished floor were handwoven too. Stephen said in reply to Gran's questioning that these had been made at the hospital in the therapy ward and that the light cream curtains embroidered in cross stitch, at the small deep-silled windows, were made from 'kaffir sheeting'.

At each end of the sitting room were two round rooms, four altogether, all with pointed thatched roofs, so that from the outside the building looked rather like an old-fashioned pepperpot. These were a bedroom for Gran, Vicky and Susan and the fourth one was a small neat kitchen. The bathroom, Vicky discovered later, was a closed-in part of the stoep.

'Where do you sleep?' Susan asked Stephen.

'I have a rondavel fairly near the hospital so they can call me easily in an emergency, but I'll share meals with you when

65

I can.'

The plain deal table was set with plaited grass mats and white plates and Vicky noticed that someone had put a few blooms of red geraniums into a blue jug. She realized whose tribute this was when she was introduced to Selina, a gentle, fine-featured African woman in a long blue dress sprigged with white flowers, and wearing a black turban and black satin apron.

'Selina will look after you here,' said Stephen, as she smiled with eyes modestly downcast. 'Ask her for anything you need. She has hot soup and cold meats and salads waiting for you, she says. I suppose you'll want to clean up after the journey. I'll join you in about half an hour.'

Selina brought soft rain water in a jug sprigged with roses. The towels were worn but soft, the old-fashioned counterpane thin with countless washings but dazzlingly white. Someone – Selina, of course – had put two pink roses in a glass jar on top of the small bedside table. A rather weak-powered electric light with a white shade hung from the central beam of the roof. Beyond this Vicky could see the wooden struts rising to the middle in a shadowy pattern upon the thatch.

Outside the small window in the gathering darkness she could just make out a hibiscus bush, flaunting its huge red blossoms in startling contrast to the simplicity within. There was a quiet peaceful atmosphere about the little room that made Vicky feel happier than she had been for a long time.

She moved towards the wooden chest of drawers, topped by a mirror, with the intention of doing her hair. But, a yard away from it, she stood motionless. If there had been a snake coiled upon the woven mat her heart could not have beaten more quickly. A white envelope was propped against the mirror and the large, familiar, once dear handwriting proclaimed to her that it was from David. She opened it hesitantly.

'My still beloved Vicky,' she read, 'I'm deeply sorry if I offended you the last time we met. Blame it on the wine . . . blame it on your dear alluring self, but please forgive me. I found out your address from the hotel, and I'm longing to see you again to show you I'm not as unfeeling as you think. And now . . . lovely surprise . . . I find that some time in the near future I may have to come your way on some business of my own. Wish upon a star for us, my darling, for this affair may mean an end to my financial worries and a new beginning for us. No more now. Yours ever, David.'

'Vicky! Vicky!'

She put the letter into the top drawer as Susan called. She would think about it later. Susan came running in, her face alight with joy. She was pulling a small African girl by the hand, a child a little older than herself, dressed in a blue and white checked dress.

'Look, Vicky, this is Tandiwe, Selina's little girl. She's going to be my friend.'

Tandiwe covered her face with her hands and giggled shyly. The novelty of finding a child shyer than herself seemed to have worked upon Susan like a charm. For once she was very self-possessed and spoke to Tandiwe with confidence.

'Look at Vicky, Tandiwe. I want you to see her. There's no need to be shy.'

'What a pretty dress, Tandiwe,' Vicky said. 'Did your mother make it?'

'*Ewe* ... yes,' said Tandiwe, speaking first in Xhosa, then in English. She lifted large trusting black eyes to look at Vicky, then lifting her diminutive skirt, with pride she showed the fluffy panties underneath.

'Selina's going to give me my supper in the kitchen,' Susan announced. 'Then I'll read a story to Tandiwe. You don't mind, do you, Vicky?'

Vicky was surprised and pleased at Susan's new-found independence, as the little girls ran hand in hand to the kitchen.

Vicky had changed from her rather travel-worn suit into a simple high-necked dress of a cream-coloured material woven in self-coloured stripes of alternate plain and lacy weave. With this she wore an intriguing belt made of tortoiseshell rings linked with gilt and her ear-rings were of dark topaz set in gold.

Gran had also discarded her tussore suit and changed into a pale blue flowered dress that matched her eyes. Waiting for Stephen, they both had a festive feeling of celebrating their arrival with this first meal in their house. Though neither of them said so, it was a relief to be rid of Olivia's rather over-whelming presence. Free of the need for social chit-chat, Gran and Vicky discussed their future housekeeping arrangements and were both in full agreement about how charming they found their simple living quarters.

Soon they saw Stephen crossing the lawn with his long stride, accompanied by an equally tall man with wavy mid-blond hair, who was engaged in animated conversation, at the same time flourishing a wine bottle as he made sweeping gestures to emphasize his speech.

'Yon's a good-looking man,' said Gran. 'He must be the Viennese doctor Stephen spoke of.'

He jumped the steps on to the stoep and strode forward with outstretched hands and beaming smile to be introduced to Gran and Vicky. At close quarters, his eyes were a startling vivid blue, almost violet, and with his golden brown face, finely cut features and dazzling smile, he looked far nearer than Stephen to Susan's description of 'an advertisement for cigarettes.'

'Stephen, Stephen, what a dark pony you are!' he exclaimed when he was introduced to Vicky. 'You see, Miss Scott, I know good English idiom . . . dark pony, dark horse . . . what does it matter?' (this impatiently to Stephen's murmured correction). 'When you said you had engaged a governess for Susan, I imagined someone . . .' He mimed a frowning teacher with pince-nez. 'You never told me you had brought a young lady so lovely, so *gentille*.' He flung his arms wide as if words failed him to express his admiration.

Vicky blushed but could not keep from smiling. There was something so light, flirtatious but likeable about his manner. He kissed Gran's hand and her eyes sparkled with pleasure.

'A little wine perhaps to celebrate the homecoming,' he suggested, brandishing his bottle. 'I gave Selina some wine glasses. I know you won't have supplied them, Stephen. It will be amazing, Mrs. Grant, if you have enough knives and forks in your kitchen. If it was left to Stephen, he would eat from a bowl with his fingers.'

Stephen did not seem to mind his teasing.

'The Africans do, Anton, and they're none the worse for it. What does it matter? The fewer appurtenances of civilization one has the better, I think.'

'What a man!' sighed Anton. 'I myself like to live well with good wine, good food, good music . . .'

'And good women, I hope, Dr. Buchner,' said Gran mischievously.

Anton nodded, looking at Vicky.

68

'Good women certainly – the women of your country, Mrs. Grant. There is a freshness, a simplicity about them that I find very intriguing, combined as it is with a suggestion of hidden depths.'

'But if you like a sophisticated life, Dr. Buchner, what are you doing here?'

Anton laughed.

'You may well ask, Mrs. Grant. It is a little matter of research. There are interesting cases in Africa that are not found anywhere else. An ignorant doctor like me needs further study.'

'Don't be deceived by Anton's frivolous manner, Gran. His work is brilliant.'

'Oh, Stephen, you are too good to me.' Anton turned impulsively to Stephen, obviously deeply touched by his remark. 'I am at the beginning only. However let's not be serious in front of two such charming ladies. It is time to celebrate their arrival.'

They sat on the stoep and drank the chilled golden wine as the moon rose huge and yellow from behind the mountain, dispersing the mists that with sunset had gathered in the deep valleys. Singing came from the huts below, the same tune repeated over and over in different keys, monotonous yet full of melody, plucking vibrantly at the senses in the perfumed stillness of the African night. Fluffy, silver-winged moths blundered against the lantern hanging from a beam and a sleepy dove, disturbed by their chatter, murmured to its mate in the rafters of the roof. A scent overwhelmingly fragrant swept towards them.

'What is that?' asked Gran. 'That strong, flowerlike smell?'

'It's the flowering bush below the stoep,' said Stephen. 'The one with the different coloured flowers, some purple, some mauve, some white.'

'They call it "Yesterday, today and tomorrow",' said Anton. 'An odd name, isn't it?'

'Yesterday, today and tomorrow,' thought Vicky. 'Yesterday . . . at least, a few days ago . . . I was in Cape Town. Today here I am at the beginning of a new life'

'And tomorrow,' she thought, 'who knows?'

'I do wander everywhere,' read Susan,
'Swifter than the moon's sphere;

69

And I serve the fairy queen,
To dew her orbs upon the green.
The cowslips tall her pensioners be:
In their gold coats spots you see;
Those be rubies, fairy favours,
In these freckles live their savours;
I must go seek some dew-drops here,
And hang a pearl in every cowslip's ear.'

'I like the Shakespeare you give me to read,' said Susan. 'It's much more fun than *Hamlet*.'

'Well, darling, *Hamlet* isn't really supposed to be fun,' Vicky explained.

They had set up a desk on the shady stoep. It was an unusual classroom. When they lifted their heads they could see the green valley below, with smoke rising in the still morning air from the cooking fires beside the huts and they could hear the voices of Africans singing out in clear tones from one hill to another or chanting in chorus as the field work was done.

Grey-blue doves landed upon the stoep and walked with modest bowing mien to gather up the crumbs from the mid-morning tray of milk and biscuits. Small donkeys, wearing panniers laden with sacks of mealies, trotted along the path at the bottom of the garden.

Two long legs swung over the low wall of the verandah. It was Anton approaching them with his charming, self-deprecating smile.

'A little half-hour's rest for your oh-so-diligent pupil, Miss Scott, while I show you over the hospital. You should know more about this place where you have come to live.'

'Dr. Buchner, I don't think . . .'

'Oh, Vicky, we've been working for hours. I got all my sums right this morning, and I won't be lazy while you're gone. Tandiwe has promised to show me how to make a bead neck-lace with a daisy pattern.'

'So there you are!' said Anton, smiling.

'Perhaps Mrs. Grant would like to come too,' said Vicky, rather defensively. She felt a little overwhelmed by Anton's practised charm and his undisguised admiration for herself.

'Though I should think he's like this with all women,' she thought to herself. 'But there is something undeniably attractive about him.'

Mrs. Grant was sitting in a deckchair under a tree, knitting socks.

'No, Vicky, I'm just turning the heel. Go, by all means. I'll keep an eye on Susan. She's done enough lessons for this morning and you don't have to be tied to her all day.'

Anton's charm obviously worked for Gran too.

'You need the company of someone nearer your own age, sometimes,' she said, 'and Susan has Tandiwe. Take an hour off if Dr. Buchner has time to spare.'

Between Gran, Susan and Anton, Vicky felt it would be churlish to refuse. Besides, she was most interested to see the hospital. This morning, perhaps with the idea of looking the part of governess to Susan, Vicky had drawn back her fair hair into a bun at the nape of her neck and was wearing a grey dress with collar and cuffs of white poplin.

'How charming you look this morning, Miss Scott,' said Anton, his brilliant eyes taking in every detail of her appearance. 'Like one of those grey wood pigeons you see upon the dewy grass in the early morning.'

He took her arm quite unnecessarily to help her up the steps and began to show her around the different wards. Vicky's idea of him as a pleasant philanderer changed as they progressed around the hospital. He knew his work and explained it clearly. In the children's ward he made up for his lack of knowledge of their language by his obvious good-will and teasing charm.

'Sing me the song about the butterfly,' he demanded, a nurse translating for him.

Some of the bolder children who were convalescent started to sing and then the more timid ones joined in. They sang in their own language, but the nurse obligingly translated for Vicky. It was charming to see them singing shyly and eagerly, watching each other as they performed the actions to the song.

'Good day.'

'Good day to you.' They bowed very seriously.

'Where do you come from?'

'I come from my home.' They pointed to somewhere in the distance.

'What do they give you to eat there?'

'A kind of porridge.' They all cupped their hands as if eating.

'How many people live there?'

They shook their heads solemnly from side to side.

'Don't ask me about this. There are so many people there that the butterflies fly away to the hills.'

They waved their arms pretending to be butterflies.

'And now all the butterflies lie down . . . they are so tired.' They lay down to rest in their cots, their eyes closing.

Vicky found it difficult not to show emotion when she saw the crippled children in the orthopaedic ward. Anton, watching her, saw her eyes fill with tears.

'Often it is too late by the time they are brought here,' he explained. 'Many of them are still pagans and rely upon witch doctors. They still believe illness is brought on by ill-wishing.'

'I know I'm foolish, but I can't help feeling touched, mainly I think because they look so cheerful and uncomplaining,' Vicky said as she tried to blink away the tears.

'What a tenderhearted person you are, little Vicky,' said Anton, putting an arm around her as they walked out of the room and along a passage. 'You mustn't worry. You must believe we all do our best for them.'

'Yes, I'm quite sure you do,' said Vicky, turning towards him, her mouth tremulous.

'There, if I'd known it would upset you I wouldn't have brought you,' Anton said, looking worried, and, wanting to comfort her as he would a child, he kissed her lightly on the cheek.

'Oh, there you are, Anton.'

The voice so close to them made Vicky start.

'I sent someone to look for you. I need you in the office for a moment to check one of your records. Good morning, Miss Scott. Has Susan finished her lessons early today?'

The grey eyes were icy, but it took more than Stephen's disapproval to disturb Anton.

'Ah, Stephen, I was just showing Vicky around the hospital. And I have found out what a charming person is this governess of yours, so gentle, so full of sympathy.'

'Yes, so it appears,' Stephen said coldly. 'But you need a little more than sympathy in a hospital such as ours. A practical nature is more necessary. There's little time for sentimentality, as you should know.'

They had entered the office and there sat Olivia looking cool and efficient in a plain sleeveless dress of turquoise blue.

'Oh, Vicky, how nice to see you!' She smiled sweetly. 'Have you been having a pleasant time with Anton? He knows so well how to make things interesting, don't you, Anton?'

'I'm glad you think so, Olivia.'

Anton's face was grave and Vicky sensed some undercurrent of hostility between the two of them. Olivia smiled at Stephen and placed a hand upon his arm.

'Stephen is worrying about our high accounts. Really, it's awfully difficult to make ends meet here. If we could only find a rich patron! I do my best, but ...' She shrugged.

'Olivia has done wonders in getting people interested in the hospital,' said Stephen. 'But it's not enough. We need more facilities. If only I could find some way to raise money.'

Olivia smiled very sweetly, very sympathetically.

'Darling Stephen, don't despair. We'll make a plan, you'll see.'

Vicky remembered the night in East London, the words overheard, the passionate embrace. Gran spoke of Stephen as a confirmed bachelor, but she had hardly seen what influence Olivia seemed to have upon him. Vicky felt sad. She could not like Olivia. And as for Stephen ... well, really, why should she worry about such a strict, priggish person? What did it matter if he got a wife who seemed hard and self-centred? But there was Susan. She could not bear to think of Susan having to live with a person like Olivia. Yet perhaps she was hardly being fair. She knew so little of Olivia, and it was true she seemed to work hard for the hospital although she seemed not to need a salary. Perhaps she was misjudging her.

Anton broke into her thoughts.

'That little matter is cleared up now. I'm taking Vicky to the outpatients' clinic before she goes back, Stephen. Is that all right with you?'

'If she wishes to use her lunchtime in that way, it's no business of mine,' said Stephen. 'But perhaps you will return to give Susan a little tuition later on, Miss Scott?'

By his formal way of speaking, she sensed that Stephen was deliberately setting out to annoy. He emphasized her surname as if to reproach Anton for his easy familiarity. He was probably furious with her for taking up Anton's time.

'I'll be back with Susan almost immediately, Dr. Nash,' she said, trying not to sound as ruffled as she felt.

Olivia looked up smiling from her desk.

'Vicky dear, Anton is a very busy doctor. Don't keep him too long.'

This remark seemed to disturb Anton's good nature at last. He looked dignified and remote, and Vicky had a sudden vision of a courtier casting down his glove when challenging someone to a duel.

'Trust me to manage my own affairs, Olivia, if you please. Come, Miss Vicky.'

To Vicky the clinic was the most interesting part of the whole hospital. Here the outpatients were examined, and most of them were dressed in tribal costume. A visit to the hospital was a social occasion and many of the patients, accompanied by their friends, wore not perhaps the full regalia used for special parties and celebrations but the clean red-ochred skirts and blankets they used every day, with the addition, however, of a good deal of ornamental bead wear. This Vicky found breathtakingly beautiful.

'Where do they get it from?' she asked Anton, astonished that such humble people, who seemed to have been by-passed by civilization, should own such beautiful beadwork.

'They make it themselves, buying the tiny beads from the traders. But the wearing of beads goes back for hundreds of years. The Portuguese mariners used beads to pay for gold and ivory when they made their voyages around the Cape.

'It all has a meaning, doesn't it, Trifena?' he added, addressing one of the neat, white-capped nurses.

'Yes, Doctor. Beads are often used instead of letters for sending messages.'

'Really?' asked Vicky, most intrigued. 'But how?'

'They are in the form of small squares woven so that they look almost like tapestry, attached to large safety-pins so that the boy-friends can wear them as ornaments,' Anton informed her.

'So it is the girls who send the messages to the boys?'

'Yes. When they are old enough to take an interest in boys then they start sending this form of love letter. The colours symbolize different meanings. That's so, isn't it, Trifena?'

'Yes, Doctor. For instance, the first message a girl sends to her sweetheart is probably made of white beads which can mean, "My heart is pure and waiting for you to write on it. My soul says I am grown-up now". Then when they start thinking of marriage, they might use blue as the main colour, and

74

that might mean, "I envy the dove that picks up mealie grains at the door of your mother's hut." Perhaps she might weave a little piece of grass into the message, meaning "I could make a very nice mat for you. I could help you to build a hut for us." '

'Do any of the beads have sad meanings?' asked Vicky.

'Yes, black stands for sadness and loneliness. A black pattern with white spots can mean that the girl is lonely and tired of waiting: "I will fly away like the guinea fowl which has white and black spotted feathers".

'But these are messages for unmarried people,' Trifena added. 'The most important necklace for a grown-up man is the *isigcina ntliziyo*.'

The nurse looked around at the chattering red-blanketed crowd, then she singled out an elderly man and called to him to come over to them. Around his neck he was wearing a square of white bead tapestry, heavily fringed, and inlaid upon this was the figure of a woman picked out in navy and pink beads. He greeted Anton and Vicky with grave courtesy and showed them the necklace, explaining about it to the nurse.

'What does it mean?' asked Vicky.

'It is known as "The Keeper of the Heart". A newly married wife makes it for her husband because from now on she is the Keeper of his Heart. It is a kind of portrait of her,' Anton informed her.

'It must show her exactly as she is,' the nurse added. 'If she doesn't tell the truth with it, her friends will say, "No, that is not really you. You aren't like that!" '

She spoke again to the dignified old man who wore the necklace. The little figure upon the square had a skirt with five diamonds upon it.

'This shows she has had five children,' Trifena explained. 'Her arms are long and placed downwards, which shows she is busy and hardworking.'

'But she has no feet,' said Anton. 'Why is that, Nurse?'

Trifena spoke to the man and then laughed.

'He says she still likes to dance, but her feet are worn out. A figure with hands raised and feet placed sideways means the wife is a beautiful dancer,' she added. 'If the legs are turned to walk it means she likes to run around gossiping instead of getting on with her work, but running feet mean she is a busy woman.'

'What a lovely idea it is,' Vicky said, somewhat wistfully. 'How good to be able to say to someone, "This is me, as I am. This is the one you love." Lovely not to have to pretend to be anything else but yourself and not to have someone trying to make you into something different.'

Anton looked quizzically at her.

'Who has wanted to change you, Vicky? What a foolish man not to be satisfied with you as you are!'

Vicky blushed furiously. She had not intended to show her own emotion so plainly, but now felt she had betrayed herself in her interest over 'The Keeper of the Heart'.

'I must go,' she said hastily. 'Susan will be waiting for me. Thank you for showing me around.'

She walked quickly away across the grass, but Anton with his long strides caught up with her in a few seconds. He took her arm so that she was forced to stop.

'What are you afraid of, Vicky? Who has hurt you so that you shy away like a startled deer when I try to tell you how charming I find you?' He smiled. 'But there, I won't ask you for confidences. That may come later. Meanwhile, will you forgive my curiosity?'

Vicky smiled at his concern.

'Of course, Anton, there's nothing to forgive.'

'Now I know I am forgiven because you use my name, but to show that it really so perhaps you will consent to have dinner with me soon. We can go to Mrs. Honeywell's hotel. It is not the Ritz, but it is adequate.'

'I don't know yet what free time I'll have or when Dr. Nash might want me to stay with Susan.'

'Oh, Stephen is not such an ogre as to keep you sitting in every evening. He would not begrudge me your company. After all, he himself dines with the charming Miss Chazal quite frequently.'

'How stupid I am to hesitate,' thought Vicky. 'Anton is charming. Why shouldn't I enjoy an evening with him?'

'Very well, Anton,' she said. 'I'd love to come with you.'

'We'll make it soon,' promised Anton.

CHAPTER FIVE

'STEPHEN is going to have supper with us. Isn't that grand?' asked Susan, bursting into Vicky's room with a very small apology for a knock. Vicky thought that the happy child with brown sunburned limbs and short shining hair bore little resemblance to the shy, restrained little girl she had first met in Cape Town Gardens.

It was the friendship with Tandiwe that seemed to have wrought the miracle. They were always together, running around the hospital grounds looking for adventure or sitting on the stoep while Tandiwe taught Susan to thread bead patterns or weave small mats, or Susan gave Tandiwe information about Scotland and their travels.

'I'm glad Stephen can come the nicht. It's little enough we see of him,' said Gran when Vicky joined her later. To honour Stephen Mrs. Grant had changed into an embroidered blouse and a black velvet skirt, and wore her cornelian necklace.

'He has a hard time of it at the hospital, I'm afraid,' she said, shaking her head.

They were sitting upon the stoep watching a silver moon rise above the tall blue gum trees. The pale barks of the trees were luminous in the gathering light. Vicky wore a printed silk dress in delicate pastel shades. Her hair hung loose and shining, making her look very young.

'To see him now, worrying his heart out about these primitive tribes in this wild country, you would never dream that once he seemed destined for a very different kind of career, would you?'

'What kind of career, Mrs. Grant?'

'Och, only a couple of years ago, people were saying he was the most brilliant young surgeon the hospital had ever had. Gradually his name was becoming known in medical schools all over the world. But it all came to naught.

'It's a hard life for any young doctor, especially when there's not much money available,' Mrs. Grant continued. 'His aunt lent him the money for his fees, and little enough he had extra. He had to scrape and struggle. Whiles he looked as if he

77

wasna even getting enough to eat, but he was too proud to accept the little help I could offer. Then, when it was all finished, and he had done well, he still had to repay his aunt and manage on his intern's pay. He was just getting on to his feet, able to manage without scraping, when he met this girl.'

Vicky was surprised by a painful emotion that she found difficult to analyse. What could Stephen's past romance matter to her?

'A girl? Yes, I remember, you mentioned he had been disappointed.'

'He had led a life without any gaiety from when he was a boy, so when he fell in love for the first time, it took him by storm. In some ways he was younger than his years, unsophisticated and idealistic, I suppose you would call it, and he thought she was the most wonderful girl in the world.'

Vicky sat quietly thinking of the young Stephen in love, vulnerable and sensitive like Susan. In those days he would not have had the set mouth, the sad expression, only the charming smile.

'They became engaged, but she was young too, a feckless, impatient girl, too attractive for her own good, who thought dances and parties much more important than study. She knew he had a brilliant future, but it seemed too long to wait. Besides, he was never really interested in making money. He preferred to be a low-paid surgeon at a medical school where he would gain experience rather than to go into private practice where he would have made more money.

'You know how it is with a doctor. Often he had to put off arrangements at the last minute and she didna like that at all. She wanted her bread buttered both sides, for him to have a brilliant career and yet dance attendance on her. He was aye with his nose deep in his books and he didna see the danger signs. It was a sad shock for him when she suddenly told him she had decided to marry a wealthy business man.

'It hit him harder than I would have expected. He threw up his work at the hospital and came out here. I must say he seems to find the work very suited to him. But I feel sad sometimes when I think of the opportunities he flung away because of a lassie that would never have been any good to him. And there's no getting away from the fact that it hardened him. He's not the same person he was, for he seemed to become mistrusting with women.'

'Not so mistrusting as not to be caught in the web of Olivia's charm,' thought Vicky, but felt it wise to keep silent.

'Yes,' said Gran, 'money, or the lack of it, is responsible for a mickle lot of worry. I really don't know what to wish for Susan. You may know that her grandfather left her some money and the rights to an unworked emerald mine in Rhodesia. He cut her father out of the will, ye ken, because he was aye good for nothing. In any case, no one knew whether he was alive or dead. They still have to find out whether the mine has any value. At any rate Susan will never have as hard an upbringing as Stephen, though she has had a lot of changes up to now, poor child.'

'But she needs love more than money,' thought Vicky. 'More love than Stephen seems prepared to give. Gran can't be here for ever. Nor I. What is to happen then? And what if he marries Olivia?'

Stephen came striding across the lawn, his dark hair glossy in the moonlight. He subsided into a verandah chair, flinging himself down and sweeping his long fingers over his eyes as if he were deadly weary.

'A hard day?' asked Gran softly.

'Oh, sorry, Gran,' he started as if roused from sleep. 'How are you all? Yes, it's been pretty sticky today. A little more trying than usual. A child with a congenital heart disease. The mother carried him on her back for twenty miles. We thought we were going to lose him, had to work on him for hours. But he'll live – this time.'

'Can't he be cured properly, then?' asked Vicky.

'He'll recover a bit. Then he'll be back again. He needs a heart operation. We need more equipment to carry out the kind he needs and his mother won't consent to his going far away. We get a grant from the Government, but we rely to a large extent on donations and the demand is endless.'

Susan came on to the verandah, her eyes shining, dark hair brushed and glossy, cheeks pink with excitement. She put her arms around Stephen and kissed him.

'Susan, how many times must I tell you you're not to kiss me?' Then, as she looked crestfallen, 'It's not that I don't want it, my dear. It's just that I meet so much illness, I'm scared of passing it on to you.'

'Och, Stephen, the child's fond of you. It doesn't do to be that careful,' said Gran.

'What a contradictory mixture he is,' thought Vicky. 'He tells me I'm too careful with her and yet he's even more cautious. Or is it that he can't stand anyone being demonstrative?' A thought leaped out unbidden. 'He doesn't seem to mind if it's Olivia.'

'I have something to show you,' said Susan. She produced three oxen made of clay and a necklace of small beads fashioned in the shape of flowers. 'I made them with Tandiwe.'

Stephen examined them carefully, looking thoughtful.

'Well, at least he's taking an interest in something that Susan has made,' thought Vicky thankfully.

'Does she play with Tandiwe a great deal?' he asked Vicky.

'Oh, yes, they're great friends.'

'She's my best friend,' Susan assured him, a statement that had pathos for Vicky, because Susan did not even know any other children.

The evening passed pleasantly enough, although Stephen was restrained and quiet. Shortly after supper he declared he would have to go. Susan had already gone to bed and, to Vicky's surprise, he asked her if she would accompany him a little way. The night was almost as clear as day; a huge moon shone across the landscape glinting upon the metal tips of the round thatched huts and disclosing a scene of rolling grey-blue countryside. In the deep valley far below they could see small pinpoints of flame, the African cooking fires that had not yet been carried inside the huts for the night.

'Early mariners used to call this country "Terra del Fumos", "The Land of Fires," because they could see grass fires and the African cooking fires from out at sea,' said Stephen. 'I would like Susan to study early South African history. How is she getting on with her lessons?'

'I find her a bright, interesting child,' said Vicky.

'I'm glad of that. What Shakespeare play did you decide she should read?'

'*A Midsummer Night's Dream.*'

'Oh, well, I suppose that's all right for a start. Never cared for it myself – rather too much romance. Later she must study the great tragedies.'

They were still looking across the moonlit valley and now he turned to look at her. Was it a trick of the moonlight or did his expression change and become less aloof, more human? He smiled.

'Susan looks well, Miss Scott. She seems to be very happy with you.'

'Not only with me but with 'Tandiwe. It's done her all the good in the world to have another child to play with.'

'Oh, yes, Tandiwe ... that was another thing I wanted to mention. I'm very anxious that Susan's education should be of a high standard. You don't think she's wasting her time with these oxen and beads? It seems a rather childish interest for a girl of her age.'

Vicky had been feeling rather pleased with his comments, but this was now swamped by a wave of indignation.

'But, Dr. Nash, surely as a doctor you must know ... I mean one of the most elementary facts is that children, like young puppies, kittens, all young animals, have to play. It educates them for adult life.'

He looked at her as if she had made some world-shaking discovery.

'I suppose you may be right. I never thought of it like that before. I don't remember that I played at all when I was a child.'

All at once, Vicky felt the same compassion for him that she had felt for Susan so often.

'So you think shaping oxen out of clay and threading beads will fit Susan for her future place in society?' he added.

'Of course, put like that it sounds ridiculous, but, Dr. Nash, she can't read Shakespeare all the time. She must have some pleasure.'

All at once he laughed heartily, and Vicky's hostile feelings vanished.

'So reading Shakespeare isn't classed as a pleasure. Shame on you, Miss Scott! I thought you were a dedicated teacher.'

He was teasing her as he teased Gran, but a small flame of happiness burned bright in Vicky's mind. Turning towards him, she stumbled over a tuft of grass and he put out his hand to steady her. It was only for a moment, but a trembling excitement possessed and astonished her and she turned quickly away to look out across the moonlit valley. Trees were etched in a delicate tracery against the rim of the hillside and a white owl flew by on silent wings, absorbed in nocturnal hunting.

'This is a lovely country!' she exclaimed impulsively.

'I'm glad you think so,' said Stephen, 'because tomorrow I intend to show you more of it. How do you feel about coming with me to the coast for the day? I have to go to a remote clinic. The district nurse will be there, but I need someone to accompany me to take notes and so on.'

'I'd love it,' said Vicky enthusiastically ... and was foolishly dampened when he added:

'Olivia usually accompanies me, but she has another engagement tomorrow.'

'Hot pies!' said Mrs. Honeywell, propelling her large bulk down the pathway of the hotel garden with surprising lightness. She wore a bright purple slacks suit, emerald green shoes and swinging ear-rings of mauve and green. Her face was even more florid from her recent exertions in the kitchen, but as usual her thick blonde plaits were wound in elaborate convolutions with not a hair out of place. She had caught sight of Stephen and Vicky as they were buying petrol and had rushed out with a steaming basket.

'I've just made some of my mutton pies. It's my old ma's recipe I always use. Take them and welcome. Where are you going to, dear?' she said, addressing Vicky. Stephen had wandered into the garage.

'To the clinic at the coast. I'm not quite sure where it is,' said Vicky.

'That's nice. Always does a person good to have a little outing. Nelson!' she yelled to one of the Africans. 'Ask the barman for a couple of bottles of cider. Now see you eat those pies. Doctor Stephen forgets to eat half the time. No wonder he's as thin as a stick. He works too hard.'

'I suppose most doctors do,' said Vicky.

'Worries himself sick over a lot of Africans who haven't got two cents to rub together. Wonder what her ladyship really thinks about that?'

'Who do you mean?' asked Vicky, although of course she could guess to whom Laetitia referred. She glanced around, but Stephen was some yards away, deep in conversation with the garage owner. He was to drive a borrowed Landrover to the coastal clinic and was asking advice about it.

'Olivia Chazal, I mean.' Laetitia gave a meaningful sniff. 'Mark my words, honey, it'll be a sad day for this part of the world if Miss Hoity-toity Chazal gets her hooks into him.'

Vicky felt uncomfortably that she should not be gossiping about Stephen's affairs out here in the street.

'Miss Chazal seems to work hard at the hospital,' she said rather weakly.

'Don't let that fox you,' Laetitia replied adamantly, shaking her heavy blonde coiffure. 'Oh, I admit, it's all sweetness and light now and "Oh, how wonderful you are, Stephen darling, how kind to the poor needy Africans!", but once they're married, it'll be a different story. Her brother was in the bar the other evening – he'd been to some rugby match – and when he'd had a few drinks, I heard him telling someone that this Olivia reckons Stephen should take an important place in the medical world. Next thing she'll have him back in London, you mark my words.'

'But perhaps that would be a good thing.'

'Not with her for a ball and chain, it wouldn't.'

Mrs. Honeywell's expression was so fierce that Vicky felt inclined to smile, but at the same time she felt a warm sympathy with the large woman's feelings. But Stephen came along just as she was wondering what to reply.

'By the way,' Mrs. Honeywell informed him, 'that fellow who was inquiring for accommodation is coming next week.'

'I remember you said he was interested in the hospital, but I haven't heard anything about him yet. What's his name?' asked Stephen.

Laetitia snapped her fingers.

'My head's like a sieve these days. I can't think of it. I remember it reminded me of a book.'

'A book?' asked Stephen, somewhat amazed, because somehow you did not connect Laetitia Honeywell with books.

'Not a book I've read lately. As a matter of fact, dear, I'm no great reader. I just look at the newspapers and the pictures in the magazines these days. No, it was one of those set books we used to have to read at school. You always remember them better because they drum them into you for exams.'

'And what was this book called?'

'Well, of course, it's a good few years since I went to school,' said Laetitia, smoothing her blonde plaits. 'Now this man's name reminded me of that book, but now I can't even remember what the book was called. All I can remember is that it had something to do with the Battle of Waterloo.'

'How extraordinary!' said Stephen, laughing.

They drove out of the village laughing companionably about Laetitia's book. But soon the road became rough and

Stephen had to concentrate on his driving. Vicky started to think over the conversation with Laetitia. 'So people do think they'll marry,' she thought with an odd sense of despair. She glanced at Stephen. He was concentrating on avoiding the potholes of the rough road, his long brown hands lightly grasping the wheel, his face serene in spite of the fact that he had to master the unfamiliar gear changes of the Land-rover. She looked around at the wild lovely country, the pastoral scene almost biblical in its simplicity.

'Happiness is here for him,' she thought. 'Not in a city, not as a famous surgeon, not as a wealthy husband to buy furs for Olivia.'

She looked at his long slender body, the thin boyish face with its high cheekbones and aquiline nose, the straight black hair with the errant lock falling over the forehead.

'Not as handsome as Anton,' she thought. 'Nor even as good-looking as David, but with something more . . .' She sighed.

'Very bored?' asked Stephen.

'Oh, no,' she denied. 'Just thinking.'

'Still missing that handsome, possessive, young man of yours?'

'He's certainly not mine any more,' said Vicky.

'Oh, well, maybe Anton's attentions will make up for that. He's a great charmer, but a wily one. He has been married once, of course. Did he tell you?'

'No,' said Vicky, rather sharply. 'In any case it's none of my business.'

Stephen was smiling as if remembering something amusing.

'They came first to Tanzania. Poor Anton. She developed an immense interest in wild life. Anton says he was interested too, but not at such close quarters. She kept a leopard in the lounge. It used to sit in Anton's favourite chair and snarl at him. They had a pet hyena roaming around the house at night, keeping him awake with its howling. He got scared to open any tin or shoebox in case she was keeping a snake in it.'

They both laughed at the thought of the fastidious Anton having to cope with these difficulties.

'What happened in the end?' asked Vicky.

'She left him for a nature conservationist and now they take tourists on wild life expeditions. Anton is determined that, if he marries again, he must find someone who's only happy on city pavements.'

'Pity Gran is too old for him,' said Vicky.

'Yes, poor darling, she really has settled down remarkably well, but she misses her TV, and her little shopping jaunts.'

The road started to twist and turn, descending between tangled trees, and again Stephen had to concentrate on his driving. Vicky had hardly thought of David for a few days, but Stephen's mention of him brought his picture vividly back again. She thought of the contents of his letter. Did he really intend to visit her in the near future? And these mysterious plans he spoke of? What could alter his present circumstances? He had implied that they might be able to marry. Had he then some prospect of becoming wealthy? She knew that otherwise he would not give up his present plans. That much had become clear. She dreaded the thought of having to face him again after the disillusionment and sadness of their last evening together.

The road was still descending at a steep angle. Stephen had to put the vehicle into low gear and the hum of the engine resounded over the countryside. Small donkeys munching grass at the side of the road scrambled up the steep banks, and African children with small scraps of blanket for their only covering waved and shouted 'Molo!' – 'Good morning!' Vicky was charmed to see tiny girls balancing small bundles of sticks or cans of water on their heads in proud imitation of their mothers, who carried huge bundles with a nonchalant tripping step, while large-eyed babies were wedged firmly against their backs.

Now on each side of the road there was indigenous forest, bush and trees with trailing flowering creepers. Grey monkeys frolicked across the road or gazed curiously from the low branches. Then the country became wide and rolling again and far below them beyond the grassy mounds they caught a glimpse of pure blue sea.

There was a collection of round huts a little way from the road, and a small thatched church with a bell in the steeple. They turned off the road and made their way towards this, bumping over the rough ground and trying to avoid large anthills. As they drew to a clattering halt, the small settlement exploded with life. Small herdboys left their work and dashed screaming towards them, and women who were tending the three-legged cooking pots or pounding corn with pestle and mortar seized their babies and came. All around Vicky could hear something that sounded like 'Ee Dokertor!'

The clinic was held in the small church hall. The nursing sister, a fat smiling African woman, had already arrived and the little room resounded with the cries of babies being weighed on a kitchen scale and the chattering of mothers as they waited with their small tins for the distribution of dried milk, baby food and soup powder.

It was Vicky's duty to write down weights and do various clerical tasks. She was amazed at Stephen's patience. When he found a child who showed obvious signs of undernourishment, with the help of the nurse, he would cross-examine the mother or grandmother, who were often suspicious and reluctant to give information. His smiling manner however soon reassured them.

'On what are you feeding this child?' he would ask.

'On food.'

'On what food?'

'On all food.'

'Do you give it milk?'

'Milk?'

'Yes, do you give this child milk?'

'No.'

'With what do you feed it?'

'With the water in which maize is boiled.'

So it went on, with Stephen giving advice and medicines for the worst cases. But there were happy incidents too. Vicky was enchanted when some of the toddlers danced for Stephen. The mothers clapped their hands and the toddlers started to dance in time, posturing and prancing, their small feet stamping, strings of beads jogging upon their fat stomachs.

Stephen was kept busy for the whole morning and Vicky found herself roped in for weighing and for distributing food. Most of the children were obviously poor and ill-fed, but there was a bubbling joyousness in their laughter and an obvious sweetness of disposition that made up for their ragged looks. Those who had behaved well and been brave were rewarded with sweets, but Vicky noticed that they immediately shared them with those less fortunate. She was amazed that children who had so little could be so generous.

At last it was finished and they drove away to the accompaniment of farewell shouts and the barking of lean dogs chasing the Landrover.

'You did well, Miss Scott. You were a great help,' said Stephen.

Vicky felt a glow of pleasure. It was the first time he had ever seemed to approve of her.

'Do you think ... would you mind calling me Vicky?' she asked rather timidly, and wondering whether she was being too rash. But he grinned and said, 'Yes, Vicky, but in that case it's got to be Stephen too. I thought we'd drive down to the sea and have lunch there. It's a beautiful beach.'

Tangled trees and bush stretched right down to the edge of the beach, so that it was only when they descended from the Landrover that Vicky could see the circular bay with its green wooded headlands on each side. The little river which they had crossed on the road by a narrow bridge could now be seen widening out to reach the sea in a broad though shallow lagoon, bordered by wild palm trees.

They parked the vehicle under a tree, and to Vicky the utter silence was a relief after the clattering noise of their journey, but Stephen lifted his hand indicating the trees, and said, 'Listen – Christmas beetles.'

She was all at once aware of a high singing hum, shrill, sweet, dinning persistently upon the ears.

'What are they?' she asked.

'Cicadas,' said Stephen. 'They call them "Christmas beetles" here because that's the time that you hear them most – in high summer. They're brown insects, just like the bark of the trees and very difficult to see.'

'Well, they certainly aren't difficult to hear!'

Vicky found that after the hard morning's work she was ravenous, and the mutton pies and cider were demolished very quickly.

'Would you like to walk along the beach?' asked Stephen.

Vicky was wearing dark brown slacks and a pale yellow shirt almost the same colour as her hair. She took off her shoes and rolled up her slacks in order to walk on the soft sand. Stephen, who was wearing a khaki safari suit, discarded shoes and socks. Vicky felt happy and carefree as she trotted along the beach trying to keep up with Stephen's long strides. He hardly spoke to her, seeming absorbed in his thoughts and the task of keeping his pipe alight.

A slight cool breeze lifted the heat of noonday, and the sun cast a glittering brilliance of sparkling light upon the blue water. Some distance away upon the flat rocks, African women were collecting seaweed. Groves of wild banana palms came right down to the sand. The scene was infinitely wild, yet peaceful. In one place there was a kind of cliff, and water gushed down the rocks from a spring at the top, forming a cascading waterfall, fringed with maidenhair ferns, like a curtain of water in front of a cave hollowed out in the rock.

'There's a fossil of a prehistoric lizard here,' said Stephen.

The weird image of this creature, thousands of years old, seemed to Vicky to give the scene its final touch of fantasy.

'How lovely it is here!' she exclaimed. 'Oh, look, there are some steps cut in the rock.'

'Yes, they lead to the cottage we use when we come down for weekends or holidays. Would you like to see it?'

They climbed the steps and reached a grassy plateau where a log cabin stood. From here the view was tremendous. Standing upon the headland one could see miles of coastline receding beyond the sweep of the bay.

An old African caretaker, called 'Jackson', let them into the cottage and Vicky admired the long living room with its stone fireplace made of boulders and its simple furnishings of old easy chairs and grass mats. There was a deep cushioned settee in front of the window that looked out over the bay. The fireplace was piled up with dry logs.

'It's very cosy here with a big log fire and the wind howling outside,' said Stephen.

Jackson offered them tea and Stephen directed Vicky to the lean-to that served for a bathroom.

'Every drop of water has to be carried from the spring and the plumbing arrangements are adequate but antiquated,' he said. 'It really was only a fishing cottage, but there have been various improvements carried out lately.'

The old caretaker seemed anxious to show her into one of the bedrooms when she had finished washing and she was surprised to find that the white-painted furniture and pale blue curtains and fluffy rugs in this room gave a more luxurious impression than she had received from the rest of the house. She combed her hair at the large frilled dressing table and felt puzzled that this pretty room, with all amenities, should exist in a simple beach cottage.

Old Jackson brought tea in thick white cups on a battered

tin tray and Vicky sat beside Stephen on the settee to pour it. She found herself chattering naturally to him, telling him about her life with her aunt, and he listened with interest, a quick smile transforming his face when she laughed at her own reminiscences.

'When we met,' he said at last, his grey eyes intent upon her face, 'I had an impression of worldliness about you which I find now seems wrong. Why was that?'

'Oh, Stephen,' said Vicky, laughing, 'I was trying to look worldly, as you call it. Evidently from your point of view I'd succeeded too well. It was just that . . .'

'That this young man to whom you were engaged preferred you that way.'

The smile left Stephen's face and it was like a cloud hiding the sun.

'Something like that,' Vicky admitted. 'But I realize now I was wrong to try to alter myself.' She turned to him eagerly. 'Have you seen those necklaces the African women give to their husbands to wear – the Keeper of the Heart?'

'Yes, I know about them.'

'That's what one should do. It's stupid to try to change yourself. I should have said, "Here I am. This is how I am. Love me for myself".'

She flung her arms wide and laughed at her own thoughts. She could not realize that at this moment she presented an alluring picture, brown eyes appealingly vivid, mouth warm and smiling, golden hair like a nimbus of shining light.

Stephen involuntarily put out his arms.

'Vicky,' he said. And then he stopped as a knock sounded upon the door and Jackson shuffled in carrying a small wickerwork cage. The moment of intimacy had vanished almost before it began. Jackson spoke to Stephen eagerly in Xhosa as if describing something.

'Jackson says he found a young bush baby the other day. He kept it because it seemed too young to manage for itself, and now he's wondering whether we would like to have it for Susan,' Stephen explained.

It was a small fluffy animal with enormous golden eyes and the most delicate of little feet and hands.

'They make a lot of noise at night,' Stephen warned, but it was too late. Vicky had fallen irresistibly in love with the tiny creature. They returned it to its cage and to the accompaniment of squeaking noises made their way back to the car.

The sun was setting as they drove home. Figures of women carrying water were silhouetted against the streaks of red and gold, and oxen dragging primitive sledges carried home firewood. Vicky was filled with a deep feeling of contentment. She looked at Stephen sitting beside her, happy, relaxed, his brown hands loose upon the steering wheel. He seemed to sense her gaze and his eyes met hers in a smiling acknowledgement. Then his attention was back on the road where in the half-light a bewildered rabbit was caught in the beam of their headlights. He stopped to let it escape and as if by chance his long brown fingers took her hand and held it for long seconds. A stifling breathlessness seemed to take possession of her.

'Have you enjoyed today?'

'Yes, oh, yes! It's been one of the most lovely days I've ever had.'

With an intense, meaningful gaze, for a moment the grey eyes shattered her tranquillity. Then it was over, and at once she felt she had imagined it. He dropped her hand as if he barely knew he had taken it and then he was driving again towards the fast darkening sky.

'We'll stop at the inn to give Laetitia her basket,' he said as they drew near to the village.

He came out chuckling from his encounter with Mrs. Honeywell.

'Laetitia has remembered the name of that book. Somehow I suspect it's the only book she's ever finished. But she still can't remember the name of the man. So it wasn't much help.'

'What book was it?'

'*Vanity Fair*,' said Stephen.

Vicky felt as though someone had dropped ice down her back. Her reading with her aunt had made her sufficiently conversant with the classics to remember that the book *Vanity Fair* was written by Thackeray. And that was David's last name!

CHAPTER SIX

'MAY I interrupt your work for a few little seconds, Vicky? I promise I won't keep you long. Susan looks most absorbed. What are you doing so earnestly, darling?'

Susan quickly covered her drawing with her arm and scowled belligerently.

'Oh, dear,' thought Vicky. 'Why is she always at her very worst with Olivia?'

The vivid green woven dress Olivia was wearing emphasized the emerald colour of her eyes, and an antique pendant swinging on a chain from her neck matched the intricate bracelet at her wrist. A subtle fragrance wafted towards Vicky as Olivia seated herself on one of the wicker chairs.

'May I go to see if Tandiwe is in the kitchen?' asked Susan. 'Just for a few minutes, Vicky?'

Vicky gave her consent and Susan ran away without a backward glance.

'Quaint – this friendship with the little African girl. Aren't you afraid it might have a bad effect on her manners, Vicky?' said Olivia, implying, Vicky thought ruefully, that Susan's manners needed improving already.

'Tandiwe's manners are really better than Susan's,' she said.

'Yes . . . well . . . Susan's don't seem perfect by any means. Though I'm sure that's not your fault, Vicky dear.

'I'm so glad you were able to go with Stephen, yesterday,' continued Olivia in the same saccharine tone. 'He begged me to come, but I can't always fall in with his wishes when I have other commitments, so I suggested he should ask you.'

'That was kind of you. I enjoyed the day,' Vicky replied equably, though she did not relish feeling obliged to Olivia for her happy excursion.

'He argued at first, of course. He hates a change of plan, but I said I was sure you would be most efficient and he says you were. He says you even weighed babies and did some of Sister's work. My dear, you are enterprising. I would never dream of interfering with Sister.'

Vicky's pride in her work of yesterday collapsed like a pricked balloon under Olivia's barbed remarks. Had she taken too much upon herself? Had Stephen conveyed to Olivia that he had thought she was too interfering?

'Some of the records you filled in will need a little adjusting, but on the whole, Vicky dear, I think you managed remarkably well, considering you'd never done the work before, and I told Stephen that too. I said "Don't worry at all if there are one or two teeny mistakes. I can easily put it right," but he does so hate it when he has to manage with a different assistant.'

'He didn't seem too perturbed,' said Vicky, determined not to show she was upset by Olivia's remarks.

'No, he has a remarkably calm temperament when it has anything to do with his work. He has learned to be patient of course, working as he does with Africans.'

The implication was clear that he had needed to be patient with Vicky. 'Surely I wasn't so bad?' she thought. She hated the idea of Stephen and Olivia discussing her together.

'How did you like our cottage?' asked Olivia.

'It was charming,' Vicky replied warily. 'Our cottage?' she thought.

'It belongs to my brother. It was just a fishing camp, but since I came back I've gradually tried to make some improvements. I have all kinds of ideas for it. Did you go into my bedroom?'

'Yes,' said Vicky, light suddenly dawning concerning the one luxurious room. Of course, Olivia would take care that her own room was improved first of all.

'It's fairly rough, of course. I couldn't bear to stay there for long in its present state, but Stephen and I have spent many happy hours there together.'

Olivia glanced at Vicky's face and seemed to be satisfied with what she saw there, for she changed the subject abruptly, declaring that she must stop gossiping and tell Vicky why she had come.

'I'm giving a party – a day-long one – at the weekend, to welcome Gran and Susan and you, and introduce you all to the neighbourhood. Stephen and Anton say they hope to be free. We'll have a glorious day, swimming, playing tennis, riding – and eating, of course. You haven't seen my house yet, have you? I've had such fun planning it and furnishing. It's almost perfect now. At least I think so.'

She looked critically at the granolithic stoep upon which

they were sitting, as if seeing it in contrast to her own home.

'You should ask Stephen to have a black and white pavement made here,' she suggested. 'It would improve it tremendously.'

Vicky watched her slender green figure walking gracefully away against the background of blossoming hibiscus, flaunting their scarlet flowers in the tall hedge. The bright bloom had vanished from the memory of the day with Stephen. Obviously, discussing her with Olivia, he had considered her just a makeshift assistant and rather a hindrance at that. The happiness she had felt had been hers alone. The intimate moments had been figments of her imagination.

The day of the party arrived and Vicky went in search of a reluctant Susan. She found her giving the bush baby his morning meal of mashed bananas. He had been named Sinkwe because Tandiwe said this was the African name for the little creature. When Susan saw Vicky she let him go and he leapt nimbly around the lawn catching grasshoppers and stuffing them greedily into his mouth, his little hands with their long thin fingers trembling with excitement. Replete, he came back to Susan and scrambled into her arms, his great golden eyes gazing intelligently back at her as she crooned endearments to him.

'Come, Susan,' said Vicky. 'You must put him in his cage. We must get ready to go to Olivia's.'

'I don't want to go to Olivia's house,' said Susan.

'Neither do I,' thought Vicky, but she forced herself to say briskly, 'Nonsense, Sue, you'll have a wonderful time. We'll play games there and have lovely things to eat and drink. Stephen and Gran are coming too. Stephen will help you to swim and ride.'

'Yes, I know,' said Susan. 'But, Vicky, I don't swim well and I don't ride well.'

'Of course you don't, because you're still very young.'

'It's not that,' said Susan with a wisdom beyond her years. 'Sometimes I think I'm just not made right for swimming and riding and playing games.'

Vicky smiled, because this was the way she had often felt about herself, but seeing Susan's woebegone expression she hastily suppressed her amusement.

'Well, do your best, Susan. That's all anyone can ask,' she said, hearing echoes of her aunt's advice when she herself was a schoolgirl.

Olivia's home was something of a showplace in the neighbourhood.

'It's a very grand house,' commented Gran as they entered the circular driveway.

A small piccanin in spotless white uniform was posted at the beautiful wrought iron gate, to open and close it, for, on the outer side of the gate, sheep and cows and donkeys strayed, and one could imagine what devastation they would cause if they entered Olivia's lovely garden. Numerous windmills showed that there was a good water supply from bore-holes, and willow trees with green graceful branches gave an impression of coolness on the edge of the terraced lawns.

Small stone walls edged each lawn with narrow beds of trailing green plants, scarlet zinnias and red petunias. Water bubbled amongst rocks to fall at length into a pool where goldfish lurked below the yellow and pink water-lilies.

The house itself was built of stone, with a roof of dove blue slate, and a large paved patio shaded by a huge bougainvillea plant, covered with so many clusters of red blossom that it was difficult to see any foliage. Elaborate cane chairs and couches padded with bright floral cushions furnished the patio while bright umbrellas, upon the emerald lawns, shaded mosaic-topped and leather padded seats. Inside the house, Gran and Vicky admired the velvet chairs in antique gold, the shining yellow-wood floors, the jewel-like Persian rugs. Everything spoke of a luxurious taste that had been indulged without thought of cost. Olivia, in a slacks suit of violet coloured silk, seemed the perfect hostess. The whole house was a setting for her dark beauty.

Vicky was astounded anew by the fact that Stephen seemed drawn to Olivia. He, who did not seem to have a material thought in his head, apart from worry about money for his hospital, seemed singularly unsuited to a woman who appeared to need luxury as a cat needs cream.

Tea was served upon the terrace. Neighbours had come from far and near, traders, magistrates, and other officials from small Transkei villages, as well as doctors who were in private practice. Some were playing tennis on the two hard courts beyond the lawns. Others were disporting themselves in the large blue kidney-shaped swimming pool. Vicky was surprised to see Laetitia Honeywell dive in, then surface like a whale. She was wearing a costume in a floral pattern of brilliant scarlet poppies and her plaits were covered by an enormous headpiece looking like a whole bed of roses.

She waved gaily at Vicky and later came to sit by her, draped in an emerald green towelling cloak. She accepted tea and bit cautiously into a *koeksuster,* a kind of fried pastry dripping with syrup.

'Wonder who made these for Olivia?' she asked. 'It's quite an art.'

'I heard her telling Gran she had made them herself,' said Vicky.

Laetitia snorted.

'Never! Don't you believe it. Olivia wouldn't spend hours making things like this if she could get anyone else to do it. But I mustn't speak ill of my hostess, must I?' And she proceeded to expound to Vicky on how much Olivia had spent on the house.

'I wouldn't be surprised if she isn't spending more than her brother can afford. They tell me he's been drinking more than usual lately. That's a sure sign that he's worried. Look at the place! You'd think it had been built for a millionaire. I'm sorry for Anthony Chazal. Before she came to settle with him he was doing well in a modest way. All he cared about was his horses, but now I hear he's quietly selling some of his best stock. You can't spend money like water as she does without someone suffering for it.'

They watched Stephen diving like a seal into the pool and gaily encouraging Susan to swim. He looked so carefree for once and Susan was so brown and happy. Vicky felt a thrill of warm pleasure as she looked at them both.

'I'm sorry for Dr. Stephen,' said Laetitia. 'That Olivia seems to get anything she sets her heart on. She's drained her brother dry, so now she sees Stephen as a good way to get away from here before the rot sets in.'

'But I don't think he has any intention of leaving,' Vicky protested. 'This is his life. He doesn't seem to want any other.'

'If she decides he's got to go, I guess he won't have much choice.'

'Oh, Laetitia, he's not foolish. He has a singularly strong will of his own. I shouldn't think he could be persuaded to do anything he doesn't want to.'

'Anyone can be persuaded to do anything if they're in love,

or think they are,' said Laetitia dogmatically.

The warm feeling that Vicky had experienced a few minutes ago evaporated. She noticed a cool wind was blowing across the lawn and that Susan was coming towards her looking sulky and Stephen was sitting on the edge of the pool with Olivia, whose beautiful olive brown body was displayed to perfection in a bikini like the silver-green wings of a dragonfly.

'Excuse me,' she said to Laetitia, and went towards Susan.

'Olivia says I should try to dive in the deep end, but I don't want to, and Stephen is cross.'

'Well, come and change and get warm,' said Vicky, who believed that in Susan's case a little spoiling did more good than too much discipline.

'Olivia says I must put on slacks for riding,' said Susan, her face a picture of misery.

'Put them on, and come down to have lunch first,' Vicky instructed, not liking to interfere with Stephen's plans for Susan's entertainment.

'The horses all look so big,' said Susan, walking slowly away and shivering a little in her wet costume. She looked small and frail and Vicky was tempted to run after her, but felt she must not fuss.

'Ah, Vicky, I hoped I would find you!' Anton dropped into the seat recently vacated by Laetitia. 'How charming you look in that pale green . . . what material is it?'

'Voile,' said Vicky, amused as always by Anton's interest in clothes.

'You look like a cool, sweet . . . what can I call you that is green?'

'A cabbage?' suggested Vicky.

'Now you make fun. A water-lily, a greenish white water-lily with a heart of golden stamens. That is your hair.'

'I didn't know a doctor could be so poetic.'

'Only a doctor from Vienna. Do water-lilies eat?'

'They get absolutely ravenous,' Vicky assured him as the guests were summoned to lunch by the silvery sound of a bell.

Mounds of crayfish tails with their sweet nutty flavour were served with all kinds of exotic salads, pineapple, green pepper, avocado pear. Succulent fried chicken, duck baked with slivers of orange, large whole fish baked and decorated, and sucking pig golden and crisp, made it difficult to choose what to eat next.

Chilled rosé wine of a delicate pink colour was served in long thin goblets and the final course was Baked Alaska, borne in triumphantly by the white-gloved servants; it was made of ice cream and crushed strawberries topped with meringue and baked so that the palate was astonished by the mixture of heat and cold.

Susan ate very little. She was quiet and paler than usual.

'Why aren't you eating, Susan?' asked Stephen.

'I'm not hungry,' she said, swinging her arms self-consciously.

'A good ride on one of our ponies will sharpen up her appetite. How about it, Susan?' said Olivia with a rather poor imitation of joviality, or so Vicky thought.

'Stephen, I don't like——' Susan, paler than ever, gazed imploringly at him.

'Olivia has offered to improve your riding, Susan. Once you get the hang of doing it properly, you'll enjoy it.'

'I'll take you now,' said Olivia. 'We'll go together, just the two of us.'

All her charm was in her smile and she put her arm coaxingly around Susan. Susan stiffened, then said reluctantly, 'Do you want me to go, Stephen?'

'Yes, of course I do.'

'Do you, Anton?'

'Well, yes, it is good to be able to ride. In Vienna they have beautiful horses that can dance.'

'Do you, Vicky?'

'Yes,' said Vicky, though she felt a qualm of guilt as if she had betrayed the child.

'Then I will.'

She had an expression of dour determination which reminded Vicky of Stephen, as she and Olivia vanished in the direction of the stables.

'Why do you make her do things she hates?' demanded Vicky, touched anew by the small, rigid, receding back. Stephen looked surprised.

'But, Vicky, you can't let her turn her back on everything she's disinclined to do. She'll get pleasure from riding later on when she's used to it.'

'You don't seem to realize how sensitive she is.'

Anton was listening to the conversation with a smiling face. Now he flung his arms wide.

'This little Vicky, she is so *gentille*, so *sympathique*. If the Africans portrayed her in a necklace they would have to put middle larger than head to show she has a big heart.'

Stephen looked annoyed at the interruption.

'That's all very well, but sentimentality is wasted upon children. They must learn to do what's best for them in their future life.'

Vicky's gentle nature was stung to retort.

'If they portrayed you, Stephen, I think they would give you a heart of stone. You're so unfeeling with Susan. I suspect even the children in the hospital are just so many cases to you!'

She knew this was grossly unfair because she did not really know much about his attitude to his patients, but she wanted to lash out at him, hurt him as he had hurt her. She felt bruised by the constant coldness he seemed to display in his behaviour with Susan. This time spent at Olivia's house had obliterated all thought of the lovely day they had enjoyed at the coast.

'He's impossible,' she thought. 'What am I to do? If I leave Susan, I'll feel I'm deserting the child. But I can't stay here when he's so opposed to everything I feel about Susan's need for tenderness and love.'

When Susan returned, the sun and wind had whipped a little colour into her cheeks, but she was quiet and very thoughtful. Later when Vicky supervised her going to bed, she looked tired with heavy blue shadows around her eyes. She seemed withdrawn into a world of her own and there was none of the gay chatter to which Vicky had become accustomed since Susan had got to know her well.

She lay flat on her pillow, her slight small body scarcely raising a curve in the sheet. Tonight all the benefits of the last few weeks seemed to have vanished. There was a lost look about her that tore at Vicky's heart. At last she said, 'Vicky, if someone makes you swear not to tell a thing, must you never tell, not even to someone you love?'

'Well, I suppose it depends upon what it is, but a promise is a promise. You shouldn't break it. There must be some reason if you're asked not to repeat a thing. Repeating things you shouldn't leads to gossip.'

Vicky felt Stephen would have approved of her uncompromising reply to Susan.

'Olivia said it's secret, but I thought perhaps I could tell you.'

Vicky's mind shied away from the disclosure Susan seemed about to make. Could Olivia have told the child that she and Stephen intended to marry? If so, she did not want to hear it until they were prepared to announce it publicly.

'You mustn't tell me,' she said. 'If Olivia told you it was secret then you must keep it so. Now try to sleep.'

Susan closed her eyes obediently. The blue veined lids looked tender and vulnerable.

'Why did I ever meet her?' thought Vicky. 'How can I break these ties that bind me to her now? Why did I meet either of them?'

CHAPTER SEVEN

'AH, how elegant you look. Laetitia will think some lady from Paris has come to dine at her hotel,' said Anton waving his hands in admiration.

Vicky was wearing the dress that flashed like a blackbird's wing. Iridescent crystals shone at her throat and ears, and her hair was swept upwards into a topknot of cascading curls.

'Have a good time,' said Gran, beaming. 'Take care of her, Anton.'

Anton kissed Gran's hand.

'If only you were a few years younger, Mrs. Grant, I would not look at Miss Vicky!'

'Och, away with you! Aren't you ashamed to use your Continental manners on a plain old Scots wifie?' Gran scoffed, but her faded blue eyes twinkled and Vicky admired anew Anton's overwhelming charm that attracted small sick children and old ladies as well as young women.

'And you, Miss Susan, in a few years' time those large grey eyes will be breaking hearts.'

'I will never marry, Anton. I will stay with Stephen and Gran always,' said Susan adamantly.

A shadow passed across Gran's bright expression.

'Always is a long time, Susan, my bairn,,' she said.

Anton helped Vicky into his sleek black Mercedes and they drove slowly through the hospital grounds.

'Do you mind?' said Anton. 'I'll have to stop a moment at the hospital. I want to give Stephen a message about one of the children.'

When Stephen heard the car he strode out of one of the wards on to the verandah. He looked a little startled when he saw Vicky in the car, then he walked across and stood near the driver's side. Anton gave him some technical details and he nodded.

'How is Mofolo?' asked Anton.

Stephen shrugged. 'Bad,' he said. His face was bleak as, without expression, he looked at Vicky, seeming to examine her finery as if she were an inhabitant of another planet.

'Does not our little Vicky look elegant tonight?' asked the

irrepressible Anton. 'Even you, Stephen, must admit how attractive she looks.'

Vicky's fine skin flushed as Stephen's grey eyes met hers.

'Her dress has the iridescence of a peacock's feathers, yes?' said Anton.

'Women's dress is not one of my hobbies, Anton, but fine feathers have a romantic purpose, I've always understood, and beautiful dresses are worn with just one object, to attract the victim.'

'Victim?' laughed Anton. 'What a word! Am I your victim, my Vicky?'

'I suppose if Stephen had his way, women would go round in sackcloth and ashes,' Vicky snapped fiercely.

Anton laughed delightedly. 'Come, Vicky, let us leave this barbarian. You can be certain that I for one appreciate your good taste.'

Anton glanced once or twice at her set face as he drove the powerful car smoothly over the country road. Then he took one hand from the wheel and gently touched her cheek.

'Forget Stephen and his lack of tact. Think only of the delightful evening we are to have together, darling Vicky.'

'He's impossible,' said Vicky vehemently. 'Sometimes he seems friendly, then, only a short while later, everything I do is wrong.'

'No, no. And even if this is so, he is like that with all women – a difficult temperament. But beneath, believe me, there is the warm, the loving heart. I see it in the hospital, day after day. He conquers the Africans' mistrust. They all love him.'

'I find it difficult to believe you. It's your own warm heart that only sees the best in people. He's so cold, so clinical. He doesn't seem to see people as people.'

'I don't want to argue with you, my Vicky, but some day you will find you are wrong.'

Vicky shrugged impatiently.

'Let's not talk about it any more.'

'With pleasure, Vicky. Let's talk about ourselves, such interesting, charming people, no?'

Laetitia was ensconced at the reception desk of the hotel, her thick plaits coiled like a crown on her head, and gleaming like golden syrup, her black crêpe dress glittering with an intricate pattern of silver beads.

'So here you are! Well, Vicky, you look smashing. Anton

phoned to say you'd be here and I made you a special starter – but wait and see!'

'Join us in an aperitif, Laetitia,' pressed Anton.

'Thanks ever so, but I can't manage it, lovey. I've got such a crowd of visitors this weekend, passing through to the coast, besides the usual commercial gents. By the way, that fellow who phoned did come, Vicky. He's here now.'

'Here in the hotel?' asked Vicky, feeling as if someone had deprived her of movement.

'Well, I don't see him around at the moment, but I expect he'll be in for dinner.'

Vicky felt bewildered. Surely David would have let her know if he was coming? But then again perhaps not. He might have suspected she would try to forbid his coming.

They sat at a small table upon the green lawn enclosed by the long low single-storey hotel. Anton set himself to amuse with stories of his student days in Vienna, and soon Vicky was laughing in response as she sipped the dry chilled Martini, the concoction of which Anton had carefully supervised.

She felt more relaxed now. It could not be David! Why had she not asked Laetitia for the visitor's name? But she had been scared to confirm her suspicions. As soon as she saw Laetitia she would ask her. But Laetitia had disappeared in the direction of the hotel kitchen from which every now and again you could hear her booming voice, a clatter of dishes, and odd fierce exclamations in Xhosa.

A white-coated waiter summoned them to the dining room. Obviously Anton had ordered very special service, for the table was set with cool pale green bone china and glittered with cut glass. Yellow roses in a small crescent-shaped arrangement glowed in the light from three white candles in a silver container.

'How charming you look by candlelight, Vicky,' said Anton. 'Your eyes are like those brown velvety pansies that Laetitia has in her flower border.'

'What flattering things he says,' thought Vicky. 'I can't imagine Stephen . . . no, I mustn't think of him.'

One swift glance around the room had confirmed the fact that David was not here. Vicky gave herself entirely to enjoying the evening. It was foolish to worry so much about something that she had merely surmised.

Laetitia's promised 'starter' proved to be a crayfish dish cooked in a creamy sauce with cheese and mushroom and served brown, sizzling and delicious in scallop shells. This was followed by Laetitia's own version of Cordon Bleu Steak, tender fillet sliced thinly and stuffed with ham and cheese, the whole served with a wine sauce. Meringue with a filling of strawberries soaked in kirsch and topped with cream followed, and at last they arose from the table and returned to the grassy lawn to order coffee and liqueurs.

Vicky felt happier and more relaxed. When Laetitia came by, she would ask the name of the man who had come to stay, but by now she was convinced that she had made a foolish mistake. Why had she become so convinced that the visitor was David? There was no cause except her own vivid imagination and Laetitia's vague remark about *Vanity Fair*.

The swing doors to the kitchen swung wildly and Laetitia came rushing along the verandah. For a big woman she moved remarkably quickly.

'Now I can ask her,' thought Vicky, but when she saw her face all thought of her question was banished.

'Quick, Anton!' Laetitia called. 'I hate to interrupt you, loves, but there's been a fight in the servants' quarters. A strange boy came there to see one of the waiters' girl-friends and Nelson has been stabbed. He's bleeding badly.'

Anton got up immediately.

'Can I help?' asked Vicky.

'I don't think there's any need. I'll send for you if I need you. Meanwhile, Laetitia, phone the police and the ambulance service. Sorry to leave you on your own, Vicky. I'll try not to be too long.'

'Don't look so pale, honey,' Laetitia reassured her. 'These things are always happening.' And she hurried off to the phone.

Vicky sat quietly, feeling a little useless, but mainly rather drowsy from the good food and drink. The sound of footsteps were muffled by the grass and she sat up with a start when she became aware of a figure standing beside her chair.

'May I talk to you, Miss Scott? George Osborne's the name.'

He turned his face towards the light, and with a feeling of incredulity Vicky recognized the stranger they had met on the mountain in Cape Town.

'Do you mind if I sit down?' And with that he took the chair that Anton had vacated.

Vicky's brain was working furiously. George Osborne – of course, she remembered Laetitia's mention of *Vanity Fair*. Obviously she had not been thinking of Thackeray, the author. One of the characters, Amelia's husband, the one who got killed at the Battle of Waterloo – he was George Osborne.

Momentarily, such was Vicky's relief that the visitor was not her former fiancé that she did not give a thought to the real significance of the stranger's name.

'Doesn't the name ring a bell, Miss Scott?' asked the man. He was dressed more carefully than before, but she remembered the slightly irritating, ingratiating manner.

'No, should it?' asked Vicky. 'I remember of course that we met before upon Table Mountain.'

'Ah, now, Miss Scott – and I thought you were such an intelligent young lady. Hasn't it struck you that your young pupil has the same name?'

'The same name . . .' Vicky's mind felt blank.

'Naturally, because, Miss Scott, I happen to be Susan's father. That surprises you, doesn't it?' He observed her start of dismay with a kind of satisfaction. 'I've been trying to get in touch with you since that time in Cape Town. When I saw tonight that you were alone, I decided I wouldn't wait any longer before venturing to approach you.'

'But what are you doing here? What do you want?' asked Vicky rather sharply.

'Miss Scott, there isn't much time. That foreign doctor friend of yours will be back soon. I must explain quickly. I need your help. You've maybe heard talk about me. I left Susan's mother when we were both young and foolish. Oh, I'm not trying to make excuses for myself. I'd never been used to responsibility and I thought the world owed me a living. But I've knocked around since then and rubbed off the rough spots while I've been doing it. I'm steadier now, but up to this I've been moving from place to place, and there's been no room in my life for a child.'

'You want Susan?' whispered Vicky faintly.

'You may think it strange for a man who discarded fatherhood almost before it had begun, but I've never forgotten that somewhere in the world I had a daughter, and now the time has come when I can settle and make a home, a thing

I've never had and always longed for.'

'But you're a stranger to Susan,' said Vicky.

'No more a stranger than Dr. Nash was. She's only known him a little while.'

'And how can you make a home for her on your own?'

'I won't be on my own. I intend to marry again.'

Vicky gazed at him, turning over his statement in her mind, trying frantically to weigh this unexpected development.

'My future wife knows about Susan. She's willing and eager to care for her. She is a charming, cultured person. Susan will have every advantage in her upbringing. Think of it, Miss Scott, wouldn't it be to Susan's advantage to have a normal home life?'

'I suppose it would,' Vicky admitted. 'But she's happy enough here.'

'Can you honestly say that it's the best life for her, being brought up by an old woman of eighty and a busy doctor who can't call his soul his own, let alone look after a small girl?'

'She has me,' said Vicky hesitantly.

'For how long? You can't tell me you intend to stay here for ever, Miss Scott. This job is only a stopgap for you, isn't that so?'

'I suppose it is,' thought Vicky sadly. 'Certainly I won't be needed or wanted if Stephen marries Olivia and neither will Susan. Susan is so fond of Stephen, but he treats her so coolly, and after he marries Olivia ... If Susan lived in town she could go to school, meet other children ...'

'What do you want me to do?' she asked aloud.

'That's better. I thought you would be sensible. Just to explain to Dr. Nash why I'm here and ask if he'll see me. It will smooth the way for my approach if you would do that for me.'

'He's scared of Stephen,' thought Vicky. 'Well, I can't blame him. Come to think of it, so am I.'

'I don't know whether I can,' she started to say. 'I really have no influence with Dr. Nash.'

'But you have my daughter's welfare at heart, I could tell that the first time I met you on the mountain.'

Vicky shuddered when she recollected the confused fear she had felt on that day when Susan had vanished into the mist with this man. But she had experienced the same panic when Stephen had held her over the high bridge at Storms River. It could have been due to her own nervous, overwrought state of mind.

George Osborne would never have sought her out if he had not been thinking of his own affection for his daughter and her future welfare. Perhaps she had found the solution to the problem of Susan.

'I'll speak to Dr. Nash,' she said, 'and let you know if he'll see you.'

'Everything has arranged itself now. Sorry to keep you waiting, my Vicky. The victim had taken someone else's girl-friend. Knives provide a quick end to a dispute sometimes, but rather a messy solution.'

Anton was as immaculate as if he had just come from his brother's.

'Will he be all right?' asked Vicky.

'He'll live to fight another day. Isn't there such an English saying?' He ordered a double vodka and tossed it off in one gulp. 'That's the way the Russians drink it, like swallow-ing oysters,' he grinned. 'I needed that badly.' And he beckoned to the waiter to bring another. 'Some wine for you, Vicky?'

'No, thank you. The wine with dinner was quite enough for me.'

'What a little Puritan you are,' he smiled, but she was relieved that he did not press her any further.

Vicky was slightly worried that Anton should still be drink-ing, considering that they still had to negotiate the rough road home, but he laughed heartily when she attempted to remonstrate.

'Drink heightens my sensibilities in a very beautiful way, my lovely Vicky,' he assured her with a very wicked twinkle. 'Not to worry. I promise you will enjoy the drive back in the moonlight.'

Vicky's heart sank. Suddenly all she wanted was to be a long way from here.

'Anton, I think we should go,' she urged.

He rose quite steadily to his feet. There was just slightly more deliberation in his movements.

'Anything you say, Vicky. Yes, it would be a good idea to go.

No future in sitting here, is there?'

He took her arm as they walked back to the car, but neither of them spoke as he drove away from the hotel.

Vicky felt tired out after the emotional scene with Susan's father and all the problems it seemed to entail, and she hoped she would be able to cope with Anton in his present mood, if he decided to be difficult. But for the moment she was too weary to care, and grateful for his momentary silence.

At least he drove well. The vodka did not seem to have affected his physical reactions and there was not another car on the lonely road. The landscape was a uniform misty blue colour, far hills standing sharp against the sky, the stars eclipsed by the stronger light of the moon.

'Da-da, da-da, da-daa, da-da,' carolled Anton, humming variations of Strauss waltzes. 'Why such a space between us? Why that cold exquisite profile turned towards the moon and away from me? Don't you like me a little, Vicky?'

Anton leaned across and drew her towards him, encircling her with one arm and caressing her shoulders while with the other he guided the car, carelessly, expertly, his fingers tapping out the waltz rhythm. He was like a small boy demanding sweets. Vicky found it hard to be cold to him.

'You're incorrigible!' she said, trying in vain to sound cross and to draw away from him.

'What means this so long word?' demanded Anton, his accent becoming more Continental as it suited his purpose. 'Amorous, affectionate, attractive, these I hope I am, all these I understand, Vicky, but not this incorri– what is it?'

'Hopeless,' sighed Vicky.

'Oh, no, no, that I am not. I am very hopeful, my Vicky, I am very hopeful that soon you are going to like me very much. You like me a little, *nicht wahr*?'

'Perhaps,' said Vicky.

'Ah, you know the old saying that when a woman says "no" she means "perhaps" and when she says "perhaps" she means "yes".'

The hospital appeared to be asleep when they arrived there, moonlight shining upon the corrugated iron roofs, and the white walls luminous. Anton drew to a halt a little way from the cottage, working the mechanism of the car to lower the roof. They sat bathed in moonlight, not even a breeze disturbing the mellow warm air.

'Your hair is like spun silk,' said Anton, leaning over to touch it. 'What very beautiful eyes you have, Vicky. Like two dark stars.'

Then without wishing it, she was in his arms, his face above her, shadowy, blocking out the moonlight, handsome, infinitely attractive. His lips were seeking hers and his body was hard and muscular as she endeavoured in vain with all her strength to push him away. She was gripped in a strong tender trap from which there seemed no escape. The kiss was long, everything a kiss should be. Then suddenly it was over. He withdrew from her gently and lifted her chin so that she was forced to look at him.

'It's no good, is it, Vicky?'

She shook her head dumbly.

'There's someone else you love.'

'No, no!' she denied vehemently.

'What a fool I am not to have seen it before. Of course, it's Stephen.'

She shook her head, finding her voice with difficulty.

'I love nobody, Anton. I don't want anything to do with men. I'm through with love. As for your last suggestion, it's idiotic. If Stephen were the last man in the world, I'd never want him. He's cold. He hasn't got a loving thought in his head. He's impossible.'

Anton kissed her hand. The effect of the vodka seemed to have disappeared completely. He was his nice, charming, but utterly unreliable self again.

'Nothing is impossible. That's what my English nanny used to say to me, very very long ago.' He lifted her hands to his forehead. 'Beautiful, cool hands!' he said. Then he placed them gently down again. 'But not for me. Go, then, little Vicky, before I am carried away again by those huge dark eyes and that small straight nose and the mouth that tries so hard to be prim but is made for passion.'

He accompanied her to the steps of the verandah, then, after kissing both her hands, he withdrew. She watched him go, feeling rather sad, though she did not know why.

It was impossible to settle down to sleep, tired though she was. Vicky took a shower, dusting herself with a fragrant talc that smelled of lemon verbena, brushed her hair vigorously, then pinned it up on top of her head, but she could not yet face lying down and having the waiting thoughts rush at her like so many flittering bats. She put on a mandarin trouser suit of white silk which fell about her slight body in cool folds. The intricate silver embroidery upon the jacket made it seem too exotic for the simplicity of her life here at the hospital, but tonight the coolness of the material was infinitely soothing in the close still air.

Hearing a noise in Susan's room, she went in. Sinkwe, the bush baby, was awake, made restless by the moonlight flooding through the small window. At any moment now, Vicky knew, he would start his pathetic wailing, like the cries of a young baby. Not wanting Susan to be disrupted, she lifted him carefully in her arms and, taking his box as well, she quietly let herself out and sat on the moonlit grass. She released him and he leaped around grabbing at moths with his soft paws, scuttling back every now and again to nestle in her arms.

Vicky gazed over the valley, where the shadows of trees and rocks looked more substantial than the objects they reflected. She had been shaken but not shocked by Anton's behaviour. Of course he would make love to any moderately attractive woman given the opportunity. She had no illusions in that respect. Dear Anton, charming, apparently brilliantly clever and quite serious where his work was concerned, but utterly irresponsible about women. He could not resist trying to charm any female, even old ladies and children.

But this was accompanied by a delicacy, a sensitiveness to feminine reaction which was often lacking in men of a more masculine outlook. He had sensed her cool withdrawal almost before she had realized it herself. What nonsense he had talked! How could he think she was interested in Stephen when obviously Stephen only had eyes for Olivia? Surely working with them as he did in the hospital, he must know of their intention to marry? But he himself seemed so cool towards Olivia that perhaps he could not imagine Stephen being seriously in love with her. That was one woman he did not go out of his way to charm. Or perhaps he had at some time tried to do so and had been rebuffed.

Her eye was caught by something a little unusual to the right of her. Slung between two trees was a hammock. Susan sometimes took her afternoon rest there and occasionally Gran used it, though she usually declared it was too unstable for an old lady.

Someone was lying there, face turned upwards to the sky, white coat dappled by a tracing of shadows from the branches above. Vicky was alarmed. The figure lay so still it was almost as if . . .

She glanced behind her at the white walls and blank windows of the sleeping cottage. She did not consider herself very courageous, but for Susan's sake, for Gran's sake, she must investigate the still form beneath the trees. Placing Sinkwe in his box, she rose quietly and walked softly across, her bare feet making no sound upon the dew-wet grass.

He lay with a lock of dark hair brushing his forehead, his white jacket open at the throat, eyes open, dark and shining in the silver light. He seemed unaware of her presence even though she was standing less than two feet away. It was his rigid, almost trance-like attitude that alarmed her.

'Stephen,' she said softly, putting out a tentative hand to touch his arm. His eyes flickered and he uttered a deep sigh, almost a moan of pain.

'What is it?' she asked.

He sat up, shaking his head, and swung his long legs over the side of the hammock, stretching his lithe body as if scarcely conscious of what he was doing. His indifferent glance swept over the silk mandarin jacket, the folds of the trouser suit, and rested briefly upon her brown eyes which were warm and concerned.

'What's happened, Stephen?'

'Nothing that concerns you, Vicky. Nothing to worry anyone really. Merely another African child has died, and what is there in that to worry anyone? It happens every day.'

'Was it Mofolo?' asked Vicky.

He nodded.

'Mofolo . . . died from cardiac failure. His mother walked many miles over rough country carrying him on her back, because she hoped I could play God. I tried everything . . . but what use was it? He was doomed from the beginning, from the moment he was born.'

'I'm sorry,' said Vicky.

'Yes, I'd forgotten. You were the one who said I should be portrayed with a heart of stone. I wish you were right. A heart of stone would be a very useful thing to have in our profession.'

'Please forgive me,' said Vicky. 'I was annoyed at the time.'

'Annoyed? Oh, yes, because you think I'm unkind, unfeeling to children. You, with your fine sentimental feelings about children ... how do you think it feels to see a child dying, to know there's nothing you can do except relieve pain a little? Stupid women used to say to me it must be wonderful to be a doctor, wonderful to save lives. All nonsense! When you have people who live from hand to mouth, who have empty stomachs most of the time, coming usually too late in any case to a hospital that lacks money, lacks equipment, you're liable to lose more lives than you save.'

'Stephen, please, please listen to me.' Vicky was half scared, half in awe of this tall, bitter stranger. 'You do far more good here than you seem to realize. The hospital couldn't go on without you. You do save lives, and the Africans love you. Anton says so.'

'Anton? Oh, yes, I was here this evening when you parted. Quite a pretty picture! Anton is quick enough to find diversions to keep his mind off any worries. And you ... you seem more than eager to provide for his entertainment.'

'Don't speak to me like this, Stephen!'

Vicky was torn between compassion and anger.

'Why not? Don't say you even forbid me to speak to you when both Anton and your ex-fiancé are willingly accorded other privileges? Or do you prefer this?'

All at once her small fair head was cradled in his arms and he was kissing her with a rapturous fury that left no room for conscious thought. This was different from anything she had ever known. She felt her own lips, warm, responsive, eager, returning his kisses with a passion that she had never felt before.

He drew away from her, grasping both shoulders in a grip that she could feel bruising her flesh underneath the thin silk of her jacket. She smiled tenderly, murmuring, though her voice was scarcely audible, 'Stephen, I didn't know ... I never dreamed it could be like this ...'

Something silenced her, his angry stance, the steely glitter of his eyes. She looked at him bewildered, the joyous enchantment draining away, dying.

'It's as I thought,' he said. 'Anyone will do. Frailty, thy name is Woman! No wonder the young man in Cape Town thought better of his engagement to you. He was wise. And Anton – women are his weakness. That suits you well, I suppose? You're not particular if you share him, as long as he doesn't mind sharing you, is that it? But I warn you, keep away from him. I won't have his brilliant career ruined by meeting someone like you who could only bring unhappiness. A doctor needs a faithful wife.'

'Stephen, listen to me. You have the wrong idea of me. From the beginning you've always thought the worst of me.'

'And haven't you proved me right? You denied you were sophisticated, but an innocent girl doesn't behave as you do. Casual lovemaking may be all very well to a worldly person like you, but it's not suitable – it's disgusting – in a small community like this.'

'Disgusting?' echoed Vicky, cut to the heart.

'Susan is fond of you, but that's not enough. I hesitate to leave her in the care of someone whose principles are to be doubted, a frivolous person who even at night dresses as if for a masquerade.'

He was wounding her with words, cutting her into little pieces to throw to the winds.

'You know I love Susan. I would never do anything to harm her, but you make it so difficult for me with your constant disapproval.'

'Do you expect me to approve of your light behaviour? It's as Olivia says. You have to be born in the Transkei to understand the way of life here, or otherwise to be very devoted to the people here. But your devotion, Miss Scott, seems to take too amorous a form.'

The mention of Olivia gave her the courage of anger.

'Would you like me to leave?'

Her voice was hoarse with unshed tears, but she held her head proudly high.

'Leave?' Her words seemed somehow to check his anger. 'If you do it will be by your own choice. I don't want to spoil Susan's or Gran's Christmas. I would like you to stay at least until that's over. After that you can decide for yourself. It's up to you. Meanwhile I would be obliged if you don't say a word of this to anyone. Neither will I.'

He strode rapidly away across the lawn.

Hardly knowing what she was doing. Vicky took up the bush baby from where he was chasing moths upon the grass. He gazed at her with his great golden eyes and lifted a tentative paw to pat her face.

She lay upon the hammock and putting her face against the warm grey fur wept bitterly for love offered and snatched away in a fleeting matter of moments. With sadness she realized that in spite of his contempt and bitter words, his kiss had changed her world. For to her Stephen had become the Keeper of the Heart.

CHAPTER EIGHT

'Och, really, Vicky, I don't know how I ever managed without you,' said Gran. Innocent remarks like this hurt more than anything else. They were sewing angels' costumes for Gran's Christmas concert. The haloes were made of gold tinfoil and the wings of white face tissues cut into feathers and stuck on to cardboard shapes.

'Are you tired, child? You have blue shadows under your eyes. Don't let Anton worry you. An old lady can speak frankly. I hope you aren't taking him too seriously, Vicky. He's not for you. He'd lead any poor wife of his a terrible jig. To my mind, Vicky, you deserve someone who will always think the world of you.'

'Oh, Gran, it doesn't seem so easy to find a person like that. But don't worry about Anton. I won't take him seriously.'

'There's only one person I could take seriously,' thought Vicky. 'And he despises me.'

She longed to see Stephen, but dreaded their next meeting. If she was to fulfil her promise to George Osborne, their meeting must be soon. Could she phone Susan's father to tell him she would not do it? It was all so difficult. She would decide later.

'I sometimes wish in a way, Vicky, that you were nae so bonny.'

Gran was struggling with the glue pot lid and Vicky hastened to open it for her. She looked inquiringly at the old lady.

'Because one of these days you will be getting married. A person as sweet as she's pretty won't get left for long, you may be sure, and I dearly wish I could believe you would be here with Susan until such time as she can go to school.'

Yesterday Vicky would have hastened to reassure Mrs. Grant with promises that she intended to stay with Susan for a long time. She believed Gran was half inviting this, but how could she make any promises when she had reached the conclusion that it would be better if she left?

'Whatever happens to me,' she said, 'Susan will have you until she goes to school.'

She imagined Gran looked a little hurt by her cool,

wary reply.

'That's what's worrying me a wee bit,' she said. 'I had a letter from my sister's neighbour yesterday. She said Harry isn't at all well. She is worried about her living alone and says something should be done about it. I'm thinking I may have to go back home for a wee while after Christmas.'

Vicky felt considerable dismay.

'But it all seems to point in one direction,' she thought. 'Maybe Susan would be better with her father. At least she would be more settled. I can't leave her knowing that Gran is going and Stephen is probably going to marry Olivia soon.'

When Vicky dreaded doing anything she steeled herself to do it quickly and get it over. Now she went on to the stoep where she had left Susan wrestling with arithmetic problems. She set her drawing a map. That would take half an hour at least. In that time she could attempt to approach Stephen. If he was busy with a patient of course it would be impossible. But she would have to take that chance.

Sinkwe was curled into his box in a sleek furry ball. 'He seems sleepy today,' said Susan.

'He was very lively last night,' Vicky informed her. 'You should have seen him leaping around on the grass chasing moths.'

'Last night!' her heart cried. 'When I was playing with Sinkwe, I wasn't even aware ... I hadn't even realized ...'

'He has almost finished his ward rounds,' an African nurse informed her, when she inquired for Stephen. 'If you go to the orthopaedic ward, he will be out soon. I'm going there myself, so I'll take you.'

As she approached the meshed verandah she could hear the singing voices of children. She stood to the side of the verandah from where she could see without being seen. The African nurse stood beside her rather curious to know what Vicky wanted with Dr. Nash.

He was standing with the African Sister, and a small child wearing a leg iron was in his arms. The others were grouped around him and he was listening to them playing a singing game. These were the more mobile ones. Those who were confined to their beds listened eagerly. Those joining in the game had small stones in front of them and, as it came to each child's turn, he or she held up a stone and sang. First there was a solo, then a chorus. The game seemed to entail much laughing and pointing.

'What does it mean?' Vicky asked.

'It is a game about birds, or it can be about animals,' the nurse explained.

'First they sing all together, "I am singing about a bird, a fine-looking fellow that flies in the sky. He flies so high, he almost reaches the sun." Then the doctor points to one child who picks up a stone and must describe a bird: "I am singing about the dove, fine-looking fellow, a dove that goes coo-curu in the green tree. This dove flies so high he almost reaches the sun." Each child must sing about a different bird. If they fail to name a bird, or if one is repeated, that child is out of the game.'

Vicky was surprised and touched to see Stephen in this new role.

'When Doctor finishes his ward rounds early, he sometimes plays a game with the children,' the nurse whispered.

The children were bright-eyed, smiling, and gazing at Stephen as if he were the most important person in the world. And he laughed and joked with them, his beautiful smile transforming his rather haggard face until one would scarcely have believed this was the same person who last night spoke so bitterly of the limitations of his profession.

As Vicky watched him, the pain and tumult of her own feelings seemed too difficult to endure. 'I love him,' she thought. 'He's difficult, temperamental, proud, obstinate – and yet I love him. But he loves Olivia, and what's to become of me?'

He came out of the ward laughing, disengaging himself from many small clutching hands, while the children shouted, '*Hamba gahle*' – 'Go well – go in peace,' and he replied 'Stay well.'

But his expression changed when he found Vicky waiting. A shutter seemed to drop across his sparkling eyes like a cloud over the grey water of a loch.

'May I speak to you?' asked Vicky. 'Have you time?'

'I have to go to the clinic, but you can walk there with me.'

There was an awkward silence between them. Two large dark birds with burnished wings were strutting upon the grass, digging into the soft earth with long curved beaks, but being disturbed they flew with a beating of wings into the air, shouting with harsh discordant unbirdlike cries. Vicky stopped, startled, her tender nerves jangled by the loud unexpected noise.

'They are bronze ibis, *hadadahs* as they call them here,' said Stephen, as if glad of an excuse to break the silence. 'The Africans say they shout *"Ngahamba, ngahamba!"* – "I'm going – I'm going away!" '

Tears sprang to Vicky's eyes and she turned aside. It was too apposite. The birds with their harsh, sad cry seemed to be echoing her own despair. There was a seat under a tree and Stephen indicated this.

'Sit down, Miss Scott, we can talk here for a few moments. We won't be disturbed.'

His suit of white drill buttoned high to the neck, emphasized the tanned face with its high cheekbones and dark, straight brows above the grey eyes with the startling black lashes that were so much like Susan's. She was overwhelmingly conscious of the slender brown hands, the arms that had held her in an embrace impossible to forget.

Almost as if following her thoughts, he said, 'I presume you've come to discuss what happened last night. I want to beg you to forget it. I was upset by Mofolo's death. It's impossible to get used to these things – they always hit one hard at the time, especially the death of a child. But I realize now that I had no right to criticize your private life. I suppose it really has nothing whatsoever to do with me how many men you choose to kiss.'

This was really too much for Vicky to endure.

'Nor is it anything to me how many women you choose to kiss either,' she retorted.

'What do you mean by that?'

He looked startled and annoyed, and she regretted now that she seemed to have become involved in undignified recriminations, but she stumbled on, stammering, 'In East London – that evening – I saw you and Olivia . . .'

He gave her a glance of icy contempt.

'It's absurd for you to think you can make your own behaviour seem better by lying about Olivia.'

His denial of something she herself had witnessed infuriated her.

'In any case, I didn't "choose to kiss" anyone,' she said, lashing out with the first words she thought of. 'I expected it of Anton. Anyone can see he would make love to any attractive girl. But how was I to know that you were made in the same pattern? I certainly didn't choose to kiss you!'

He flinched a little.

'I'm sorry my attentions appear to have been so distasteful to you. Odd that it didn't appear so at the time. But let's agree, shall we, to forget all about it? Certainly I have no right to any part in your life at all.'

Was he referring to the fact that he was pledged to Olivia? Obviously the embrace had meant nothing to him. It was merely an experiment, one he wanted to forget as quickly as possible.

'Perhaps it would be best for me to go away from here,' she said quietly.

'There's really no need. It wasn't I who suggested you should go. I see very little of you, and Susan likes you. But you must decide for yourself. It's all the same to me whether you go or stay, but I should be grateful if you would stay until Christmas has passed. I wouldn't like to spoil it for Susan or Gran.'

His icy indifference oppressed her more than his anger. Susan – his mention of her recalled her original purpose in approaching him.

'Stephen, can you forget our differences for a while and think about Susan?'

'Willingly,' said Stephen, an ironical smile twisting his mouth.

'What have I to lose?' thought Vicky, and decided to employ shock tactics.

'I met Susan's father last night.'

If she had wanted to startle Stephen, she had certainly succeeded.

'What?' he exclaimed.

'He's staying at Laetitia's hotel, the same man who inquired about the hospital and the one we met on Table Mountain.'

'So that was his game,' said Stephen, his eyes stormy.

'At least give me a hearing,' begged Vicky. 'He says he would like to see you.'

'Indeed? I would have thought after our last interview that that would have been the last thing he wanted.'

'When was that?'

'Ten years ago. Soon after Susan was born.' My sister was

delicate. She needed attention, but he neglected her shame-fully.'

'He says he's deeply sorry for everything that happened then. He intends to marry again and wants to provide a home for Susan.'

'What infernal impudence! Does he think he can calmly come and take Susan from us when up until now he's never worried about her existence?'

'Stephen, he's older now. He seemed quite sincere in his desire to have Susan. He intends to live in a town. Wouldn't it be better for her to have a more settled life in a real home?'

'She's perfectly happy here.'

'Is she? She has had a great many changes to face in her life for a ten-year-old and it seems that if she stays here there'll be many more.'

'Such as ...' Stephen's expression was obtuse, unhelpful. Vicky floundered on.

'Well, Gran may go home to her sister ... and I ... I may leave ... and you may ...'

'Yes? I may ... ?'

'Well, you may change your way of living. If you – if you were to marry one day, your wife might not want a ready-made family, though it appears that Mrs. Osborne's wife will welcome Susan. That's what he said.'

'Yes,' Stephen said abruptly, 'I suppose that's how most women would feel. I mean that they wouldn't want to take on the responsibility of someone else's child. You, for in-stance, would you welcome a child of ten in your home if you were newly married?'

'I ... I ...'

'If I were married to you,' her heart said, 'and the child were Susan, I couldn't ask for any greater happiness.'

'I can see by your expression you wouldn't think that a good idea, but all women are not like you, Miss Scott. I sup-pose I'd better see Osborne, little as I like the idea. You'd better phone him and tell him you've succeeded in your plan. I'll see him as soon as possible.'

'So he's come round,' said George Osborne. 'I thought he would see it was to his own advantage. A confirmed bachelor like Stephen can hardly want the responsibility of a child. And Stephen has never been interested in money.'

'Money,' thought Vicky. 'What has money got to do with it?'

'I don't understand,' she said.

'You don't have to, Miss Scott,' George Osborne replied sharply. 'Thanks a lot for your help. I won't forget it. I'll see you right, my dear, when the time comes. But from now on it's between me and Stephen Nash.'

This conversation disquieted Vicky. The old feeling of uneasiness she had experienced when she first met the man came flooding back. But it was too late now. She had made the appointment for him.

She spent the afternoon with Gran making haloes out of cardboard and silver tinfoil, with Susan and Tandiwe seated upon the floor, laboriously cutting out stars to sew upon the white calico dresses intended for the angelic choir.

'Si-lent Night, Ho-oly Night,' sang Tandiwe in a clear silvery voice, and Susan joined in with a shrill treble.

'Why can't I be in your choir, Gran?' demanded Susan.

'Oh, my girlie, you havena got the voice these little Africans have, but dinna fash yourself, for I've got a right grand thing for you to do too.'

'What, Gran?' demanded Susan, eyes sparkling.

'We're to make a tableau.'

'What's that?'

'It's to be a living picture of the stable on the night the infant Jesus was born. And you're to be Mary.'

'Me? Oh, Gran!' Susan hugged her.

'Now mind my needle!'

'What will I wear?'

'We'll go to the shop and buy a length of royal blue cotton for your veil and you can wear a long white dress.'

'You can have my mandarin pyjamas for one of the kings,' said Vicky. 'I never want to wear them again,' she thought.

'Tandiwe is helping me to cover a tobacco tin with beads for Stephen,' said Susan. 'It's to be his Christmas present. Do you think he'll like it?'

'Of course,' said Vicky.

'I must practise a bit on that old harmonium – it's older than myself and twice as wheezy,' said Gran. 'Susan, run and ask the Umfundisi to give you the key. He'll be at the church now.'

Susan jumped up eagerly. 'Come on, Tandiwe,' she cried.

The two little girls ran vigorously across to the hospital.

'Susan is looking sae bonny these days,' said Gran. 'You've done her so much good, Vicky. She's like a different child.'

'I've not really done anything,' said Vicky. 'It's just the healthy open-air life she leads here. But don't you think she'll be better when she can go to school and have more friends of her own age?'

'I dare say you're right, but it's a treat to see her as happy as she is now.'

But when they came back, the two little girls were strangely quiet. Gran went off accompanied by Tandiwe to conduct a practice with her choir and Susan mooned around, then started cutting stars in such a haphazard way that she wasted more silver foil than she used.

At last Vicky could stand the heavy moodiness and the futile snipping no longer.

'What is it, Susan? What's wrong?' she asked.

'What do you mean?' asked Susan, her mouth set in the old stubborn lines.

'Why are you in such a bad mood?'

'Why should you care?' asked Susan rudely.

Vicky felt as if Susan had jabbed a small knife into her heart. But she persisted.

'You were so happy about our plans for Christmas before you ran to get the key. What's happened to change you?'

Hot tears welled up in Susan's grey eyes and spilled over, splashing Vicky's dress as she flung herself down burying her head in Vicky's lap.

'It's you who've changed,' she accused through her sobs.

Vicky felt tears start in her own eyes. With difficulty she controlled her speech.

'How have I changed?' she asked.

'You want me to go. You don't want me any more!'

And her sobbing became even louder and so uncontrolled that Vicky became alarmed.

'Quiet, now, quiet,' she soothed, taking the child upon her knee and smoothing the warm hair, the damp tear-stained face. 'Tell me what's happened.'

It appeared that on her way past the hospital, Susan had glanced through the window of Stephen's office, and had hidden beside it planning to jump up and give him a surprise when whoever he was talking to had gone. But unfortunately the visitor was George Osborne and she overheard the conversation during which it had been mentioned that Vicky had arranged the meeting.

'Of course, I knew my father was here,' said Susan. 'I knew before you did,' she added with a sad kind of pride.

'Oh, Susan, surely that can't be true,' asked Vicky.

'Remember the day of the party when I went riding? Olivia told me he was coming.'

So Olivia was involved too. Vicky remembered how troubled Susan had seemed that evening – and no wonder!

'You wouldn't listen to me, Vicky. You said I must keep the secret. But I was worried. I wanted to tell you about my father. But you wouldn't listen, and now you want me to go away.'

Vicky was appalled that Susan should have found out about her father in this fashion, and was at a loss to find words to comfort her, not knowing what decision Stephen and George Osborne had taken.

'My darling,' she said at last, 'we don't want you to go away. We all love you very much and are only thinking of your own good.'

'It's my own good to stay here. I want to stay here for ever with you and Stephen and Gran,' said Susan. She had controlled her sobs now and apart from an occasional hiccup appeared more calm.

'Oh, my dearest Susan ...' began Vicky. What could she say? 'Nothing would please me more ...' No, not that. 'Things change all the time,' she said. 'Nothing can stay the same in life for very long. If your father loves you, it's better to have a real parent and to be brought up somewhere where you can have a home life and go to a day school and meet other children of your own age and kind. Gran may have to go back to England,' she added. 'I may have to go too some day. You know Stephen is too busy to look after you on his own.'

'I've got a wonderful idea,' said Susan, sitting up and forgetting all about her hiccups.

'What's that?' asked Vicky, glad to see signs of animation once again.

'That man' (she meant her father) 'said he could take me because he's getting a new wife. So if Stephen gets a wife, he can take me, can't he? So you could marry Stephen and then you need never go away, and I needn't either, need I? Don't you think that's a good idea, Vicky?'

'Perhaps,' said Vicky, and in her mind echoed Anton's words: 'When a woman says "perhaps" she means "yes".'

CHAPTER NINE

VICKY had heard nothing of the results of Stephen's interview with George Osborne. She supposed he thought it was none of her business and indeed, if she was going to leave after Christmas, it would appear that it was not her concern, but her heart was torn between one idea and another, and her main idea was to get a settled home for Susan before she herself left.

Gran seemed to be unaware of the conflict going on around her. Vicky supposed that Stephen did not want her to be worried, and she went on happily making her preparations for Christmas, sewing frantically, between rehearsals of her African choir, and every now and again stabbing Vicky with her affection and artlessly innocent remarks about the fact that she was quite indispensable.

This afternoon they sat sewing in the deep shade of the verandah sheltered from the glittering fury of the afternoon sun.

'It seems all wrong somehow,' remarked Gran, 'to be celebrating Christmas in midsummer.'

'Gran, that's the fifth time you've said that this week,' said Susan.

'Well, I must say there's nothing like a little frosty weather to get up your appetite for the turkey, and Christmas pudding won't seem the same served in this heat.'

'Have you put threepenny bits in it?' asked Susan.

'Five cent pieces, no less – there are no threepenny bits in this country. There used to be something called a tickey, but I believe it vanished when they changed to decimal coinage.'

'Yes, I know,' said Susan. 'Do you remember someone in the hotel at Cape Town told us that she went into a post office in England and said "I would like some tickey stamps" and the girl behind the counter told her, "Madam, all our stamps are sticky."'

Susan shrieked with laughter at her own joke, and Tandiwe smiled sympathetically, though not really understanding.

'She seems much more cheerful now,' thought Vicky. 'But of course what child wouldn't be happy two days before

Christmas?'

Stephen came walking across the lawn with his lithe springy stride. He had discarded his white hospital coat and his skin glowed brown against the cream safari suit he was wearing. He looked vibrantly alive and when Susan rushed over to embrace him he lifted her in his arms, tolerating the kisses she showered upon him.

'What do you say to a drive up into the forest, young lady?' he asked. 'I've arranged with the forest ranger to get a Christmas tree from the small plantation near his house. We can take Gran too, and Tandiwe. What do you say to that?'

'And Vicky?' said Susan.

Vicky imagined his smile faltered a little, but he seemed determined to please Susan.

'If Vicky wishes to come, certainly she may.'

'That sends the ball right back into my court,' thought Vicky. 'If I say I don't want to, I will sound churlish. In any case, if he is willing to take me, I will go. There will be one more afternoon of his company to remember.'

'Just take Susan and Tandiwe and Vicky, Stephen,' said Gran. 'It's a wee bit hot for me to go out and I have a rehearsal at five. Tandiwe can skip it. I wouldna like her to miss the treat.'

'Now I've really let myself in for something,' thought Vicky. 'Without Gran's chatter and with Susan having Tandiwe for company, it's going to be more difficult.'

But her heart denied this, whispering exultantly, 'I'm going to be with him for a whole afternoon. Whatever happens, I'll have this to remember.'

She was wearing a cool cotton dress flower-printed in pink, yellow and blue upon a background of pale green. This seemed quite suitable for a drive in the forest, but she decided to take her sun-glasses and a hat of pale woven straw that Selina, Tandiwe's mother, had fashioned for her.

'Will we be walking much?' she asked, glancing questioningly at her sturdy leather-thonged sandals.

'Not much. Your sandals will be adequate for the forest paths,' said Stephen, a curiously blank look upon his face as he regarded her slender feet and the toes tipped with pink pearl varnish.

'He probably disapproves of varnished toenails,' Vicky surmised. 'Though come to think of it, Olivia even wears gold varnish with her gold bikini, but then she seems to be a rule unto herself as far as Stephen is concerned. I should have the green eyes instead of her,' she chided herself, smiling secretly.

'What's funny, Vicky?' asked Susan.

'Just a thought,' she answered.

The countryside lay yellow-green under the fierce beat of the afternoon sun. The rains had been good this year and on every piece of ground that could be cultivated waved the tall green maize plants, the tightly wrapped green sheaths holding the fast developing cobs topped with silky strands. Between the rows of maize, vines of pumpkin grew, the large yellow flowers fading upon the late planted vines, but on earlier planted ones the huge wavy gourds were already developing. Sorghum or Kaffir corm, as it was called here, waved its brown tassels, and near the cattle kraals the tall agave plant stretched flowering yellow arms like some giant candelabrum above its base of grey-green leaves.

Beside the road, bushy plants of ragwort flaunted their yellow flowers, and occasionally sheets of yellow showed where they had taken root over the rolling pastures like flashes of sunshine fallen upon the grass.

The road led upwards and presently they found themselves at the gate leading to the forest path. At once they were in a different kind of world, far removed from the pasture land. Tall trees lined the path which wound steadily upwards against the side of the mountain.

'This part of the forest is indigenous,' Stephen said. 'But further up towards the forest ranger's house there are plantations of fir trees.'

The road was smooth, graded but not bitumenized, and as it grew steeper he had to drive carefully in low gear. On the lower side the forest trees fell away and one could see layers of leaves where the tops of the trees were level with the road, with every now and again a glimpse of a sunflecked glade.

Here and there a giant yellow-wood tree showed by its girth that it had stood there for hundreds of years. On the other side of the path the ground rose steeply and huge boulders reared themselves from the mossy ground like prehistoric monsters.

'I can imagine elephants here,' said Vicky, looking at the grey, lichenous trunks and the huge branches with their wreaths of Spanish moss.

'There might have been elephants a couple of hundred years ago.'

'Look, there are monkeys!' cried Susan. Thoughts of hypothetical elephants were banished by the sight of a troupe of grey vervet monkeys running across the path and swinging rapidly into the branches. A great grey male monkey stood guard, grunting in an admonishing way to the stragglers, while mothers, their babies clinging to their stomachs, viewed the oncoming car with squeaks of alarm.

Susan and Tandiwe were thrilled with the sight.

'I wish I could have one,' said Susan.

'Sinkwe gives us enough trouble already.'

High up in the clearing they came to the forest ranger's house, an enchanting log cabin with floors of honey gold yellow-wood and a fireplace made from natural stone. Tall foxgloves, arum lilies, and blue agapanthus grew in the small garden, which was strongly fenced. Beyond this was a tremendous view of blue mountains and valleys, but near at hand a child's swing and a line of diminutive washing gave a strangely domesticated look to the wildness of the scene.

The ranger, Tom Wood, a robust young man with khaki leggings and wide-brimmed hat, seemed tremendously pleased to have visitors. He called to his wife, Alice, who came running, plump, rosy-cheeked, smooth-haired, smiling, with two tow-haired little boys, jostling each other like puppies, a small wide-eyed little girl clinging to her skirt, and another child, a blonde blue-eyed baby, in her arms.

'Dr. Stephen!' she exclaimed, beaming. 'We were so pleased when we heard you were coming. You must have tea. I'll have it ready in seconds. How do you think your baby's looking?'

'Bonny,' said Stephen, holding out his arms to the chortling child, but not forgetting a smile for the little girl.

'I'll help you make tea,' offered Vicky.

'Well, hold Baby, there's a love, while the men go to fetch the tree,' said Alice.

The baby seized a strand of Vicky's fair hair when she tried to take it from Stephen and, in trying to free it, another strand wound itself around the button of his jacket. Stephen gently took the silky fine hair and eventually freed her, while the rest of the party laughed heartily, and the baby kicked excitedly and patted her flushed cheeks. She was glad when Alice led the way to the kitchen, for she was afraid Susan would embarrass her still further by some innocent remark.

Here there was a woven rush mat upon the flagstones, a kitchen dresser with bright crockery, a large wood-burning cooking stove, shining metal pots, and a big bright red enamel kettle. The curtains were of checked blue and white gingham, and red geraniums grew upon the deep windowsill. Alice regarded Vicky's bright eyes and flushed cheeks with frank curiosity.

'It's nice you came,' she said. 'Dr. Stephen's never brought a lady to see us before.'

'I – I came with Susan.'

'Yes?' said Alice. 'Well, it's a treat, anyway, to see another woman. It often gets a bit lonely here. Though I have plenty to do. Not much time to mope with Tom and the children to care for. I'm not grumbling, for really I wouldn't change places with the Queen of England. Do you like it at the hospital? You haven't been there long, have you? We heard about you from Laetitia Honeywell when we came into town last.'

'Yes, yes, I've been happy there on the whole,' said Vicky.

She could hardly start confiding in Alice on such short acquaintance, though her cosy manner and friendly stare invited confidences.

'He's a wonderful man, Dr. Stephen,' said Alice. 'I think the world of him. If it wasn't for him, this one,' indicating the baby, 'wouldn't be here today. He came up here in a terrific storm. We never thought he'd get through. He did the last ten miles on foot – and I wasn't even really his patient – I was supposed to go to the hospital in town, but my baby was premature. I can never repay him ever for what he did for us that night. Don't you think he's wonderful?'

'I ... I ...' stammered Vicky.

'But there, I could see you did when you were together. Ah, I can tell you, my Tom gets quite jealous when I start talking about Dr. Stephen. Any woman would love him the way he is, so kind and good when you're really in trouble. Mind you, he hasn't any time for any nonsense. When he gets in a temper, when anything goes wrong at the hospital, everyone has to look out. And he'd do anything to get money for the hospital. He's quite ruthless when he's looking for funds. But he's a wonderful man, make no mistake about it. The woman who gets him – well, she may not have a very peaceful life, but take it from me, she'll be happy.' She eyed Vicky speculatively. 'Laetitia had some idea he was interested in Miss Chazal, but I think she's barking up the wrong tree. I can't see a man with character like Dr. Stephen being taken in by such as her.' (She put a wealth of meaning into the pronoun.) 'And now I've seen you ... well, I mustn't stand here gossiping. Here are the men back and wanting tea.'

Although Vicky had hardly said one word during this long chat, she felt considerably heartened by Alice's cheerful common sense. It was only later that she thought at most Alice must see Stephen only about twice a year. She could hardly consider herself an authority upon his feelings, though obviously she thought she was.

'I thought at first that Stephen was a most unlikeable man,' Vicky mourned to herself. 'Now I find too many people love him, including me. And if you've got any sense, Vicky my girl, you'll get out of this situation as soon as Christmas is over, Susan or no Susan. For you're at the very end of the queue as far as Dr. Stephen is concerned.

'Bramble jelly!' she exclaimed when they were seated on the garden chairs having tea and scones. 'I haven't seen blackberries since I left England.'

'We have plenty here in the forest,' said Tom. 'Though only a few are ripe as yet. There'll be more towards autumn.'

When they left the forest house, they were laden with flowers and what Susan called 'English fruit' – redcurrants, blackcurrants and gooseberries that would only grow in the damp rain belt of the forested mountains. A large Christmas tree protruded from the boot of the car and was securely strapped down.

'Can we gather pine-cones for Christmas decorations?' asked Susan.

'Yes, we'll stop further down and you can get some, so long as I can have a quiet smoke and don't have to run around too,' said Stephen.

It was cooler now and the westering sun was sending long shafts of light through the trees as Stephen drew up in a clearing just off the road. The fir trees were evenly spaced here, so there was little danger of losing sight of the children. They darted around under the trees, their feet sinking into the thick carpet of fallen needles and last year's leaves, their voices and laughter echoing among the tall columns of the trees like notes of music in some vast cathedral.

Sitting next to Stephen, Vicky tried in vain not to be conscious of the silent man by her side. He sat smoking, apparently completely relaxed and not at all anxious to carry on any conversation. She thought he was looking at the children as they picked up the huge compact cones with shrieks of delight, but when she ventured a glance in his direction, he was watching her with an expression she could not interpret.

'Have you known Tom and Alice long?' she asked, confused by his limpid grey gaze, and seizing upon the first topic she could think of.

'Quite a while,' he said. 'Though I don't often see them. Alice is a gem,' he added.

Apart from Gran, it was the first time Vicky had heard Stephen praise any woman, except Olivia.

'A gem?' she queried.

'They don't come like her very often. She leads a very lonely life, but she's quite content with her home and her children. She doesn't seem to want anything else.'

'What else would she want?' asked Vicky.

He looked surprised.

'I would have thought most women would want a little gaiety, a more sophisticated social life.'

'You know very little about women if you think that,' protested Vicky. 'Why, it's as plain as can be that Alice is in love with Tom and he with her. If I had a home and children and a husband who loved me ... why, I would ...' She stopped abruptly, very confused.

'You were saying?' asked Stephen, his eyes gravely considering her.

'As if,' she thought indignantly, 'I were a specimen on a laboratory table!'

'Why,' she said lamely, 'nothing. Just that I think Alice is one of the lucky ones of this world.'

He smiled and she caught her breath as he leaned towards her.

'Vicky, do you mean ... ?'

'Look at all the cones we've collected! We've got heaps and heaps!'

Susan and Tandiwe burst open the door spilling the brown cones into the back of the car, breathless and noisily excited. Whatever Stephen had been going to say was lost, and the quiet of the forest was shattered as the two little girls enlivened the homeward journey by lusty singing of carols. *Good King Wenceslas* vied with *Hark, the Herald Angels Sing,* and *Night* in the car was anything but *Silent*.

That night there was a small, bright star close to the newly risen moon.

'I'll wish on it,' thought Vicky, smiling at her own foolishness.

'Please, please,' she asked the star, 'let us have a happy Christmas, whatever's to happen afterwards. If only it could be like it has been today,' she thought, 'for ever and ever.'

'Only for you, Gran, only for my beautiful Scots lady, would I do this terrible thing. How do you dare to risk losing me for the hospital? Don't you know that doctors are very scarce?' declared Anton.

Vicky and Susan collapsed into childish giggles at the weird sight of the usually elegant Anton, arrayed in a red Santa Claus costume, a pillow enlarging his slim middle to grotesque proportions, his bright, wicked eyes looking out over a positive curtain of white curly whiskers.

'I always understood St. Nicholas drove a sleigh through the snow, but now you expect me to climb on to the roof as if I've just landed in a flying saucer,' he protested, his voice muffled by the hirsute screen.

'Mind you speak up now when the time comes,' Gran instructed sternly. 'There's one thing – no one will be able to recognize your voice behind all those whiskers.'

'I should hope not,' said Anton. 'In any case, I am expecting to fall to my doom like Lucifer before I can even begin to speak.'

'Now bide still a wee moment while I stick on your eyebrows. Such a fussation over a wee bit scramble up on to the roof! Folks might think I'd asked you to climb Mount Everest.'

'They had an advantage over me, these climbers of Mount Everest, at least they were roped together – and you expect me to do this alone!'

'Hark at the man! A wee bairn would have more courage. There will be a ladder at the back of the hoose and a ladder

131

at the front. All you have to do is to climb over the thatch and stand upon the rooftop. Mind you stand tall and try to look twice as big as you are.'

'Vicky, you are teacher. What is this thing you have when you fear heights? Claustrophobia?'

'No, that's fear of closed spaces. Fear of heights is acrophobia.'

'That is what I have got. I have just discovered it this minute, Gran. I have acrophobia.'

'Well, prescribe a pill for yourself,' advised Gran, quite unmoved.

'Oh, what cruelty! And for my Noel gift I bought you an African love letter telling you that you are my favourite lady and worth twelve oxen. Now I must find another one to say you have no heart.'

'Away with your shenanigans!' cried Gran as Anton put his arm around her and laid his whiskers against her cheek that was wrinkled like an old red pippin apple. 'Get to that ladder. I can hear the children coming,' she admonished sternly.

They were singing as they came. Vicky thought she had never heard anything as lovely as the pure nightingale voices soaring into the warm, starlit night. Candles in glass containers cast a golden glow upon the dark faces, the shining brown eyes, the smiling mouths uttering the words with grave precision and just a trace, Vicky was touched to hear, of a Scots accent.

This morning Gran's angel choir had sung at the hospital making a tour of the wards and distributing gifts, but now they themselves were to have their reward, an evening party with Father Christmas arriving to bring them gifts. Set up in the garden, the tree twinkled with a hundred coloured lights and glistened with tinsel and gold-painted fir-cones.

As the children saw the tree, their voices died away and there were exclamations of *'Muthle!'* or 'How beautiful!' Cries of astonishment greeted Anton's arrival. There was still enough light left in the sky to see his cushion-padded silhouette, black upon the rooftop. Elder sisters reassured the smaller ones as the red-coated, bearded figure waved to them, demanding in ringing tones, 'Have you been good children this year?' They were struck dumb at first, then, with Gran's encouragement, timidly shouted, 'Yes!'

'Then I have got nice presents for all of you!'

And with that Anton descended the ladder with much grunting and groaning, and distributed sweets and toys.

'Where's Stephen?' asked Susan, jumping about, overwhelmed with excitement and impatience. 'I want him to have my present.'

'I expect he's busy at the hospital. He'll be here soon.'

'Who's talking about me?' said Stephen from behind them, and he swept Susan up into his arms.

'How different he has been the last few days,' thought Vicky. 'He seems almost to be going out of his way to charm Susan. He seems really fond of her now. Perhaps I was mistaken in thinking she would be better living with her father. I wonder what they've decided about it? But what about Olivia? Lately he doesn't seem to be so much in her company, or is that just wishful thinking on my part?'

Now the African children retired to sit upon the grass and drink cool drinks and eat bright pink cakes with highly coloured icing that Gran and Selina had baked. They had already eaten their Christmas dinner in the middle of the day, but it had not impaired their appetites.

The family party went back to the verandah to examine their own presents which Anton had distributed, after insisting that the ladies paid the forfeit of receiving a whiskery kiss from him. At last Susan was able to give Stephen his beaded tobacco tin upon which she had worked patiently for weeks. His reception of it was all that she could have wished, and Vicky marvelled afresh at his change of attitude as he hung it around his waist in the fashion of an African youth, first placing in it the expensive tobacco which Vicky had found out from Gran that he liked but seldom purchased.

She had made bedsocks for Gran and had dressed a doll for Susan in exact imitation of a red-blanketed African girl. Susan gave Gran and Vicky a photograph of herself that she had persuaded Anton to take.

'Yes,' said Anton, who by now had divested himself of his fancy dress and had changed into a blue shirt with gold cuff links and tight charcoal grey trousers, 'Miss Susan bullied me into taking it, nor was she satisfied with my first efforts. It had to be just so to please this little lady's vanity.'

'And Anton, I've bought you a beautiful present, so you'll be pleased you went to so much trouble for me,' declared

Susan, giving him a flamboyant necktie of purple and green stripes. 'Isn't it lovely?'

Anton's eyes registered shock for a second, but Vicky could not help admiring the perfection of his manners as he thanked Susan warmly and changed his own dark silk tie for the vivid object the little girl had given him. She must have bought it on an expedition into the village with Selina and Tandiwe, for Vicky had not seen it before.

'Open your presents, Vicky,' Susan demanded.

There were lace table-mats from Gran, and Vicky kissed her warmly.

'They're to start your bottom drawer, my dear, you'll be needing them one day.'

A small box was next with a plain white card with writing in thick black letters, 'A Happy Christmas and Thank you from Stephen.' She looked wonderingly at him and he turned away, pretending to admire the mohair stole that Anton had given to Gran.

'Well, go on, open it!' urged Susan.

It was a bracelet of stones they call 'Tiger's Eye', golden brown striped gems, warm and glowing in their golden setting.

'Thank you. It's beautiful,' whispered Vicky, quite overwhelmed that he should have given her this gift.

'To apologize for many things,' said Stephen. Then he added so softly that she could scarcely hear, 'They reminded me of your eyes.'

If it had been Anton she would have expected it, but compliments seemed so foreign to Stephen and therefore of infinite value. She hugged the words to herself, knowing that later she would take them out, examine them, analyse them, and, whatever happened, remember them for ever.

With a flourish Anton produced a beaded collar for Vicky that he had had made for her, but what he was most proud of was an African love letter, a flat beadwork square, worked in red, yellow, and blue upon a white background, threaded upon a large safety pin. When she exclaimed in delight, he said, 'I'll tell you what it means, but only if first I get my reward.' And he kissed her with warm affection.

'I like these English customs at Christmas time,' he assured Stephen.

'I've never heard of kissing being described as an English

134

custom before,' said Stephen.

'Well, if it isn't, it should be,' said Anton, putting his arm around Vicky's shoulders, and disregarding Stephen's annoyed glance. 'Now look, my Vicky, this letter is really from a girl to a man, but that is of no consequence. The white beads say "When I see you my heart goes white as milk, for I love you so much", and these red ones mean, "Whenever I see you my heart goes on fire and burns with jealousy", but the yellow means, "I shall go on loving you for ever".'

'I'm so glad to have it, Anton,' said Vicky. 'It was sweet of you to get it for me.'

'I knew you would like it,' said Anton. 'But I beg of you, do not take the message too seriously. Remember it is a girl's message, not a man's. "For ever" is a long time. For myself, I do not believe in love that lasts for ever, do you?'

'I think I do sometimes, Anton. At least, I like to hope it can be true.'

She was conscious of Stephen standing very near, listening to their conversation. She traced the yellow emblem with a small pearl-tipped nail.

'I shall go on loving you for ever,' she said to herself. 'It's the right message, but it came from the wrong man.'

The weather had changed and a sudden cold south-easter bowed the trees and sent the guests running for shelter. The children shepherded by African nurses went to play games in the hall.

'Now inside, all of you,' said Gran. 'Selina has the turkey cooked to a turn.'

Gran had pooh-poohed their suggestions of a cold buffet, and, with the sudden drop in temperature, they were glad she had insisted upon a 'proper' Christmas dinner. Coloured goblets contained small pink shrimps, dressed with a pink tabasco-flavoured sauce and served on a bed of pale green shredded lettuce. This was followed by a large turkey, with all the trimmings – small sausages, halved poached peaches filled with cranberry sauce, ham, mushroom and walnut stuffing, roast potatoes, roast pumpkin, tiny peas, and dark green fingers of broccoli.

The pudding, borne in resplendent with blue flame, by a triumphant Selina, gave its large quota of five cent pieces, and at last, with paper hats askew, the company retired to the arm-chairs to drink coffee and savour a cherry liqueur, which, together with the champagne, was Anton's contribution to the feast.

But Gran was still not quite satisfied.

'It doesna seem like Christmas without a wee bit fire to sit around and have a crack,' she complained wistfully.

They laughed affectionately if a little derisively. 'A fire! Gran, what will you think of next? A fire in the middle of summer!'

'It's no so hot now. The wind is quite chilly.'

'But, Gran . . .'

'I have it,' she said. 'Wait, I have just the very thing.'

They all looked mystified as she hastened out of the room.

'I know what it is,' said Susan, clapping her hands, her eyes sparkling. 'It's the peat! I've got some too. She gave it to me to remind me of Scotland.'

'The peat?' said Stephen, puzzled.

'What is this "peat"?' asked Anton.

But before anyone could answer, Gran came in carrying something which looked like a peculiar kind of fibrous mud brick.

'Where in the world did you get that from?' asked Stephen, with a teasing, affectionate smile that produced for Vicky a confusing mixture of sad and tender emotion.

'I begged it from an auld wifie on the moors, before we came away from Scotland,' Gran explained.

'But didn't you have any difficulty with the Customs officials?' asked Vicky. 'I didn't think they allowed . . .'

'Och, it didna worry me. They were nae looking for peat, so they didna find peat.'

She took some newspaper and sticks and, with Susan's help, kindled a small fire in the stone fireplace. Then she put the piece of peat upon the flames and watched with satisfaction as it developed a deep red glow. But this still wasn't quite what she wanted.

'It's the smell I'm after,' she declared.

Seizing a poker from the side of the fireplace, she cut a piece of the glowing stuff away from the main body, and swept it on to a small shovel, and walked around the room, waving the smoking odorous chunk of burning peat in all directions. The rest of the dinner party guests hastily left their coffee and liqueurs and retired to the far corners of the room, coughing and choking as the pungent smoke penetrated their lungs.

Gran was quite unperturbed by the discomfort she had caused.

'That's what I wanted,' she declared triumphantly, 'the smell of Scotland!'

'Gran dear, you seem determined to turn us all into Scots kippers,' protested Stephen. 'This may be satisfying nostalgia, but it's not very comfortable.'

'Och, away with you, it was worth it!'

'I must go,' said Anton. 'I have a case to see before I turn in.'

'Susan's half asleep already. Say good night, girlie, and go to bed,' said Stephen.

She clung to him, giving him a sleepy kiss, and he did not rebuff her as he had so often done in the past.

'I'll away too. Don't bother about Susan, Vicky. I'll see her to bed,' said Gran, yawning.

Vicky and Stephen were left alone. The smoke had gone, and a glowing mound of peat, emitting a fragrant, evocative tweedy smell, was the only reminder of Gran's longing for her native land. Stephen came to sit beside Vicky upon the small settee in front of the fireplace.

'I must go,' she thought.

After this Christmas evening, so full of simple emotion, she felt deeply scared that if she was alone with him she would somehow betray her true feelings. She started to rise, but sensing her intention he said quickly, 'Don't go, Vicky, I want to talk to you.'

There were tall red candles, festooned with ivy, upon the mantelshelf, and silver candlesticks with white candles still burning upon the table. Long shadows fell upon the white walls, but the roof beams and the deep hollow of the thatch were lost in darkness. The candlelight lightened Vicky's hair, making it shine like silver, but Stephen's features looked darker, more saturnine than ever.

'Have you enjoyed your first Christmas in Africa?' he asked, turning towards her.

His eyes were looking into hers, his arms and lips were so close, she had only to stretch out a hand . . .

'My first and perhaps my last one, it seems,' she said, rather flatly. 'How can you ask? Of course I've loved every moment of it.'

'I'm glad. Vicky, are you so set on going? I'm truly sorry about the other evening. After all, Anton is Anton. I should have realized ... and he has explained to me that he'd had a little too much to drink.'

'He has explained to you!' Really, this was too much. Vicky shrank from the idea of their both discussing her. A kind of recklessness seized her.

'So now you're satisfied that it was not my fault, but you think someone has to be intoxicated to want to kiss me?'

'No, no, you know I don't mean that at all. Oh, Vicky, Vicky, why do you always put me in the wrong?'

She gazed at him, amazed. He had turned the tables and was now complaining of the self-same thing she had always had against him. Tears sprang to her eyes and she turned aside, blinking rapidly. He took her chin in his hand and very gently turned her face towards him.

'Vicky, my dear, won't you stay? We need you so much. Gran may go home soon, and what's Susan to do without you?'

His hand dropped to her shoulder and he still kept her turned towards him so that she felt herself drawn, almost hypnotized, by his urgent gaze.

'Isn't she going to her father?' she stammered.

'Never,' said Stephen. 'Oh, Vicky, can't you see that I'm really fond of the child? It's hard for me to show affection in a demonstrative way. That kind of thing was dried out of me when I was just a boy, but believe me, I'm truly fond of Susan and do want to keep her.'

'But Susan's father is marrying again. Wouldn't it be better for Susan to have a real home life with people she felt she belonged to?'

'That's where I hoped you would help me.'

'I?'

'It's occurred to me that it would be a good idea if we were to marry.'

'I must be dreaming,' thought Vicky frantically. 'I must have fallen asleep beside the fire. This can't be true!'

'But ... but ...'

'Of course I realize it may seem a surprising idea to you at first, but really it's quite sensible. You're fond of Susan and she's fond of you. I don't flatter myself that you could love me, but you don't seem to find me altogether unpleasing. You seem to have settled here and to like the place, and I'll care for you as well as I can.

'I expect to be better off in the future than I am now, so

you needn't fear that you'll lack for life's necessities. Even, there may be a little jam with the bread every now and again, and if you become bored here when Susan goes to school, you'll be able to travel.'

'But – but – Olivia?' asked Vicky faintly.

Was it a trick of the firelight or did Stephen's expression grow darker?

'Olivia is not suited to me, nor I to Olivia,' he said. 'Besides . . .' he broke off, then continued. 'Olivia doesn't enter into this discussion. It's between you and me.'

'Dare I?' thought Vicky. The temptation to consent was overwhelming. 'I love him,' she thought. 'My feelings are hopelessly involved. Wouldn't it be better to accept his offer? That way I don't have to go. That way I can stay. I'll be with him even if he doesn't love me. He has not said one word about love, not even that he likes me. But surely there must be some tiny glimmer of liking for him to ask me to marry, but no, all he's concerned with is finding a settled home for Susan.'

Firelight and candlelight mingled to make the moment precious. She longed with all her heart to be swept into his arms, to feel again the passionate promise of his kiss, but to him, she supposed, his proposal seemed businesslike, practical, matter-of-fact. 'Can I accept half a loaf,' she thought, 'half a loaf of stale, left-over bread instead of the warm, fragrant, newly risen, whole miracle that my love demands?'

The African children were going home from their party, and the hadedahs, disturbed from their roosting place, soared into the air with clamorous cries, '*Ngahambe* – I'm going!'

'But I don't need to go. I can stay here. Stephen has asked me.'

'I would like to know your decision soon,' said Stephen.

The peat fell apart, releasing a sudden flame that flickered upon the dark, intent face so close to her own. For a moment she thought of Gran's story of the man who made a bargain with Lucifer. Then he smiled, and once again she was swept away by an enchantment from which she knew there could be no release.

'I've decided,' she told him. 'The answer is "Yes".'

He touched her hand.

'Thank you. I promise you won't regret it. We'll announce it at Olivia's party on New Year's Eve. The whole neighbourhood will be there, so it will be a good opportunity.'

CHAPTER TEN

'AND I can stay with you always?' asked Susan, her eyes alight with happiness.

'Of course,' Vicky assured her.

'By telling Susan, I've really committed myself,' she thought. 'But I owed it to the child to tell her myself before it was announced publicly.'

'Oh, Vicky, I love you, I love you!' Susan bounced off the bed and put her arms around Vicky, kissing her fervently. 'But I mustn't spoil you – you look gorgeous.' She withdrew a few steps, then tried to repair any slight damage she thought she had done to Vicky's appearance.

'Don't worry, Susan. Fortunately these pleats are un-crushable.'

Vicky was wearing a full-length dress of peach coloured pleated chiffon with slender shoulder straps of seed pearls. The colour emphasized her radiant fair hair, the glowing brown eyes and golden skin.

'You'll look like Cinderella at the ball, and Olivia will be an ugly sister.'

'Susan, you mustn't be rude about Olivia. She is our hostess, and in any case she always looks elegant.'

'Well then, she can be the beautiful, wicked Queen,' said Susan, determined to give Olivia an unfavourable role.

'Are you talking about me?' asked Gran, coming in at that moment. 'Vicky dear, can you manage to close this zipper? It's a gey long time since I wore this dress and either I've grown or it's shrunk. Why do they always put zips at the back where they're the most difficult to reach?'

Vicky zipped Gran's black lace dress, then, in spite of her halfhearted protests, she teased the silky grey hair until it fluffed around Gran's head in a silver aureole, and applied a little powder and a pale pink lipstick to her soft, wrinkled old face.

'I'm a plain Scotswoman and I've no time for such fol-de-rols!' declared Gran.

'Look into the mirror,' Vicky commanded.

'Och, Vicky, you are a marvel. You've made me look ten

years younger.'

'And why not?' asked Vicky.

'When I spoke to you in the park that day, I little thought how much you were going to mean to us all, my dear. I'm that pleased about you and Stephen. He's aye needed affection and you're the one to give it.'

'And I?' thought Vicky sadly. 'Don't I need affection too?'

She felt a twinge of guilt that they were so delighted when to Stephen it seemed a businesslike arrangement.

'I've burned my boats now,' she thought. 'Whatever happens, I can't let Susan and Gran down.'

Susan went off to prepare Sinkwe's supper of chopped fruit and milk. Then she and Tandiwe ran around the lawn trying to catch his dessert of grasshoppers. The small golden-eyed creature had charmed everyone with his appealing appearance and playful ways. He was sitting near his cage, playing with a red dahlia, alternately tossing it into the air and then meditatively chewing some of the petals.

Tandiwe and Selina were to stay with Susan while Gran and Vicky went to the party, and soon the children's shouts heralded the arrival of Anton and Stephen in the former's car. Anton was loud in his admiration of 'our two most beautiful ladies,' but Stephen, though he gave Vicky one brilliant, analytical glance, kept silent.

'We've got handsome escorts the nicht,' said Gran to Vicky, and she could not but agree. Both Anton's fair good looks and Stephen's dark, slender, almost Spanish appearance were enhanced by the tropical white dinner jackets and red cummerbunds that Olivia had demanded as suitable dress for her party.

'Two most lovely ladies,' admired Anton, bowing, and kissing Gran's hand, but coming to Vicky, he paused. For once his eyes were grave, his tone serious.

'My sweet Vicky, Stephen has told me your secret. Is it permitted to offer my very sincere felicitations?' He kissed her affectionately. 'Stephen will not object to one little kiss now, that is clear. He is to have your kisses for the rest of his life ... But what did I tell you? Did I not tell you that you were in love with Stephen? Ah, yes, Stephen, you have me to thank for furthering your suit. Did I not tell Vicky what a charming man you were, gaining love for you perhaps at the expense of Vicky's esteem for myself?'

Stephen was looking puzzled and Vicky flushed with embarrassment, wishing that Anton would not be so expansive about her emotions. She could only hope that Stephen would put it down to Anton's vivid imagination. But he was incorrigible.

'So sorry,' he said. 'Here I am monopolizing your lovely Vicky, when no doubt you wish to greet her yourself in the appropriate way on this happy Old Year's Night.'

He gently pushed her towards Stephen and there was nothing for it but to follow his wishes. Stephen put his hands on her shoulders and gently kissed her on the mouth.

'Ah, you have him well trained already, Vicky. He does not wish to ruin your make-up, but take heart, Stephen, later this evening it will not matter so much.

Gran sat in front of the car next to Anton, and Stephen took the place next to Vicky in the back. Anton's sports car had luxurious seats for the driver and front passenger but not much room for anyone else. Already shaken by the kiss that seemed a public acknowledgement of their betrothal, Vicky was breathlessly aware of Stephen's close proximity as the car raced along and they were flung together by its swift motion upon the curving road. At last Stephen put his arm around her shoulder to steady her and she leaned towards him, the feeling of security his arms gave her entirely dissipated by the knowledge of his nearness and the wild beating of her heart.

'No second thoughts, Vicky?' he asked, his mouth very near to hers as he whispered the question.

'I can't have second thoughts when I've told Gran and Susan that we intend to marry,' said Vicky, making a great effort to sound cold and full of common sense.

Stephen sighed. 'Susan seems very happy about it,' he said. 'And you . . .?' thought Vicky.

Was he regretting it already? She was still puzzled by his proposal. At first he had seemed to disapprove of her completely. It was only during the last few days that he seemed to have changed. The threatened loss of Susan seemed to have influenced his attitude to both of them. But he had not uttered one word of affection for her. Could she go on with this apology for love when she longed for his whole heart?

She was painfully aware of his arm so carelessly encircling her shoulder. Every time that the car negotiated the hairpin bends of the road, she was flung against him and her hair brushed against his cheek. At one moment she could have wished the journey would go on for ever, and at the same time she longed desperately for it to cease, so that she could gain some respite from her turbulent emotions.

Through the gloom, Olivia's house glowed like the tent of some Arabian potentate at a luxurious oasis in the desert. Flaring torches in wrought iron stands marked the route of the driveway towards the open parking place, where uniformed African guards directed the cars into some semblance of order.

Huge round coloured Chinese lamps illuminated the path through the garden and, on the terrace itself, paper lanterns took the form of strange beasts, dragons and monsters, in red, green and yellow. Olivia had chosen a Chinese theme for her party and had engaged a Chinese chef who had been flown here from Johannesburg.

Fortunately, she had not demanded Chinese costumes from her guests, but she received them in a beautiful mandarin coat of emerald silk, heavily overlaid with gold embroidery, and her dark silky hair was elaborately dressed in an oriental style, adorned with jewelled pins of flashing green and gold. As they waited to greet her, she laid the coat aside and stood revealed in a clinging gown of shimmering gold lurex, revealing much of her satiny olive shoulders and the generous curves of her perfect figure.

'Olivia's really gone to town on that dress tonight, hey?' a voice said in Vicky's ear as she waited in the crowd. It was Laetitia, herself resplendent in purple brocade, her heavy blonde hair for once unplaited and mounted in a pyramid of awe inspiring proportions.

'She usually dresses a bit plain for my taste, though her clothes cost her a pretty penny, I dare say. I will say this for her, though, she pays for dressing.'

'She looks beautiful,' said Vicky.

'I'll grant you that,' said Laetitia. 'But what gives? Her ladyship looks like a cat that's swallowed a pint of cream.'

'Sh!' Vicky felt uncomfortable at the thought that Stephen might think she was gossiping with Laetitia about their hostess. But he and Anton were talking to Gran, who was admiring the strange lanterns and exotic floral decorations.

It was true that Olivia seemed tonight to glow with a radiant, perfect beauty. As she looked at this dark, glamorous woman, Vicky felt waves of doubt obliterating all the security of her decision to accept Stephen's offer of marriage.

'Stephen, you look like an Italian prince. How glad I am I insisted on white jackets and cummerbunds for the men,' Olivia laughed into his face with an intimate, teasing gesture. 'Don't you agree, Mrs. Grant? How pleased I am that you could come. And you, Vicky, what a pretty little dress. It was kind of Stephen to release you from your duties and let you come to my party, wasn't it?'

'Indeed it was!' said Vicky, managing a smile. 'And that's put you in your place,' she told herself, thinking with dread that Stephen could not have found a worse place to announce their engagement. Perhaps she could ask him to delay it, but he had seemed so insistent, and in any case, there would hardly be an opportunity to talk to him alone between now and the time when the announcement was made.

Small tables dotted the terrace and these were set with pastel-coloured porcelain Chinese bowls and delicately carved chopsticks. Heavy candles glowed in glass bowls, holding flowers floating in jasmine-scented water. A thin, fragrant chicken soup, eaten with flowered porcelain spoons, preceded the more solid food. Though 'solid' was hardly the word for the delicious courses that followed, each one a dream of savoury, exotic taste. By the time the guests had eaten omelette stuffed with crayfish, prawns fried in batter, boned duckling, and tiny pieces of crisp pork served in a sweet-sour sauce of green peppers and pineapple, they had become accustomed to the chopsticks, even picking up the delicious savoury rice that was served with each course.

Olivia had welcomed the hospital party to the main table, but Vicky was puzzled by her rather distraite manner, for usually she was a perfect hostess, calm and gracious. She barely touched her food and seemed hardly to hear her guests' conversation. Vicky felt she must be thinking of something else.

At last the long dinner was over. Flaming plates of preserved fruits had been brought for dessert, and bowls of china tea were served with crisp biscuits of rice and honey. Olivia spoke to her brother, and Vicky, who was sitting quite near, caught the words, 'Tell him he can come now.'

Olivia's brother rose from the table, making some excuse to the guests.

'Olivia has a surprise for you,' he said. 'I don't know why

144

she has kept you in the dark until now, but she insists on doing it this way. She likes to introduce a little drama into our humdrum lives here.'

As he left to go into the house, Olivia rose and rang a crystal bell which hushed the sound of voices and laughter.

'Sorry to interrupt. I won't keep you long,' she said.

She looked warm, golden, her sumptuous dress glowing in the candlelight. Vicky thought she had never seen her so lovely. She glanced at Stephen. He was looking at Olivia with a peculiarly enigmatic expression, almost, thought Vicky, as if he disliked her.

'I'm so pleased to have all you dear friends around me on this happy occasion, for it's not only the beginning of a new year for me tonight, but, I hope, the beginning of a new life. Tonight I want you to meet someone who has become very dear to me, someone who has persuaded me to become his wife.'

A murmur of astonishment swept over the tables like the susurration of leaves being blown along the grass by the winds of autumn, and, like an intimation of first frost, Vicky felt a chill premonition, a dread of something as yet unknown, that threatened the hope of happiness she had so doubtfully grasped. And suddenly these confused emotions resolved themselves as she watched the shadowy figure of a man making his way towards the table. The flicker of the candle, the lantern overhead, both served to identify him.

'I want you all to meet George Osborne,' said Olivia, 'my future husband. We're to be married soon.' She gave a gurgling trill of laughter and leaning forward kissed him ardently. 'My fiancé is an impatient man!'

There was a surge of guests towards the table coming to congratulate the newly engaged couple, and once more Vicky found herself beside Laetitia.

'So Dr. Stephen has been pipped at the post,' she whispered. 'A lucky let-off for him, I would say. The gentleman must be loaded. Just sight that ring!'

Olivia was laughingly brandishing her left hand which was now adorned with a beautiful square-cut emerald.

'I don't understand,' thought Vicky. 'Why did her father say he wanted Susan? Olivia would never want to be saddled with a child, or do I just think that because I dislike her? And Stephen?' Laetitia's heedless words had been like a barb in her heart. 'Did he know about Olivia's engagement when he asked me to marry him? Is that why? His nature is so proud. Did he not wish to appear jilted again?'

She wanted to run far away, to be back in her own quiet room, and there to disentangle her bewildered thoughts, to dissolve by weeping the terrible pain that seemed to be lacerating a vital part of her being. But Anton had sprung up and was congratulating the happy couple in a charming impromptu speech, and who, unless they knew him very well, was to know that it was not altogether sincere?

'And now,' said Anton, 'I have another pleasant surprise. Dr. Stephen, whom we all know so well and esteem so highly, has also become affianced.' He paused dramatically while another wave of surprise swept his audience. 'To someone we have only known for a little while, but I can say truthfully that those who have been privileged to know her have learned to love her. Miss Vicky, who came to teach Susan, but has captured our doctor's heart!'

There was another round of applause and good wishes. To Vicky's surprise, Stephen produced a small old-fashioned jewel box, in which, upon a background of faded blue velvet, nestled a ring of red garnets and pearls. 'Gran wanted you to have this,' he whispered.

'Put it on. Come on, Stephen, let's see you do it properly!' shouted some of the onlookers who had drunk rather deeply of the saki wine and followed it none too wisely by the champagne Olivia had served after her betrothal announcement.

Stephen took her hand. 'Why, your hand is like ice!' he exclaimed. He slipped the ring on to her left hand.

'Now a kiss. Let's see if you can do it as well as Olivia and George!' shouted a raucous voice.

Vicky wanted to turn and run, to get as far away as possible from this travesty of an engagement, but she submitted quietly to being kissed again and even managed to smile, though her throat ached with the effort of stemming back the tears.

'Second best,' her mind kept reiterating. 'He couldn't have Olivia, so he took me as second best. But why? why? I don't understand. Was it to revenge himself upon Olivia?'

Vicky looked at her. Beneath the smiling mask she sensed ill-restrained fury. The green eyes glittered cold as far-away stars.

146

'You look frozen, child. Have you got a wrap?' asked Gran, who had come to join in the congratulations.

'Yes, Gran. It's inside the house. I'll go to fetch it,' said Vicky, seizing upon this excuse to get away.

Olivia's personal sitting room had been set aside as a cloak-room for this evening and Vicky stumbled blindly into the small perfect room with its blue patterned wallpaper, white paintwork and Wedgwood china ornaments. She sat down on a ruby velvet sofa, put her head in her hands and shivered uncontrollably. After a few minutes, however, hearing footsteps upon the paved hall outside, she pulled herself together, wrapping her fleecy stole about her and making a pretence of repairing her make-up.

The door burst open and Olivia came in, carefully turning the key in the lock. She stood there like a Chinese Empress, an imposing figure in shimmering gold and emerald, the disguise of a charming hostess completely forgotten.

'What a ridiculous farce!' she exclaimed. 'My poor Stephen – I never realized he would do anything so desperate.'

Vicky, white-faced and bewildered, felt herself caught in a tangled web, with Olivia a furious, venomous spider at the centre of the maze.

'How much did he offer you to go through with this?'

'I don't understand,' whispered Vicky.

'Don't tell me money wasn't mentioned between you, or did he capture you with his own brand of irresistible charm?'

With an effort of will, Vicky stood up. Her head was held high, her chin resolute.

'Would you explain to me, Olivia, what all this is about? I'm tired of people talking in riddles. I want to know what you're implying when you talk about our engagement in terms of money?'

Olivia gave a low laugh. Her gilded nails emphasized the expansive gesture of her long, cream-coloured hands as she turned towards Vicky.

'Surely Stephen told you the reason why he wishes to marry?' Then, seeing Vicky's expression: 'My poor child, did you think our rather chilly Stephen capable of romantic love?'

'No,' said Vicky, in bitterness of spirit. 'No, I never thought he loved me. I realized he needed someone to make a home for Susan.'

'And so you very sweetly offered yourself as a candidate for domestic bliss. How self-sacrificing of you! Especially when one considers the amount of money involved.'

The rage that shook Vicky bore no relation to her usually mild disposition.

'What money?' she demanded. 'I'm tired of all this mystery. What money are you talking about?'

'Didn't he tell you that whoever is guardian to Susan gets a considerable share of her fortune, a proportion of the rights of the emerald mine for himself?'

'No, I didn't know. But that fact would never influence Stephen.'

Olivia laughed mockingly.

'Don't you believe it, my dear. Granted Stephen is not materialistic, but he would do anything to get money for his beloved hospital.'

An echo built up in Vicky's mind, from the first day they met: 'Everybody likes money, Miss Scott. Even I do.'

'Why do you think I became engaged to George? I'll be frank with you, Vicky, there's more future in it. Even if Stephen got the money, he's too interested in the hospital to give me the life I need. If the emerald mine is workable, and it probably is, George can claim Susan and a large part of the proceeds and he will spend the money on ourselves, not on stupid hospital equipment.'

'But Stephen loves Susan. That's why he wants to keep her.'

'Don't delude yourself, Vicky. Stephen hasn't got time for personal relationships. He's only interested in Susan in relation to the money. That's why he asked you to marry him, because a clause of the will says the chosen guardian must have a wife.'

The full significance of Olivia's words burst upon Vicky.

'Then none of you love Susan for her own sake! George Osborne was deceiving me when he said he wanted her back because he repented the fact that he had left her. And Stephen . . .' In spite of herself, Vicky's voice broke.

'Don't upset yourself over Susan. You and Stephen can have her and welcome. You don't think I really want to be trammelled with a ready-made family, do you? Especially a difficult child like Susan.'

'But I thought you said George Osborne intends to claim

her in order to get the money?'

'Not necessarily. We've been thinking we may be able to get round that.'

'How?'

'We can fight the will. After all, George was his father's legal heir. He had no right to cut him out of his will. We'll see what a lawyer can do. Better to get it all to ourselves than be saddled with a child, don't you think?'

'So none of you want her,' said Vicky softly. 'All of you are just thinking about Susan's money. To you and her father, she's a burden, not a living, breathing, sensitive child. And to Stephen . . .'

'Yes, Stephen has his eye on the main chance too, but he's not as frank as George. He wraps up his desire to get the money with his love of humanity. Vicky, if you intend to marry him, I warn you that this fine idealism of his may blot out any other feeling.'

There was a loud knock upon the locked door.

'Coming!' called Olivia, her dulcet tones belying the scene of the last few minutes.

'A gentleman has just arrived,' said the African servant. 'He say he want to see this madam.' He indicated Vicky.

Shattered by the revelations of the last half hour, Vicky found it difficult to adjust her mind to the present moment.

'Who can it be?' she asked, bewildered.

'Vicky!'

The overhead light illuminated the golden head of the man who was standing upon the zebra kaross in the foyer. He advanced with both hands outstretched.

'Vicky, my dear!'

He made as if to kiss her, but she avoided his embrace.

'David! What are you doing here?'

'Didn't Dr. Nash tell you? I've been looking into this emerald mine for him. Quite a coincidence that he should have chosen our firm to do the investigation, isn't it? Fortunately Dr. Nash didn't know I was the geologist chosen to do the investigation.'

Up until this moment Vicky had had some vague hope that Olivia's accusations about Stephen's interest in the money was wrong. But this final stroke shattered any faint illusions she had left.

'It's true, then. He has no feelings for me and none for

Susan. All he's interested in is getting money for the hospital,' she thought. 'What's to become of us? We both love him so much. Susan may outgrow it, but not I.'

'So you two are old friends,' said Olivia, with an amused smile. 'I'll leave you alone. You'll want to tell Mr Thackeray the news of your engagement, no doubt.' She turned away with a wave of her long gold-tipped fingers and a rustling of stiff brocade. 'I must return to my guests. Enjoy yourselves, my dears!'

'Let's go in here,' said David, indicating the nearest door. 'I want to talk to you.'

Numbly, Vicky allowed herself to be led into Olivia's music room, a long room which seemed more decorative than practical. Small turquoise velvet chairs and fragile gold settees were grouped near the white and gold concert grand piano, beribboned mandolins hung upon the walls, and an antique gilded harp stood next to the piano upon the light shining floor that elsewhere was covered by a blue and gold carpet of elaborate Chinese design embossed with birds and flowers.

'Lovely to see you again, Vicky,' said David, putting an arm around her. But Vicky slipped out of his intended embrace and walked towards the French doors that led on to the terrace. Laughter and music echoed from the assembled party and for a moment she stood there, the tears in her eyes blurring the Chinese lanterns into a kaleidoscope of nightmare shapes.

But David was beside her, closing the doors and working the mechanism of the turquoise velvet curtains, so that they quietly drew together, and she was enclosed in this artificial room with the man whom she had hoped never to see again. How could she ever have believed she loved him? His fair good looks had blinded her to his weak, obstinate mouth and a certain hardness in the blue eyes that had once so fondly gazed into her own.

'You received my letter?' asked David.

'Yes. I didn't understand it. I don't understand it now. Why have you come here at all? Surely you could have written to Stephen if you needed to give him a report about ... about the emerald mine?'

'Well, of course.' David smiled, using all his accustomed, winning charm. 'I came to see you, darling. I said I would, didn't I?'

'We've been over all this before. You're engaged to be married, David. You must realize we have no further claim on each other.'

'Oh, that!' said David, dismissing the mention of his engagement as if it was rather indelicate of her to remind him of it. 'But, darling, I told you I must have been crazy to give you up. It just seemed expedient at the time. But since I started investigating that part of the country where the mine is, I've had several ideas. I mustn't say too much yet, but it may lead to something big, and if it does I'll leave Eve's father's firm. The prospects there are feeble compared with this business.'

Vicky felt sickened by yet another example of someone's greed overriding affection.

'But Eve seemed so fond of you,' she said.

'Oh, she is, bless her heart. But don't let that worry you. You have no need to be jealous. Ever since I saw you again in Cape Town I've realized that it's you I love.'

'You don't even know what the word means,' said Vicky sharply. 'The only person you really love is yourself. You just let other people down as it suits you.'

'Sweetheart, don't be such a little spitfire! It doesn't become you. And come to think about it, what is all this about your engagement? Did I understand the *femme fatale* who was here a while ago to say you had become engaged to the doctor fellow?'

'Yes,' Vicky said lifelessly. 'We announced it this evening.'

'Indeed? So why are you here on your own, looking, if I may say so, a little down in the mouth? Why isn't everything full of rejoicing and bliss, and where is the loving doctor? Surely he hasn't been called away already from his bride-to-be?'

David always had an astute way of finding out if something was wrong. He seemed to have a kind of sixth sense for trouble which benefited him in his business dealings. But Vicky was determined he should not know that there was a flaw in her relationship with Stephen.

'I came in for my wrap,' she said.

'And found me,' smiled David. 'Oh, Vicky, Vicky, you look so beautiful. You should always stand with that golden hair against a background of turquoise velvet.' He strode towards her and seized her in his arms. 'Now I've found you again, no one is going to take you from me. You were mine long before you met this doctor. I won't let you go.'

His mouth came down upon hers, hard, demanding, bruising her lips as if he wished to obliterate all memory of anyone else. His hands were caressing her bare shoulders as he pressed her close, striving by dominant force to break the coolness of her response.

'We seem to be interrupting something,' said Olivia's mocking voice, and her laughter tinkled like the sound of the crystal chandelier disturbed by the cool draught from the open door into the hallway. David slowly released Vicky, but still kept his arm around her shoulders as he turned to face the two who had just come in.

'So sorry, Vicky dear,' said Olivia. 'Stephen wanted to see Mr. Thackeray about this business, so I brought him along. I didn't mean to be tactless, didn't realize you knew each other so well, but after all, what's a kiss between friends? Stephen quite understands, don't you, darling?'

'Yes,' said Stephen, 'I understand only too well.'

Suddenly from the terrace a clamorous tintinnabulation of sound broke the cold silence in the gilded room. The sound of bells amplified upon a loudspeaker clashed from outside the velvet curtains, the grandfather clock in the hall boomed out twelve solemn strokes, and the elaborate gilded timepiece upon the mantel joined in with a tinkling chime.

'Midnight,' said Olivia, regarding the other three with a cool, amused stare. 'A Happy New Year!'

'I'll see you in my office in the morning, Thackeray. It doesn't seem to be a suitable time now,' said Stephen. 'Come, Vicky, Gran is tired and I think we should go soon.'

David seemed completely unperturbed by Stephen's icy manner and his anger which was obvious, though restrained. He took his arm from Vicky's shoulder and yawned hugely.

'Think I'll hit the hay, too. I'm pretty weary after the long drive on these appalling roads. I must find a hotel.'

'Don't go, Mr. Thackeray,' said Olivia graciously. 'Mr. Osborne is in the best guest room, but I'm sure we can make you comfortable elsewhere.'

'Very good of you. Are you sure I won't be putting you to too much trouble?'

'No trouble at all,' said Olivia, pressing a bell for a servant. 'We meet so few interesting people here, it's a pleasure to have a well-known geologist with us.'

David was obviously very impressed by Olivia's flattering manner and hardly seemed to notice when Vicky and Stephen withdrew. On the terrace the guests were celebrating the New Year. Streamers were flying, car hooters blaring, whistle blowing, and comparative strangers kissing as if they had loved each other all their lives.

Vicky was whirled into a social merry-go-round that at this moment was the last thing she wanted. People were kissing and congratulating her, wishing her happiness for the coming year. Anton was progressing from one group to another, champagne glass in hand, setting it down when he came to a pretty girl, and embracing her with vigour.

'I like this New Year custom,' he declared rather superfluously, as he made yet another amorous sortie. Gran trotted after him and tapped his shoulder.

'Come on, Casanova,' she said. 'Stephen and Vicky say it's time to go home.'

'So soon?' said Anton. 'Ah, one can understand that the newly affianced prefer to be alone. But wait, I have not yet greeted Vicky. Stephen, you allow?'

'Why not?' said Stephen with a frosty smile. 'You will not be the first to greet her this evening.'

'Now, now!' Anton admonished playfully. 'Jealousy will get you nowhere!' And he kissed Vicky warmly.

Almost immediately, however, his teasing manner changed and he regarded Vicky with genuine concern.

'What is it, Vicky darling? You are so cold, you are trembling. Stephen, you must look after this precious, beloved one. We do not want her to have pneumonia.'

Gran insisted that Vicky should sit in the front seat of the car, and Anton wrapped her around with a fleecy mohair blanket. Only Stephen stood aside from their solicitude, a faint, bitter smile playing across his dark face.

As they traversed the dark road back to the hospital, it was Anton alone who kept up some semblance of conversation. Gran was tired and, sitting as she was next to Stephen, could hardly be unaware of his gloomy mood.

'What a surprise Olivia gave us,' said Anton. 'Were you aware of this interest, Stephen?'

'She told me a few days ago she intended to become engaged,' said Stephen.

'So I was right,' thought Vicky. 'He knew before he made his proposal to me.'

'Where did she meet him?'

Stephen sounded irritated by Anton's questions.

'I really have no idea. Presumably they already knew each other well when she met us in East London. She had met him previously in Johannesburg and she took the opportunity of buying her new car to meet him again when he wrote to tell her he would be coming to the Eastern Cape.'

In the midst of the dark turmoil of Vicky's thoughts, a small ray of light gleamed. Could it be ... perhaps George Osborne whom she saw with Olivia that night on the balcony at the hotel? It was surprising what a lift this small fact gave to her depressed spirits. It was such a tiny thing to hearten her, and yet it seemed to put Stephen in a slightly more favourable light.

She was relieved on their arrival when Stephen said he would like Anton to take him straight to the hospital.

'Poor Vicky,' Anton sympathized. 'She is starting rather early to find out the drawbacks to being a doctor's wife.'

'You haven't forgotten, have you, Stephen, that the day after next we're going down to the cottage? We must get Vicky better by then,' Gran said. 'I'm looking forward to a sight of the sea again, and so is Susan. She's all for taking the bush baby to see his old home.'

Olivia had asked them to come to stay with her for a day or two at her seaside house. Vicky was not looking forward to it. Especially now.

'I will have to confront Stephen with the fact that I know now why he asked me to marry him,' she thought. 'I'll have to tell him that I can't accept him under those conditions, not even for Susan's sake. How strange that my disillusion in him is more complete than that I felt about David, because I always recognized David's faults, but I thought I knew that Stephen had absolute integrity, and yet when I only look at him, I forget it all and love wells up in me as strong as death.'

Next day Gran insisted that Vicky should stay in bed to fend off the threatened cold, and Vicky in her state of emotional exhaustion submitted meekly to a diet of gruel and aspirin. Fortunately this made her sleep and so her worried thoughts were quietened. By late afternoon she felt stronger and more able to cope with the situation.

'As soon as I can,' she thought, 'I'll tell Stephen that I know of his motives, and I'll say I want to leave here. He'll have to find someone else to teach Susan, or otherwise find a boarding school for her.'

The thought of leaving the child gave her almost as much pain as her hopeless love for Stephen, but she tried to make her mind blank in this regard.

Despite Gran's protests, she got up in time for the evening meal, and was relieved when Stephen sent a message that he was involved with last-minute arrangements at the hospital and would not be able to see them until tomorrow.

There was no word from David. Vicky wondered what had happened when Stephen and David met this morning, but perhaps Stephen had devoted the time strictly to the business in hand, David's investigation of the emerald mine. This was only a preliminary measure, she knew. David had said he would not be able to give the final verdict upon it for a few days.

Would David go as soon as his business was finished? There was no point in his staying any longer. Was he aware, she wondered, that they were going to the sea cottage tomorrow? He would probably hear this from Olivia. Olivia had sent two of her servants ahead to open up the cottage and unpack supplies. They were all to follow early tomorrow morning and stay over the week-end, though Anton was being left to hold the fort at the hospital.

'I can take Sinkwe, can't I?' Susan demanded next morning.

Vicky looked at the small animal, with his owl-like eyes and squirrel tail, who was draped over Susan's arm like a very domesticated kitten.

'I suppose it will be all right,' she said. 'But it would be difficult if he got lost, because the bush is so thick down there.'

'I'll look after him well, I promise. Every time I'm not holding him, I'll close him in his cage, and he'll sleep in the room with me at night.'

'Olivia may not like that.'

'Then I won't tell her,' said Susan.

Vicky could not help smiling to herself though she tried to look severe. Susan had changed so from the timid child who was almost frightened of her own shadow and had had to steel herself to be brave. The brown-skinned, sparkling-eyed little girl wearing sandals, blue shorts and a red and white T-shirt, looked very different from the quaint Alice-in-Wonderland child she had met in Cape Town.

'Selina and Tandiwe are going down in the bus. I wish I was,' Susan said.

They had decided Selina and Tandiwe would enjoy a jaunt to the sea too, but there was not room for them all in Stephen's car, and Olivia, with her new fiancé, would not want to be bothered with taking their servant and her little girl.

'But you like driving with Stephen,' said Vicky.

'And you,' declared Susan, putting Sinkwe down and winding her arms around Vicky's waist. 'Oh, Vicky, it'll be lovely to be at the sea with you and Stephen and Selina and Tandy. We'll fish and we'll find shells and we'll swim in pools. I wish Olivia wasn't going.'

'But, Susan dear, it is her cottage.'

'Yes, I suppose so. But she doesn't like me. She doesn't like you either. Really, Vicky, she only likes men.'

Vicky was amused at Susan's astute thinking, but she shook her head reprovingly and told her she should not discuss grown-up people so critically.

The gently rolling green pastures were covered by large bushes of ragged flowers, making a pattern of chequered gold as far as the eye could see. Around the beehive huts, near the cattle kraals, the tall agave aloes raised candelabra branches tipped with yellow blossom. It was just the same. Only she herself had changed. Recollecting the happy hours she had spent with Stephen, when they journeyed to the clinic on this same road, Vicky felt deeply sad.

At that time, she had not even realized her feelings for him and now, after so short a time, she must put them away from her, with not a word of love spoken. For the sake of Susan's welfare, she had been prepared to accept marriage with him even if the love was all on her side, but the thought that he was marrying simply to get control of Susan's fortune was unbearable to Vicky.

Although unfortunately it did not quench his attraction for her, she could not with integrity accept his offer knowing that affection for the child was a minor consideration to him.

'I must find an opportunity to tell him,' she said to herself, trying not to look at the dark ruffled hair in front of her, the firm brown hands guiding the car. 'Soon – very soon – and then I can go away and this life, this countryside that I've learned to love, will seem like a far-off dream.'

There had been a shower of rain the previous night and the sky was a new-washed blue pied with fleecy white clouds. Puddles by the side of the uneven road reflected the sky, except where small grey wagtails with neat white waistcoats rippled the water with bobbing dance.

Gran and Susan had a pact between them that whoever saw the sea first won a box of chocolate drops, and, as they drew nearer to the coast, every corner turned was a source of excitement. Finally, 'I can see the sea!' shouted Susan, as a tiny triangle of blue appeared between two hills.

'You've got younger eyes than I have,' said Gran. 'It isn't fair.' So they shared the chocolate drops.

A rough track led off the main road to Olivia's cottage. Their pace was of necessity slow, and small piccanins, covered only by a scrap of ochre-coloured blanket, ran beside the car waving sticks in greeting.

'They play stick games to prove their bravery,' Stephen explained to Susan. 'They duel like knights of old with a long stick and their hands bound and protected by rags of material.'

As usual, Olivia's arrangements were perfect. The cottage, which on their previous visit had had a blank, untenanted air, was now humming with life. Upon an outside fireplace, a huge iron cauldron, its lid only partly closed, revealed the feelers of several crayfish. A young African boy was plucking chickens in a cloud of feathers. Someone else was chopping wood to feed the primitive hot water geyser. At the kitchen door, an African with a bamboo fishing rod was haggling with the chef over the price of a large fish. Olivia had already arrived, but she explained that George had been delayed.

'He had to put through an important phone call, so he'll be here later. So tiresome,' she sighed.

They had crayfish mayonnaise for lunch, served with crisp salads and hot bread baked in the Dutch oven, which was on the exterior of the cottage at the base of a whitewashed chimney.

Olivia glanced slyly at Vicky, while they were sitting over coffee.

'David stayed with George, but don't worry, Vicky. He

157

may come down later. I tried to persuade him to come with me, but he said he too had business to negotiate for you, Stephen.'

She smiled radiantly, seemingly unaware of the barbs she was shedding as readily as a porcupine. Stephen did not bother to reply. It was almost as if he had not heard her.

'Can we bathe this afternoon?' asked Susan eagerly. 'I'm dying to use my goggles and flippers.'

'What a brave wee bairn it is now. A wee while back you were feared of bathing,' said Gran.

'But I'll have Tandy with me and we'll find pools with funny fish and all kinds of things.'

'You mustn't go into the sea unless a grown-up is with you,' warned Stephen. 'Vicky and I will come this afternoon.'

Vicky looked at him in surprise. She had forgotten, of course, that he did not know of Olivia's revelations made the previous night. He was still keeping up the pretence of their being engaged, as of course they still were.

After lunch they rested for a while, then, urged on by Susan, Vicky changed into the pale yellow swim-suit, cut with deep plunging back, that flattered her golden tan.

'Why not wear your new bikini?' demanded Susan, skipping about in a neat red two-piece costume which Anton had given to her for Christmas.

Vicky glanced regretfully at the exiguous costume in gay green checks which she had bought on impulse during the journey from Cape Town.

'I'm afraid I might get too burned in it, until I'm more used to the sun,' she explained hurriedly.

'I can't face Stephen in that costume,' she thought. 'He would disapprove of me even more.'

She slipped on some orange-coloured sandals and, wearing a short jacket of yellow towelling dotted with gaily coloured sea-horses, she joined Stephen who, in black swimming trunks, was waiting at the head of the steps that led down past the waterfall to the beach.

The lean brown body, the lock of dark hair falling across his forehead, gave him a young, little boy look. Already he was less taut, more relaxed, and his welcoming grin was so frank and sweet that Vicky felt bitterly sad. She would soon have to disturb his calm.

'How can he seem so simple sometimes and yet have been so devious in his behaviour?' she thought despairingly.

The bay swept in a great curve and, in the distance, forest came right down to the water's edge. The beach was not as deserted as it had been that other time, for during the Christmas holidays many people came to stay in their cottages. However, there was such a long stretch of sand and rock that the scattered figures only seemed to emphasize the vastness of sea and sky. The tide was low and the exposed rocks gave up their secrets in deep pools where children played and sometimes Africans dived for seaweed.

Anglers were silhouetted against the brilliant light as black shadows beside the foaming sea, and in the lagoon at the river's mouth, men were throwing nets with curving precision, pursuing the leaping silver mullet that would be used for bait.

Small children upon unsteady legs tottered beside their African nannies and dogs chased sandpipers along the water's edge. Large ladies in brightly coloured culottes struck an incongruous note on this wild beach, and yet they were at home, supremely confident in a way of life that they had known for years, the annual exodus, accompanied by servants, from their Transkei villages to the sea.

Susan was not unique in having an African companion. Small boys were accompanied by 'ghillies' the same size as themselves and they fished together in companionable silence, baiting up each other's hooks and comparing catches.

Susan and Tandy found a pool just deep enough to swim in, and they were able to use goggles to gaze at the fascinating underwater world that was revealed to them below. Anemones unfolded predatory petals of orange and red. Pink seaweed made a delicate tracery of pattern against the rocks, and schools of small zebra fish striped in black, or moonfish with round, flashing silver bodies darted in and out of crevices. while on the bottom curly shells seemed to have a weird mobile life of their own until one realized they were the homes of hermit crabs of all shapes and sizes.

Soon Selina arrived to keep an eye on the two little girls and Stephen suggested a bathe for himself and Vicky in the sea.

'Would you like to try swimming underwater?' he asked. 'There's a reef not very far out to sea. It's very calm there – not more than ten feet of water and there are lots of fish.'

'This will be the last time I am with him,' thought Vicky, 'Before I tell him that the plans for our life together are

159

over. Let me enjoy one lovely afternoon before the storm breaks over me, tearing me away from him.'

'I'm a fairly strong swimmer,' she said. 'I would like to try, though I haven't any experience of underwater swimming.'

Stephen helped her to fasten her flippers. His dark head bent so near filled her with anguished longing. She quickly put on her mask to hide from him the expression of her eyes and adjusted the breathing snorkel to fit into the hole at the side. As they flapped with duck-footed gait into the water, Susan came running to see them.

'You look like people from Mars,' she exclaimed.

'I would say we look like primitive lizards with very pre-historic feet,' Stephen suggested. He had a belt with a knife and a speargun with which he was hoping to catch fish.

'When we reach the breakers, swim straight through each one before it actually breaks,' he told Vicky. 'There's calm water underneath the wave and you'll find you go straight through to the other side. Breathe deeply first before you go under.'

They were waist deep now and the pull of the water was quite strong. He held her hand firmly, waiting for an opportunity to negotiate the breakers.

'Now!' he called out, and they dived through the emerald wall of water that was topped with foam. In a moment they came up to the surface and found themselves beyond the wave, then they swam near together on the surface until they had to face another one. Joy invaded Vicky's being once more. The flippers, so heavy to wade in, now made her light and buoyant. Here there was no time to think of anything else but this lovely world of green, glittering water and wide, sunlit sky.

Beyond the breakers, the sea was calm and they could see a low line of rocks breaking the surface. Stephen hoisted himself upon a flat rock and pulled Vicky after him.

'Not cold?' he asked.

'No,' she assured him.

'I'd forgotten that Gran thought you had a cold threatening.'

'That was nothing.' ('Merely a disillusioned heart,' she thought to herself.) 'The water is marvellously warm. The Indian Ocean in midsummer is certainly different from the Atlantic or the North Sea.'

'It seems clear enough to use the goggles. I think you will find it's fun floating on the surface or just underneath with the snorkel taking in air. There should be plenty to see.'

He lowered himself from the rock and for a moment held Vicky in his arms, smiling all his charm. He seemed to have put behind him his grudge against David and the scene of the night before.

'How I wish I could forget about it too,' thought Vicky. 'Why does he choose today to be so nice to me, when he knows in his heart it's all pretence?' And again there welled up in her a deep resentment that he could pretend to like her and yet use her and use Susan to further his own ambition.

'Breathe deeply and we'll go under,' said Stephen.

The water was clear, pale green underneath. Vicky felt as if she was in a different world. It was all so tranquil that her worries seemed to recede into the distance. It was a world of gently waving seaweed and strange small sea-creatures. Black and white angel fish gracefully trailed their winglike fins, and down below a cerulean blue parrot fish nibbled at a shellfish with its hard horny beak, while schools of blacktail performed a ceaseless ballet.

It was a shock to come back to the ordinary world again. Vicky was reluctant to leave this haven of the sea. But Stephen was adamant.

'Gran won't forgive me if you catch a fresh cold,' he said. 'Do you think you'll be able to get back to shore while I try to catch a few fish? It's much easier to get back – the breakers carry you in.'

'Yes, I'll go soon,' Vicky promised, and sat upon the rock watching him dive in search of fish. Presently he swam further down the reef and she was alone except for stray seagulls swooping down to take a closer look at her. She supposed she should start swimming towards the shore and yet she was reluctant to break the spell cast by the calm blue sea, the arching sky with its fleecy clouds, the lovely bay enclosed by its arms of land. Here life seemed suspended in a peaceful dream. Once back on shore every moment would bring her nearer to the time of parting.

She cast herself into the lapping waves and floated quietly along. 'I'll stay here for a while,' she thought. 'I needn't go back yet.'

In her dreamy state she failed to realize that she was floating away from the reef and when she did she decided it would be quicker to swim directly to the shore. She turned over and started to swim with strong strokes, but it seemed amazingly difficult to make any progress towards the receding shoreline.

What she did not realize was that, while she had been floating, she had gone beyond the calm water enclosed in the bay by the reef and was being pulled further out to sea by a powerful offshore current. The water beyond the reef was much more turbulent and the gentle lift of the waves was transformed now into a deep swelling motion, making it much more difficult to swim.

'Only a little way,' she assured herself, 'and I'll be in the calm water again.'

But it seemed as far away as ever.

'I mustn't panic,' she thought. 'It's absurd. I'll soon be back on shore.'

A few minutes ago she had wanted to stay in the tranquil ocean. Now all she longed for was to be upon dry land. She could feel herself tiring and turned upon her back trying to float, but it was impossible to keep on the surface with the great swells battering at her. Several times she was inundated by a mountain of green water, and incredulously she examined the thought: 'I'm going to drown!'

A particularly huge wave swamped her and she felt herself being dragged down, down to the very bottom where her limbs were scraped upon the jagged rocks. 'This is it,' she thought. 'What a stupid way to die!'

A darting thought flashed upon her reeling brain. 'The cuts from the stones are probably bleeding. It will attract sharks!' And at that moment she felt herself seized by the arm in a powerful grip. Blinded by water, she wanted to scream, but did not even have the strength. Then she was on the surface again and a voice said, 'Vicky, my dearest, hold on to me.'

'I thought . . .' she spluttered.

'Don't talk, just kick a little.'

His arms were strong and comforting as he towed her away from the dangerous water. Within the reef the waves were their friends, speeding them towards the shore. She let herself drift into unconsciousness that had been threatening during the last dangerous moments. With Stephen there nothing else mattered.

When she opened her eyes the wild motion of the water

had ceased. She was in Stephen's arms and his mouth was upon hers, breathing air into her exhausted lungs. The sand was warm beneath her cold limbs, but a large piece of driftwood sheltered her from the sun. When Stephen saw that her eyes were open, he took his mouth from hers, but his arms still held her cradled against him.

'Vicky, my crazy darling,' he said. 'How did you get out there? You should be spanked for giving me such a fright!'

And once more his mouth was upon hers and it was like that night in the moonlight when she had first realized she loved him, but this time it was she who thrust herself away from the security of his arms.

'How can you kiss me like this, when this whole stupid farce is one gigantic lie?' she asked, blurting out in her overwrought state what it would have taken her hours to come to in cold blood.

'What is it, Vicky? My poor sweetheart, I shouldn't have worried you in your exhausted state. Let me fetch your wrap. The whole world seems to have gone up to the cottages for tea. Just as well we were alone. First aid is difficult with people crowding around.'

She watched him as with long strides he went to fetch the towelling wrap. She felt exhausted, but buoyed up by a terrible anger. A small voice said, 'He saved your life.' But she ignored it. 'Dr. Stephen Nash,' she thought, 'I'm tired of your playing with my feelings. I'm going to end things now.'

She struggled into the warm coat. The sun had revived her, and the weak exhausted feeling was disappearing. He embraced her once more.

'Oh, Vicky, Vicky, when I saw you going down below the waves, I thought I was going to lose you. I realized then . . .' and he started to kiss her again with a tenderness shadowed by latent passion.

Blossoming like a hidden flower, she felt her love for him imbue her whole being with fervent emotion. But before her heart could betray her into an ineffaceable surrender, she drew away from him.

'I must end this now,' she thought, 'or give away my integrity to this man who plays with my feelings like a musician striking dissonant chords.'

'It's no good, Stephen,' she said. 'You see, I know.'

'What do you know, my dear?'

His teasing smile faded as he saw her serious expression. 'I know the reason you asked me to marry you.'

'Then I didn't conceal my feelings as well as I thought I did. When I asked you to marry me I was afraid you would refuse. You must have known I was only using Susan as a means to an end.'

'You admit that!'

'Naturally,' said Stephen, smiling again.

'You admit now that you used the child for your own ends, and yet you can still make love to me like this . . .'

'But, Vicky, I knew you loved Susan. It was the easiest way to get you to consent to marry me.'

Vicky lost her temper very rarely, so when she did it was all the more thorough.

'Because you had to get some poor, silly, simple fool of a girl to fall in with your plans!' she shouted, beside herself with trembling anger. 'Olivia had refused you, but you had to get Susan's money somehow. So you chose the first person to hand because you simply couldn't bear to have Susan's rights to the emerald mine fall into someone else's hands. All along it wasn't Susan you cared for. It was your precious hospital!'

Stephen's blanched face disclosed that her words had found their mark. She should have felt pleased when she saw his stricken expression, but she found it difficult to sustain her anger.

'So that's what Olivia told you last night. And you believed it. You thought I'd asked you to marry me simply to ensure that as Susan's guardian I would get my share of the profits!'

'What else could I believe?' cried Vicky, her voice breaking at the piercing condemnation in his grey eyes. 'You commissioned David to investigate the mine. You asked me to marry you when you heard of Olivia's engagement!'

It was out now, but she felt no satisfaction. Stephen's expression frightened her, but she stared defiantly at him even while she felt that something inside her was slowly bleeding to death.

'So that's your opinion of me. You think I'm capable of using Susan, of using you, for material gain.'

He looked so strangely unhappy that her heart smote her. Had she inflicted this hurt?

'I know . . . I know . . .' she stammered, 'that it's for the hospital, not for yourself.'

'So your first observation, the one I heard you pass in Cape Town, has proved right. You believe me so fanatical that I'll go to any extremes.

'Had it occurred to you,' he added, 'that it was only sensible to investigate the value of the mine, simply for Susan's sake? Especially since her father, who had been so long lost, was now showing an unhealthy interest in it?'

She stared at him, her thoughts a medley of confused regret. His direct manner was one of anger rather than guilt. Had she wronged him in thinking his ambitions for the hospital had guided his every action?

'Stephen, I'm sorry if I was wrong about the money. It all seemed so true. I was puzzled. I didn't know why you had asked me to marry you. I couldn't believe you had any feeling for me. You've never . . .'

Stephen turned coldly away.

'I prefer you when you're angry to being apologetic, Vicky. Go on believing the worst of me if you wish. Let's leave it, shall we? You've made it very plain to me how despicable I am to you. You're tired and overwrought, and true feelings come out in those circumstances. Naturally I release you from your promise to marry me. As you say, it was never anything but a farce anyway.' Angrily he swung her up into his arms.

'What are you doing?' asked Vicky frantically.

'Don't disturb yourself. You're too weak to negotiate the steps. I propose to carry you, or would you prefer me to go up and see if David has arrived?'

In a confusion of bitter emotion, Vicky leaned against him as he carried her towards the cottage. What had she done? Had she really been mistaken in his motives? But then if they were not what she had thought, why had he asked her to marry him? Simply to provide a home for Susan? Or could it be . . .? She glanced at his dark face. It was set and stern. Whatever his feelings had been before, it was too late now.

CHAPTER ELEVEN

VICKY had done what she had been steeling herself to do since the night of Olivia's party. So now it was over. She should have been feeling relieved and justified. Stephen had said she was free to go whenever she wished. It was just a matter of breaking the news to Susan and Gran, and then she could take her leave. 'South Africa is a big place,' she had remarked to David once. It would be easy to place plenty of distance between herself and the man who could still fill her heart with anguished longing.

When she thought about it sensibly, she felt she must surely have been fully justified in her accusations. So why did she continue to feel regret, as if she had found a rare flower that had struggled for survival upon unpromising ground and had deliberately torn it up by its roots?

She tried to make herself feel angry again. 'How dared he make love to me when he didn't really mean it?' But the memory of his kisses were engraved indelibly upon her heart, and she could not hate him.

She had managed to get back to her room without anyone seeing her, and had slipped under the handwoven coverlet to try to rest, but her head throbbed painfully. She supposed she should take some kind of tablet, but she could not bring herself to get up and ask for one.

Thoughts whirled in a mad kaleidoscope around her aching head and sharp pains thrust themselves from the base of her skull like a burning tracery of lightning. She heard Susan and Tandiwe burst into the adjoining room with an ear-splitting clatter. The door was warped by the sea air and usually stood permanently wedged open, but for some reason they were trying to close it, wrenching it squeaking inch by inch until it broke free of the floor and they were able to slam it with ear-shattering force.

Then there was silence, but not for long. Piercing whispers were interspersed with high-pitched giggles until Vicky felt her aching head would burst. She lay there becoming more and more tense, the pains at the back of her head extending downwards to her neck and spinal column, while black tadpoles waltzed before her eyes.

A pulsing hoot of laughter from Susan broke what little control she had left over her nerves. Painfully she arose and stumbled towards the interleading door. She heard Susan and Tandy pushing something under the bed with much rustling and scraping, but when she looked in, they were sitting quietly, their large eyes, grey and dark brown, round and innocent like a parody of the bush baby's. He was also staring with his golden eyes as he perched upon the back of a chair.

Their pretence of innocence, the obvious attempt at deception, irritated her beyond bearing and she could hardly recognize the voice she spoke with as her own.

'What are you hiding under the bed?'

Susan's eyes were wide and frightened now.

'It's crayfish.'

'Crayfish?'

'We . . . we thought of a funny joke.'

'What was it?'

Susan hesitated, but she was not used to concealment.

'We . . . we were going to put them in Olivia's bed.'

'What! Susan, how could you think of such a thing? I would never have dreamed you could be so naughty. Take them away, and for heaven's sake, go somewhere else to play. I have a splitting headache and I just can't take any more of this stupid chatter and giggling!'

'I'm sorry, Vicky. We were only playing. We wouldn't really have done it.' Susan's eyes were frightened, her face pinched. She looked shocked and scared. Vicky was inescapably reminded of Stephen's face when she lost her temper during the scene on the beach.

'What have I done?' she thought, but the drums in her head were beating up to an excruciating crescendo.

'It's ridiculous to stay in the bedroom anyway. This is no place to play when you have the whole of the beach to play on.'

'Stephen said we mustn't go there by ourselves.'

'Oh, for heaven's sake! Stop arguing, Susan, and go! I've had more than enough of argument for one day.'

Very subdued, the two little girls shuffled out of the door, and Vicky lay down again upon the bed. Sheer exhaustion conquered her pain and she drifted into a deep sleep that was only interrupted an hour or so later when she was awakened by the sound of a car stopping with a slamming of doors, and the noise of people talking.

Her headache had disappeared, but she felt drained physically and mentally.

'Tomorrow I'll go,' she thought. 'I've even hurt a child because of my own mixed-up feelings. One episode like that could undo all the careful patience I've used with Susan. How could I have been so unkind to her?'

She poured rain water from the flowered jug into a basin and splashed her face and hands, then put on a pink dress with which she hoped to bring colour to her pale cheeks. From the verandah on the front of the house came the sound of male voices, interrupted occasionally by Olivia's incisive tones. There was the clinking of glasses and the hissing of a soda siphon.

'Oh, there you are, child. Stephen asked me to fetch you,' said Gran. 'Why, what is it, Vicky? Don't you feel well?'

'It's nothing, really. Just a bit too much sun, I think.'

Stephen had evidently not mentioned the underwater diving episode, or the fact that she might be going to leave them. She supposed he would find some excuse for that later.

'You must be careful, my dear. You aren't used to this heat yet, are you? Susan evidently thrives on it. She and Tandy were as noisy as a basket of monkeys today. But they seem to have quietened down a wee bit now.'

'Where are they?' asked Vicky.

'They've gone down to the beach with Selina to fetch some water. The cook insists on sea water for boiling the crayfish. Poor wee creatures, I suppose they may as well meet their death in their own element. Though I can't feel too sentimental about the weird, clattery things. They taste much better than they look. But come, Vicky, more visitors have arrived. Olivia is entertaining her fiancé and Stephen's geologist man. They're having drinks on the stoep. Oh, I forgot, of course you know Mr. Thackeray – he's the man we met at Groot Constantia. He seemed very pleased to know you were here.'

There was nothing else for it but to follow Gran out on to the stoep. The three men sprang up, and cordial meaningless greetings were exchanged. But conversation seemed to be at a premium. Stephen answered when he was spoken to, George Osborne seemed lost in a brown study, and only Olivia and David kept up a kind of flirtatious badinage that was as natural to them as breathing.

Olivia was wearing a sailcloth dress of bright emerald decorated by outsize zips on the pockets and front opening. Her hair hung loose and she looked very young and gay. Beside her vivid charm, Vicky in her present mood felt about a hundred years old.

'Ah, Vicky,' she said. 'Let me get you a drink.'

It was so unusual for Olivia to lift a finger in domestic matters that Vicky was quite taken aback. Olivia laughed, 'I must look after my guests. I haven't had a chance to speak to you since you came, you've been so involved with Stephen. Come with me and you can see how I mix my special fruit cup.'

Vicky followed her obediently into the long living room where an array of drinks was flanked by plates of olives, cucumber, sliced peaches, cherries and small decorative cocktail sticks. Olivia made a great show of pouring a drink, clinking ice, ladling in cherries and cucumber until there was hardly room for any liquid. Then she turned around and looked directly at Vicky.

'You look rather pale, sweetie. But you can stop fretting. We aren't going to take Susan away from you. It seems the famous emerald mine is not workable. The child won't get a penny from it, nor whoever is her guardian, naturally.' She paused as if to let Vicky digest the news. For one who had apparently lost a chance of a fortune, she looked remarkably cheerful. 'So it seems Stephen won't get his share for the hospital after all. Nor will we. But not to worry, there are plenty more fish in the sea, and I could never have tolerated the brat anyway.'

'Does Stephen know about this?'

'Yes. I must say he had more sense than us. In fact I think he suspected it all along.'

'But you said . . .'

'Oh, that!' said Olivia, laughing. 'You mean that Stephen was going to marry you to make sure of Susan's money? You didn't take me seriously, did you? No, darling, I'll be frank – all girls together and so on – no, that was just a bit of green-eyed jealousy, dog in the manger and all that jazz. I always thought Stephen was mine, if I lifted a finger, but you see, I didn't really want to lift it.'

'So you never really believed what you said?'

169

'No, my dear, did you? Surely you know Stephen well enough to realize he would never ask anyone to marry him unless ...'

'Unless?'

Olivia's laugh trilled.

'Well, unless he was deeply attracted to her, as of course he is to you.'

'But – but –' Vicky stopped. She could not discuss Stephen and her feelings with Olivia. She could not tell her that she was convinced Stephen did not even like her, especially now.

'Don't think I mind, dear. I couldn't care less. These idealistic types don't really appeal to me. I like the things that money can buy far too much to barter my chances in life for an existence at an African hospital in a thatched hut.'

'Are you girls going to be all day?' asked David, coming in with an empty glass. 'We're all set to do some serious drinking.'

'Isn't he a dream?' said Olivia, kittenishly putting her arm in David's and nestling up to him. Over her head, David glanced at Vicky, his eyebrows raised quizzically in mock despair.

'All the same, he seems to be enjoying Olivia's attentions,' thought Vicky.

She was surprised by the signs of fast growing intimacy, especially since Olivia had only two days before announced her engagement to George Osborne. But, when she saw Olivia with David, she felt not the slightest qualm of jealousy, for all her thoughts, all her feelings were centred on Stephen, in spite of the scene of this afternoon.

She was still trying to think about Olivia's denial of her previous assertion that Stephen wanted to marry to obtain his share of the emerald mine. But whether Stephen were innocent or guilty of a desire for wealth, as far as she was concerned, it was too late now. Whatever his feelings for her, and Vicky thought that Olivia's present opinion was as exaggerated as her previous accusations had been, it was clear that he now hated and despised her.

She excused herself from the company, saying she wanted to give Susan her supper and went in search of her, finding her sitting at the kitchen table eating bread and milk from a blue and white striped bowl.

'Selina made my supper,' Susan explained with a guarded look at Vicky. 'Are you better now?'

'Quite better, thank you.' She put her arm around Susan and the child passively submitted to her embrace for a few seconds, then said, 'My milk will get cold.'

Vicky dropped her arm.

'Shall I help you to get to bed?'

'No.' Susan's reply was sharp and decisive. 'Tandy will help me. I promised to read her a story.'

She was obviously not eager for Vicky's company, so with a small sigh Vicky left her alone. It was obviously not the time for a reconciliation. She went into her room.

But some time later Susan came hesitantly in.

'Vicky, have you seen Sinkwe? I forgot to put him in his cage.'

'When was that?'

She glanced at Vicky and looked away.

'When you were cross with us.'

'But he must be in the room somewhere.'

'No, I didn't close the door. I was afraid to slam it because of your head. And Sinkwe was afraid of the crayfish. I suppose that's why he ran out.'

'One more addition to the worries of this dreadful day,' thought Vicky. They searched through their rooms and the surrounding area, but the little animal with the fuzzy tail and endearing ways was nowhere to be seen. They listened carefully. At first only the piercing hum of the cicadas and the shrill note of the grasshoppers came to their ears. Then somewhere in the house they heard Sinkwe's cheerful squeakings.

'We didn't go into Olivia's room,' suggested Susan, running quickly.

But before they could reach there, Olivia had entered from the stoep with the intention of repairing her make-up before dinner. Her gasp of shocked dismay hastened Vicky's steps. Sinkwe was perched upon the dressing table, surrounded by clouds of face powder, spilled cosmetic jars and smashed perfume bottles. As Vicky stood in the doorway, Olivia seized hold of Susan's arm in an angry grasp.

'You little fiend!' she shouted. 'How dare you let your wretched animal loose in my room? You did it on purpose, didn't you?' And she slapped at Susan and shook her in a violent paroxysm of rage. Then, letting the child go, she seized Sinkwe from the dressing table and flung him down upon the floor.

With a squeak of dismay, the little animal fled limping through the outside door. Susan, gulping down sobs, ran after him, but she was too late. In spite of his dragging foot he managed to propel himself into a nearby bush, leaped from there to the next one, and was soon lost to sight in the foliage.

'Oh, Vicky—' Olivia tried to speak calmly, but was still shaking with rage. She had only just become aware of Vicky and did not realize she had witnessed the whole scene. 'Just look at the damage this wretched animal has done. Really, it's too stupid to allow Susan to keep such a wild pet!'

'I'll come to help clear up in a little while,' said Vicky, though she was shattered by the ugly scene she had just witnessed, and Olivia had already rung for a servant. 'I must go to Susan.'

She ran out to the tangled seabush nearby where, in the gathering dusk, Susan was searching for her pet. They searched for an hour, finally using torches to try to attract the little creature home. But it was no use. He had vanished into the bush from which he had originally come. Fireflies glittering like stars were the only moving things to be seen amongst the wild banana palms and grey, twisted, wind-wracked trees.

'He'll come back,' Vicky assured Susan. 'In the morning, when he's hungry, he'll find his way home.'

'But he doesn't really know his way around here, and Olivia frightened him,' sobbed Susan.

'You must come to bed now. We've done all we can. I'll get up at first light and come to look for him,' Vicky promised.

Reluctantly Susan allowed herself to be persuaded to come back to the house. Vicky had missed dinner, but she could not bear to leave the worried child until she was asleep. She sat quietly talking to Susan until, worn out with shock and exhaustion, the little girl fell into a troubled sleep, broken by heartrending quivers of breath.

Vicky had returned to her own room when Stephen knocked at the door. It was only when he seemed to look surprised that she was conscious of her bedraggled appearance.

The hunt for the bush baby had been extensive and through wild shrub. Her hair was tangled and full of leaves, her pink dress covered with green stains, her bare brown legs scratched and bleeding from the thorny undergrowth. In contrast, he was immaculate in white polo-necked shirt and close-fitting dark trousers that made him look like a matador.

'I came to see if you needed any attention. We wondered why you didn't appear for dinner,' he said abruptly.

So much had happened since her misadventure in the sea that she had almost forgotten about it, but he was evidently referring to that and did not know of the scene with Olivia, or at least, it appeared, only as much as she allowed him to know.

'I had difficulty getting Susan to sleep. She's upset about the bush baby.'

'Olivia said something about the bush baby getting amongst her things. It's fortunate she took it so well. Most women would have been livid!'

Vicky felt her surprise must make her look positively idiotic. Once over her first anger, Olivia must have presented to Stephen a pretty picture of a sweet, forgiving hostess. And it appeared Susan had been placed in the role of an obstreperous child.

'If Susan wants to keep a pet, she should take better care of it. It can't be allowed to wander around doing damage.'

'It was my fault it got out. Now it's lost and Susan is heartbroken.'

'Olivia didn't tell me it was lost.'

'She evidently only told you what she chose you should know.'

'Really, Vicky, there's no need to be spiteful about our hostess. I thought she was very forbearing about the damage done to her possessions. But she did say it would be a good thing when Susan could be sent to school, and I must say I quite agree with her. All this consideration for Susan's feelings is making her thoroughly spoiled.'

'How can you be so blind! She's a sweet child who perhaps exaggerates her affection for things like the bush baby because she has never had the love of parents or brothers or sisters. At one time I hoped you were becoming fond of her, and when her father came, I believed him when he told me he wanted her back, but it seems none of you loved her for her own sake, only on account of the wretched emerald mine – and now it appears that dream has gone for all of you.'

Stephen was white with anger.

'So we're back again where we started and you're still accusing me of greed and deception and heaven knows what else!'

'What else can I think? – when you're so harsh and unkind about Susan directly after hearing the emerald mine is no good!'

In her heart Vicky knew she was being unfair and that she did not truly believe what she was saying, but she had a primitive urge to lash out at him, to hurt him as much as he was hurting her.

'You're being quite ridiculous, Vicky. And it's just as well, perhaps, that this whole farce of our engagement has come to an end.'

'Yes, I agree, it's just as well. Let's put an end to it now, finally. When would you like me to go?'

Stephen was pale under his tan.

'When were you thinking of going?'

'Well, since you seem to think I have such a bad influence on Susan, it seems the sooner I go, the better. I'll make arrangements first thing tomorrow morning.'

'Very well,' said Stephen, and strode out of the room.

So it was really all over now. Vicky stood for a moment near the window. She opened it wide in case Sinkwe should choose that way to return. The night was full of stars. The Southern Cross with its two pointer stars hung like a jewelled ornament above her, and out at sea a solitary coaster showed its green starboard light. Far down the coastline, the lighthouse flashed a rhythmical beam, and on the brow of a hill a troupe of Africans, returning from a party, sang the same line of tune over and over with repetitive harmony.

'Vicky!'

The small voice broke across her sad thoughts. Susan! Had they wakened her? Vicky lit a candle and went into the other room. The little girl was lying flat on her back, her face flushed with weeping. But she was not crying now. Her voice and expression were solemn as she asked: 'Are you going away?'

She must tell Susan the truth.

'Yes, I am.'

'Why?'

'Stephen wants me to.'

'But I thought you were going to marry him.'

She must give her some explanation.

'It was all a mistake. Sometimes people find they don't like each other as well as they thought at first.'

'Oh.'

Susan lay for a while considering this, her long, dark lashes fluttering nervously over the large, grey eyes. Vicky thought she should attempt some consolation.

'Gran will look after you again, until you go to school. You'll meet other children there. It will be more fun.'

'Yes.'

She accepted Vicky's statement without comment, almost as if she brushed it aside because she was thinking of something more important.

'Don't you like Stephen, then?'

Vicky felt she could not lie to the child.

'Yes, yes, I do like him.'

'But you're going away.'

'He doesn't really – he never has – liked me the way people do when they marry,' she told Susan sadly.

'But what will happen now to Selina's necklace?'

For a moment Vicky thought the child was wandering in her thoughts.

'What do you mean?'

'Selina made me promise I wouldn't tell, but I guess it doesn't matter now if you're going away. I'll show it to you if you like.'

She got up and rummaged in a drawer to find a fancy chocolate box where Vicky knew she kept all her treasures. For that reason Vicky would never have dreamed of looking in it. She insisted on taking it everywhere together with the packet of Scots peat Gran had given her. From the bottom of the box, she produced a beaded square of the type Vicky had seen the old Pondo wearing that day at the hospital clinic.

But this one was new, fresh and beautiful. Not quite finished yet, its background was white. The small figure in the middle, dressed in a pale blue dress with floating yellow hair and dancing feet, held out its arms as if to embrace the world.

'It's you,' said Susan. 'Stephen asked Selina to make it for you. He knew you liked them and he said, when Selina told him, that it didn't matter if it was usually the wife who gave it to the husband. He was going to give it to you on your wedding day, or perhaps sooner, just when you found out, he said, that you were the one who was the Keeper of his Heart. He laughed when he said that and we all laughed too, but he really meant it, Vicky, I know he did.'

Like the beam of the lighthouse, a moment of revelation lit up all the dark, obscure, bitter thoughts in Vicky's mind. The small figure in the blue dress blurred before her eyes.

'He loved me,' she thought. 'He loved me and I never even knew. But it's too late now. By my accusations and my lack of understanding, I've spoiled it all. He was hurt once before and he's gone back into his shell again. He'll never forgive me now.'

She said good night to Susan almost in a dream. She would talk to her tomorrow and try to make her understand that it was best for her, Vicky, to go, and that as soon as possible.

Vicky slept badly that night, but towards morning she fell into a troubled sleep interrupted by nightmare dreams. She seemed to be struggling through bushy country as she had done the previous evening in search of Sinkwe, but in her dream it was not only the bush baby she was looking for. Sometimes it would be Susan, sometimes Stephen. She would see them at the end of a path, but as she ran towards them with joy, they would disappear. Then she would be in the sea again, but it was Susan and not herself who was drowning.

After one particularly vivid dream, she woke with a start. She felt heavy-eyed and weary, but could not face dreaming again, and forced herself to get out of bed and get dressed. Putting on navy slacks, a yellow cotton sweater and flat canvas shoes, she glanced into Susan's room to see if by chance the bush baby had returned. Susan was not in her bed. She also must have wakened early and gone to look for her pet.

She did not suppose the child had gone far, but it was odd that she had not come in to waken Vicky to accompany her. Remembering the events of the day before and the fact that Susan had overheard her conversation with Stephen, Vicky felt vaguely troubled. But when she went to the kitchen, Selina, stirring porridge, informed her that the two little girls had gone out together.

'They said they might not be back for breakfast,' she said.

'I gave them some sandwiches and apples. They took some sausages to cook. They said they were going to make a fire.'

'I hope they don't go very far into the bush looking for Sinkwe,' said Vicky.

'Tandiwe will look after Inkosikasi,' Selina assured her.

'I hope so,' said Vicky, thinking that Tandy was no bigger than Susan and did not constitute a very efficient guardian. She took a pair of binoculars and went out into the bush near the house, but could see no sign of the children or of the bush baby. The wooded area made a natural barrier between the beach and the grassy clearings where the cottages were built, but in places it developed into a kind of forest, dense and wild in the clefts of the hills.

The shortest way to the beach was down the steps and past the waterfall, but now Vicky chose the roundabout path through the trees, hoping she would see signs of the children or of Sinkwe. Sunlight glittered on dark green, shiny leaves and on huge dew-spangled spider webs strung from branch to branch, but in the sting of the sun there was a promise of heat to come, and beyond the vivid blue of the sky that was nearby, heavy clouds massed themselves out at sea, totally different from the fair weather clouds that usually hung in a drifting bank above the Mozambique current.

The beach was deserted save for one or two African fishermen and their wives who were gathering driftwood in great bundles. Most of the holiday people seemed to have departed yesterday evening, for the statutory holidays were over, and shops and trading stores must be opened again.

'As soon as I can do it without fuss, I'll pack and get a lift back to the hospital,' thought Vicky. 'Then I'll get a bus from there and try to make my way back to Cape Town.' She did not know when the others would be going, but she knew Stephen could not leave the hospital for long, and she wanted to go from the hospital before he came back. She could not bear the thought of seeing him in his own setting again, seeing him being welcomed by patients and nurses, seeing how they loved him.

She had come through the bush to the end of the beach near to the lagoon, where an inland river widened its mouth as it reached the sea. At low tide the water was so shallow that you could walk across on to the beach beyond, and Vicky saw two figures walking on the other side apparently deep in earnest conversation.

She lifted her binoculars, curious to know their identity. Through the powerful lens, the man and woman sprang into vivid life, David in a white polo-necked shirt and narrow checked slacks, his blond hair gleaming in the sun, and Olivia, in a vivid red blouse and white shorts. As she looked, the two figures merged in a passionate embrace. Vicky lowered the binoculars, rather shaken by this new development.

She had not meant to spy, but even at this distance there had been no mistaking Olivia's exultant smile. Why was she embracing David when her engagement to George Osborne was a mere three days old? Vicky turned and quickly made her way back, hoping to see the children, but there was no sign of them.

Back in the kitchen, Vicky begged a piece of toast and cup of tea from Selina. She could not face meeting Stephen at breakfast, but from her room, as she packed, she saw his tall figure striding along the path that led to the small trading store. She knew he had arranged that from there he would make a daily telephone call to the hospital to get a report.

David and Olivia had not returned, but George Osborne sat on the stoep, looking out to sea in a rather bored and gloomy fashion.

'Where is everyone?' he asked on seeing Vicky. 'Come and talk to me. This quiet life is getting me down.' She sat down reluctantly at his insistence.

'Have a drink,' he said, helping himself to Olivia's brandy, and then when Vicky refused: 'No? Well I need one, I tell you, after all our disappointing news. Too bad about the emerald mine, isn't it?'

'Yes, I suppose it is, from your point of view,' Vicky replied coldly. 'Though wealth might not have brought happiness to Susan.'

'Oh, yes – Susan. Keep forgetting I have a daughter. Not that I have really now. Stephen asked me if I would sign adoption papers and I said I would.'

'When . . . when was this?' faltered Vicky.

'Last night when our geologist friend had broken the news that the mine was no good. Must be nice not to mind about money. He was the only one who didn't seem to care. He just laughed and said, 'What does it signify anyway? Now I suppose you two won't object to my keeping Susan. That's all I care about. It would have been good to have extra funds for the hospital, but we'll get along – we always have.'

'Then he asked you about adoption?'

'Yes. Olivia said "I suppose this is one of Vicky's ideas," but he said "No, Vicky has nothing to do with this. It's going to be a matter between me and Susan." So I said I had no objection, and I haven't. She'll be better off with you two. Olivia was never wildly keen to have her with us, although she pretended to be at first.'

'How mistaken I was!' thought Vicky. 'How could I have been so blind?' She thought of how the Africans regarded him. 'The humblest patient at the hospital realized his true nature and I didn't.'

'Will this make any difference to your wedding date with Olivia?' asked Vicky tentatively. She knew it was perhaps impertinent, but she could not resist satisfying her curiosity.

A sly smile flitted across George Osborne's face and he helped himself to another brandy.

'It doesn't do to have all your irons in one fire or eggs in one basket ... which is it I mean? Olivia's a clever one and that David's pretty smart too. We have another scheme in hand – you'd be surprised.'

He shook his head mysteriously, trying to look knowing, but only succeeded in appearing stupid, as the drink began to affect him.

'Wonder where Olivia's got to?' he asked Vicky. 'Talking things over with David, I dare say. There's lots to discuss. But we must decide soon. Think I'll have a little kip. Excuse me.'

His head nodded forward and in a moment he was sound asleep in the comfortable wicker chair. Vicky rose and walked away, scanning the surrounding landscape to see if she could see any sign of the little girls returning.

Her eyes were covered by the binoculars and she did not see Stephen until he was close beside her. He spoke in an abrupt, businesslike fashion, the way she had occasionally heard him speak when he was giving orders.

'We may have to go home later today. There've been storms upcountry and they say the river may come down.'

'What does that mean?' asked Vicky.

He shook his head impatiently as if irritated by such a stupid question.

'These South African rivers, apparently so shallow, can change to roaring torrents in a matter of hours when there's been a storm in the catchment area.

'The bridge across the lagoon is the only link between us and the road, and in a few hours it may be under water. They're going to phone me later with information as soon as they get it. In the meantime I think it best if we pack up in case we have to go. Where's Susan?'

'She went out early with Tandiwe to look for her bush baby. They took sandwiches, but said they would be home by lunchtime.'

Stephen frowned. 'She's too little to go off on her own like that. I'm surprised you allowed it.'

'She went without my knowledge. But Tandy knows her way about this part of the country. Her grandmother lives near here.'

Vicky hoped she sounded more confident than she felt. She did not want to pass on her uneasiness to Stephen, but she wished very much that the children would come home. It was stiflingly hot and great towering cumulus clouds banked themselves upon the horizon, as if somewhere out in the ocean a sea-god had set off half a dozen atom bombs.

Gran was sitting knitting in the shade of a tree, but she came in to help pack upon hearing Stephen's news.

'At least,' thought Vicky, 'I need not tell her yet that I'm going. If we all have to leave here together, I can delay the news of my departure until we're at the hospital.'

The blue sky was gradually disappearing, and a wild south-wester began to keen around the thatch.

'I must find those children,' thought Vicky. 'They should be nearby. Surely they would have turned back when the weather became so bad.'

Again she made her way through the bush, calling loudly, and when she came to the edge, she scanned the whole length of the beach. The sea was a churned-up maelstrom of steel grey waves and small jagged caps of foam. The horizon was invisible. Olivia and David were struggling along the beach, the wind whipping Olivia's dark hair into snakelike tendrils.

'Have you seen the children?' shrieked Vicky.

They shook their heads, apparently not very concerned. But

when she told them of Stephen's phone message, they looked at each other significantly.

'We'd better hurry,' said Olivia. 'The servants can pack and follow later. If the river is coming down, we must get going.'

Vicky had not thought Olivia would be alarmed about the river because in any case she had intended to stay for a few more days, and the bridge would be passable long before that. Stephen had to get back to the hospital, but she could not understand Olivia's alarm. Wearily she made her way back to the cottage. She must confess her fears to Stephen. The children should have been back long before now. As she returned he was coming back from another visit to the trading store.

'The river is coming down for certain,' he said to the others. 'I'll have to get back to the hospital while the bridge is still open. Sorry to have to cut our visit short, Olivia, but I'd better take Susan, Gran and Vicky while there's still time. In any case, Vicky wouldn't want to stay here. She has other plans.'

He did not bother to explain this statement.

'But, Stephen darling, we must go too,' said Olivia. 'I'll leave the servants to clear up. They can come later.'

'There's no need for alarm, Olivia. You'll be quite all right here. I thought you'd intended to stay until next week.'

Olivia looked at David. 'Shall I tell him?'

David shook his head slightly.

'No, perhaps not. It's just that we have important business to settle. We must go.'

It was starting to rain, great torrents of water blowing across the misty sea. Vicky could no longer restrain her fears.

'Stephen, what about the children? I've looked everywhere. They should be back by now. They have the sense not to stay out in this weather.'

'Do you mean to say they're still not back? Well, there goes our journey. We can't go until we've found them. Olivia and David, could you take your car and go along the road to look for them while we search the bush. Go and call Mr. Osborne, Vicky. The more people we can get to look for them the quicker we'll find them.'

'But, Stephen,' said Olivia plaintively, 'surely you don't expect David and me to risk not being able to get across? I thought I'd explained. We have very important business to negotiate. We have to be in Johannesburg by tomorrow evening. Let the servants go out and look for them if you feel uneasy. But I'm sure they can't be far away. They're probably hiding. It would be just like the mischievous little monkeys.'

'Hiding in this?' said Stephen, looking at the rain driving against the window. 'Olivia, have some humanity. We must find the children. There's hardly anyone left in the other cottages who could help us. The river isn't coming down immediately. You'll still have time to get across even if you help us.'

'What a fuss about nothing! Take the servants, but David and I are going straight away. I'm not even going to bother to pack. When you know what it's about you'll understand, Stephen. Come, David.'

She flounced into her room, and David, glancing rather shamefacedly at the two of them, turned to follow her.

'You see how it is, old chap,' he said to Stephen. 'Must strike while the iron's hot ... sorry and all that ... sure the kids will turn up safe and sound.'

In another five minutes the sound of Olivia's powerful car reverberated through the cottage, then there was nothing but the purr of the gears as she negotiated the steep hill and roared across the bridge. George Osborne stood in the doorway of his room, yawning and rubbing his eyes.

'Weather looks a spot dirty. What's all the commotion? Did I hear Olivia's car?'

'You did,' said Stephen grimly.

He quickly explained the circumstances. 'So, Mr. Osborne, I hope you at least will be willing to join us in a search for your daughter,' he added.

'Susan ... oh, yes, you said she hasn't turned up yet.' George Osborne seemed to have something else on his mind. He was red in the face. 'The dirty doublecrossing ...' a look at Stephen's face warned him off using the word in front of Gran and Vicky. 'You know where they've gone, don't you? They've gone to stake their claim to the emerald mine!'

'But that's nonsense. It's been proved that the mine is worthless.'

'That one – Susan's one – yes. But during the investigations David found another one in the neighbourhood previously unknown. He confirmed the results yesterday by phone. It seems highly workable, they think, but he had to take up his option and get all the business papers signed by tomorrow. They offered me a share in it. We signed an agreement of sorts. And now they've gone! To think they've doublecrossed me in this way! I should have known better. Engaged to me – and there she was making eyes at David all the time. I should have realized she was always after the main chance. And what about the engagement ring I gave her?'

He stormed into Olivia's room, returning with a note. 'She must have scribbled this before she left,' he said. ' "You must know I could never marry a poor man. Sorry, George darling, you lose. I'm going to marry David by special licence as soon as we get to Johannesburg. Then we'll go up to the mine immediately. Here's your ring back – I'm going to have all the emeralds I want very shortly".'

'I'm going after them,' George Osborne declared, crumpling up the letter and stamping on it. 'I'll show that bitch she can't get away with it. I'll make them give me a share in the mine if it's the last thing I do! My car may not be as fast, but I'll catch them up in Johannesburg if I have to search the whole town for them.'

'Aren't you forgetting something?' Stephen asked quietly.

'What?' snarled George.

'There's a storm about to break; the river is coming down, and your small daughter is alone with an African child in God knows what kind of danger. Doesn't that count more than petty revenge?'

'Susan? Look, old chap, she's managed without me for eight years. You can hardly expect me to sacrifice the chance of a lifetime for her. She'll come back. They're probably sheltering somewhere. I'm going to get into that car and drive like the hammers of hell, and I'll force a share of the mine from that woman even if I have to knock David's teeth in!'

He slammed out of the cottage, floundering through the mud, and in a little while they saw his car lurching over the grass until it reached the main track.

'Let's not waste any more time,' said Stephen. 'The children may be sheltering, but I'll feel much better when we've found them. I'll organize the servants to search on this side of the river. We'll send someone to the shop to ask for more assistance. You say you've been through all the bush nearby? They must have strayed further.'

At the last moment Gran came running out with some blankets and a satchel containing a flask of hot coffee and a packet of sandwiches.

'The bairns will be frozen and clemmed by now,' she said. 'They'll need a wee bite.'

They left instructions that she should light a fire in the grate if there was any news, so they would see the smoke. Then they took the car and drove to the bridge. The sky was dark now and squalls of rain swept across the white-capped waves. They had found fishermen's oilskins and sou'westers in the cottage, and as they walked along the shore of the lagoon, water poured from the yellow coats in a continuous stream.

'Do you think they could be on the other side?' asked Vicky.

'It seems probable. There's much thicker woodland there and if they were looking for the bush baby it seems a likely place to search.'

The river was deeper now than it had been this morning, but they crossed the bridge without difficulty and plunged into the natural forest on the other side, following the path and watching carefully for any sign of the children.

'If we don't find them soon, I'll go back and phone the police,' said Stephen. 'It's a long way for them to come, but they might be able to bring police dogs.'

'We'll find them soon,' Vicky assured him. 'They can't be far away.'

'If they'd been on this side, we would see some sign of footprints on the path,' said Stephen. 'I think we're wasting our time here. We'd better go across the bridge and see if the Africans have found anything.'

On the bridge, the wind between the walls of cliff had reached gale force. Vicky, hampered by the heavy oilskins, tottered as the full strength of the weather battered against her, driving her towards the wall with its dangerous gaps. At once Stephen seized her in his strong arms and, clutching Vicky to him with one arm while guiding himself along the side cable with the other, he sidled across the seemingly endless space with a crablike gait that in any other circumstances would have been ludicrous.

But to Vicky, drenched in rain, thrashed by the howling tempest, a kind of happiness came again like a watery beam of sunlight through dark clouds. She was with Stephen. His arms were giving her strength, and the storm was endurable.

They had paused for breath, turning their faces to the sea and against the wind. A little way up river, a spit of land, that ended in high ground covered in trees, had already become an island with water swirling around the place that usually connected it with the mainland. Through the veils of rain, all around them from the bush on each side came a mushroomy odour of damp undergrowth and the bitter fragrance of crushed leaves, but Vicky, her senses vibrantly alert, was aware for a moment of another smell, familiar and haunting, but not in this setting.

Into her mind flashed the memory of Christmas night, and of the peaceful time with Stephen sitting in front of the fire, before he made his astonishing proposal.

Fire! That was it. The haunting fragrance that came upon the stormy wind was the smell of peat, and only yesterday Susan had shown her the piece she had begged from Gran and said she and Tandy would use it some time.

'They must be somewhere nearby,' she said to Stephen, explaining her theory. They scanned the river banks, but the wet landscape returned nothing unusual to their anxious gaze.

'There,' said Stephen. 'There on that rising ground – do you see anything?'

It seemed for a moment as if a wisp of blue smoke, scarcely to be distinguished from the misty cloud, rose above the spit of land where on the rising ground there appeared to be an African hut.

Vicky almost cried with disappointment.

'It's only an African's wood fire,' she said. 'I must have imagined the smell was the same.'

'No,' said Stephen, 'that hut is deserted. We looked at it long ago. The Africans left it because the river was constantly sweeping away their crops. And you're not mistaken about the peat. I can smell it now. There's no mistaking it.'

'But how are we to get there?' asked Vicky.

Stephen had started hurrying back across the bridge and down the river bank, sliding and almost falling in the muddy red ground, with Vicky breathlessly trying to keep up with him.

'If the children are there they've already been cut off by

the rising tide. They probably walked across before the ground was covered. But there's an old boat somewhere along the bank. It was used as a ferry boat before the bridge was built. At one time we had to leave the cars on this side and carry all the supplies across. I think it's still kept in good repair because it's used for fishing.'

Anxiety seemed to make their strength superhuman. Usually the boat was yards above high water line, but now it was already afloat, its mooring post almost under water. Stephen climbed in helping Vicky to clamber up. She had discarded her shoes and her bare feet squelched in the thick slime of the river bottom. But she managed to get in at last and, taking an oar, they both paddled away from the bank.

'There's quite a strong current here. You can let her drift,' said Stephen. The river caught them, propelling them swiftly towards the island, where Stephen guided the boat and they ran aground with a sickening jolt.

'Up this path,' said Stephen, when they had pulled the boat further up the bank. Again they plunged into a wilderness of dripping trees. Rain had washed out whatever trail of footsteps there might have been. The path led steeply upwards through thorny branches and with the red mud sticky underfoot.

No sound came to them save that of running water, and beyond, seeming far away the sullen boom of the sea. At last, just below the highest ridge, hardly distinguishable from the uniform brown and grey of the surrounding woods, there came into sight a round African hut. It was in a state of disrepair, the wooden poles of its basic structure showing through the crumbling mud, and the thatch tattered and unkempt.

But from the broken metal peak of its roof, smoke filtered into the clearing. The door whined noisily on its rusty hinges, as they pushed it open. In the small, smoke-filled room the children were sitting one on each side of a tiny glowing fire, built upon the centre hearthstone. They were kneeling down like small devotees of some household goddess. Susan was holding Sinkwe and appeared to be telling Tandy a story, but when she saw Stephen and Vicky, she slowly stood up, her eyes wide and as expressionless as those of the little animal who was looking at them too with eyes like small yellow moons.

Vicky went towards her. 'Susan, my darling! Thank goodness you and Tandy are safe. We've been looking everywhere for you.'

For a moment Susan stood rigid in Vicky's arms, then she was crying and Vicky was weeping too.

'Vicky, we found him. He was here in the bush. Some Africans told us they'd seen him here. But then, when we found this hut, we thought we'd stay here for a while and play houses. Then when we tried to get back the river was too deep. We ate all our sandwiches hours ago and we're so hungry.'

Vicky started opening the satchel to feed them, but Stephen stopped her.

'They can't eat now,' he said. 'We must get them back. The river is rising all the time and it will be harder to get across from here because we'll have to row against the current.'

'What's that?' asked Vicky.

Above the sound of the wind in the trees and the water rushing down the slopes was a strange sound, that seemed out of place in these wild surroundings.

'It's like a train,' said Susan, her tears forgotten and her expressive face sparkling with excitement. But Stephen's face was grim.

'It's the river,' he said. 'It's coming down. It's too late, we'll never get across now. We must just hope the water doesn't reach this hut, for we'll have to stay here.'

Noise was all around them now. Through the trees they could see the wall of water rushing in its angry flood between the high banks, carrying in its furious course great logs, carcasses of animals, pitiful remnants of crops, stalks of corn and pumpkins wrenched from some land that had been worked with painstaking labour only to be devastated by the raging river.

Higher and higher the water rose. They could see it lapping through the trees below like some savage beast let loose and prowling through the forest. There was nothing they could do but disguise from the children and each other the fear they felt. The hut was almost on the highest ground of the island. If the water reached them, there was nowhere else they could hide, and no one could hope to survive more than a few minutes in the seething flood.

Tandy and Susan jumped up and down, highly excited, not even realizing they were in any danger.

'If the water comes much nearer we'll have to make our way

to the highest ridge,' Stephen said quietly. He wrested pieces of timber from the broken walls of the hut with his bare hands and, with Vicky's help, started lashing them together with monkey ropes from the surrounding trees.

'What are you doing?' asked Susan.

'I'm trying to make some kind of raft in case we have to swim for it,' he answered.

'What fun!' cried Susan, not in the least perturbed. 'Just like Robinson Crusoe!'

Vicky realized that the idea of a raft was rather a forlorn hope. If it rose higher, nothing could save them from the seething maelstrom of water that was pounding towards the sea. But it occupied their minds as the floodline crept towards the high ground.

The water was lapping scarcely twelve feet below them when suddenly they sensed a change.

'I think it's over,' said Stephen. 'The water's going down.'

Slowly, almost imperceptibly, the level of the flood was dropping.

The sun was setting in a fiery conflagration of red clouds when they ventured out further down into the woods to investigate their situation.

'We're like Noah and his family on Mount Ararat,' said Susan.

'But unfortunately we don't have a dove to take a message to Gran,' said Stephen. 'I'm afraid she'll be worried, but there's very little we can do. We'll have to stay here until the river is negotiable again, and I think that means until morning. Your peat has all gone, Susan, but is there any dry wood left?'

Fortunately the children had gathered plenty during the day, and when the fire was stoked and Vicky had rolled the children in blankets and given them hot coffee and sandwiches, the old hut seemed quite cosy. They were soon asleep, worn out by their adventures, and Vicky poured coffee for herself and Stephen. She handed it to him where he was sitting with his back against the hut wall, then went back to sit beside the sleeping children.

Her hair was tangled, her face dirty. He looked across at her and laughed. 'Vicky, Vicky, how lovely you look!'

She regarded him uncertainly. 'Don't make fun of me, please.'

'Come and sit near me.'

Slowly she walked over to his side and sat down. He put his arm around her, drawing her close, and she rested her head wearily upon his shoulder. In her exhausted state it did not seem to matter whether he knew of her love, or of her knowledge that he had once felt affection for her. From the pocket of her slacks, she drew out the Keeper of the Heart necklace.

'Stephen, your knowledge of African customs isn't very good, you know.'

'Why, my dear?'

'It's the wife who gives the necklace to her husband. He is the Keeper of the Heart. She makes the portrait of herself and gives it to him, and what it says is "Here I am – I don't disguise my faults – this is me, and you must love me for what I am because you have my whole heart".'

As she said this, Vicky handed the necklace to him. He put his arms around her and her mouth was very close to his.

'Vicky, do you mean that?'

She put her lips to his and kissed him with great gentleness.

'I've been so wrong, Stephen, but I could never truly believe all the awful things I said to you. Please, forgive me. I wanted to believe those things because I wanted to be cured.'

'Cured?' asked Stephen.

'Of loving you. And even you aren't a clever enough doctor to accomplish that.'

It was done now. She had told him. Pride had disappeared and in its place was a desire to let him know she loved him, without thought of self.

'I'll go away tomorrow, if you wish,' she said. 'But at last I've told you the truth, even if you despise me for it.'

'Go away? Vicky, my sweet, foolish Vicky, how can you be so blind? Don't you know I've loved you since that first day in Cape Town when you looked so beautiful, so haughty, so entirely the kind of girl I never intended to fall in love with.'

'And now?' said Vicky.

'Now I know you're warm and loving and utterly beautiful with your tangled hair and dirty face, and I love you more than I ever thought it possible to love anyone.'

His lips were upon hers, demanding the ardent kisses for which they had waited so long. The necklace of the Keeper of the Heart fell unnoticed to the ground, for its message was no longer needed.

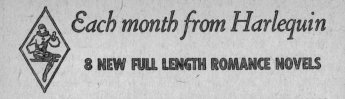

Each month from Harlequin

8 NEW FULL LENGTH ROMANCE NOVELS

Listed below are the last three months' releases:

1857	CRUISE TO A WEDDING,	Betty Neels
1858	ISLAND OF DARKNESS,	Rebecca Stratton
1859	THE MAN OUTSIDE,	Jane Donnelly
1860	HIGH-COUNTRY WIFE,	Gloria Bevan
1861	THE STAIRWAY TO ENCHANTMENT,	Lucy Gillen
1862	CHATEAU IN PROVENCE,	Rozella Lake
1863	McCABE'S KINGDOM,	Margaret Way
1864	DEAR TYRANT,	Margaret Malcolm
1865	STRANGER IN THE GLEN,	Flora Kidd
1866	THE GREATER HAPPINESS,	Katrina Britt
1867	FLAMINGO FLYING SOUTH,	Joyce Dingwell
1868	THE DREAM ON THE HILL,	Lilian Peake
1869	THE HOUSE OF THE EAGLES,	Elizabeth Ashton
1870	TO TRUST MY LOVE,	Sandra Field
1871	THE BRAVE IN HEART,	Mary Burchell
1872	CINNAMON HILL,	Jan Andersen
1873	A PAVEMENT OF PEARL,	Iris Danbury
1874	DESIGN FOR DESTINY,	Sue Peters
1875	A PLUME OF DUST,	Wynne May
1876	GATE OF THE GOLDEN GAZELLE,	Dorothy Cork
1877	MEANS TO AN END,	Lucy Gillen
1878	ISLE OF DREAMS,	Elizabeth Dawson
1879	DARK VIKING,	Mary Wibberley
1880	SWEET SUNDOWN,	Margaret Way

These titles are available at your local bookseller, or through the Harlequin Reader Service, M.P.O. Box 707, Niagara Falls, N.Y. 14302; Canadian address 649 Ontario St., Stratford, Ont.

Have You Missed Any of These *Harlequin Romances?*

AA-1

Have You Missed Any of These
Harlequin Romances?

☐ 941 MAYENGA FARM
Kathryn Blair
☐ 945 DOCTOR SANDY
Margaret Malcolm
☐ 948 ISLANDS OF SUMMER
Anne Weale
☐ 951 THE ENCHANTED TRAP
Kate Starr
☐ 957 NO LEGACY FOR LINDSAY
Essie Summers
☐ 965 CAME A STRANGER
Celine Conway
☐ 968 SWEET BRENDA
Penelope Walsh
☐ 974 NIGHT OF THE HURRICANE
Andrea Blake
☐ 984 ISLAND IN THE DAWN
Averil Ives
☐ 993 SEND FOR NURSE ALISON
Marjorie Norrell
☐ 994 JUBILEE HOSPITAL
Jan Tempest
☐ 1001 NO PLACE FOR SURGEONS
Elizabeth Gilzean
☐ 1004 THE PATH OF THE
MOONFISH, Betty Beaty
☐ 1009 NURSE AT FAIRCHILDS
Marjorie Norrell
☐ 1010 DOCTOR OF RESEARCH
Elizabeth Houghton
☐ 1011 THE TURQUOISE SEA
Hilary Wilde
☐ 1018 HOSPITAL IN THE TROPICS
Gladys Fullbrook
☐ 1019 FLOWER OF THE MORNING
Celine Conway
☐ 1024 THE HOUSE OF DISCONTENT
Esther Wyndham
☐ 1048 HIGH MASTER OF CLERE
Jane Arbor
☐ 1052 MEANT FOR EACH OTHER
Mary Burchell
☐ 1074 NEW SURGEON AT ST.
LUCIAN'S, Elizabeth
Houghton
☐ 1087 A HOME FOR JOCELYN
Eleanor Farnes
☐ 1094 MY DARK RAPPAREE
Henrietta Reid

☐ 1098 THE UNCHARTED OCEAN
Margaret Malcolm
☐ 1102 A QUALITY OF MAGIC
Rose Burghely
☐ 1106 WELCOME TO PARADISE
Jill Tahourdin
☐ 1115 THE ROMANTIC HEART
Norrey Ford
☐ 1120 HEART IN HAND
Margaret Malcolm
☐ 1121 TEAM DOCTOR, Ann Gilmour
☐ 1122 WHISTLE AND I'LL COME
Flora Kidd
☐ 1138 LOVING IS GIVING
Mary Burchell
☐ 1144 THE TRUANT BRIDE
Sara Seale
☐ 1150 THE BRIDE OF MINGALAY
Jean S. Macleod
☐ 1166 DOLAN OF SUGAR HILLS
Kate Starr
☐ 1172 LET LOVE ABIDE
Norrey Ford
☐ 1182 GOLDEN APPLE ISLAND
Jane Arbor
☐ 1183 NEVER CALL IT LOVING
Marjorie Lewty
☐ 1184 THE HOUSE OF OLIVER
Jean S. Macleod
☐ 1200 SATIN FOR THE BRIDE
Kate Starr
☐ 1201 THE ROMANTIC DR. RYDON
Anne Durham
☐ 1209 THE STUBBORN DR STEPHEN
Elizabeth Houghton
☐ 1211 BRIDE OF KYLSAIG
Iris Danbury
☐ 1214 THE MARSHALL FAMILY
Mary Burchell
☐ 1216 ORANGES AND LEMONS
Isobel Chace
☐ 1218 BEGGARS MAY SING
Sara Seale
☐ 1222 DARK CONFESSOR
Elinor Davis
☐ 1236 JEMIMA
Leonora Starr

BB